A Wedding
on
Ladybug
Farm

Center Point
Large Print

Also by Donna Ball and available from
Center Point Large Print:

*Christmas on Ladybug Farm with
    Recipes from Ladybug Farm*
Vintage Ladybug Farm
The Hummingbird House

A Wedding
on
Ladybug
Farm

DONNA BALL

CENTER POINT LARGE PRINT
THORNDIKE, MAINE

This Center Point Large Print edition is published in the year 2014 by arrangement with Donna Ball.

The text of this Large Print edition is unabridged. In other aspects, this book may vary from the original edition. Printed in the United States of America on permanent paper. Set in 16-point Times New Roman type.

ISBN: 978-1-62899-342-4

Library of Congress Cataloging-in-Publication Data

Ball, Donna.
A wedding on Ladybug Farm / Donna Ball. —
    Center Point Large Print edition.
pages ; cm
Summary: "When Bridget, Cici and Lindsay left behind their safe suburban lives for a stately old mansion in the Shenandoah Valley, they redefined the concept of family. Now Lindsay is marrying Dominic and the foundation of their life together will be tested"—Provided by publisher.
  ISBN 978-1-62899-342-4 (library binding : alk. paper)
  1. Female friendship—Fiction. 2. Weddings—Fiction.
    3. Life change events—Fiction.
    4. Shenandoah River Valley (Va. and W. Va.)—Fiction.
    5. Large type books. I. Title.
PS3552.A4545W43 2014
813′.54—dc23
                                                    2014030131

CHAPTER ONE
ೞ
On Matters of Life and Death

The church was packed to overflowing, and those who were unfortunate enough to arrive less than forty-five minutes early were forced to stand in the vestibule, where the air-conditioning was less than ideal, or even beneath the shelter of the portico outside. They did so gladly, because on an occasion like this the important thing was to be able to say you had been there. The Baptist parking lot was filled, as was the adjacent fellowship hall lot, and the Methodist parking lot across the street. Cars lined both sides of the street for two blocks, and even as the organ music began to play, latecomers dressed in their Sunday best made their way up the sidewalk toward the assembly. They would be among those who ended up standing against the walls or crowding the vestibule.

There were roses everywhere. Baskets of them lined the church steps, the aisles, and the altar, along with the usual selection of potted plants and ostentatious arrangements of lilies. Cici, the practical one, wondered what in the world they were going to do with all those fresh flowers when the service was over. It was too bad no one was giving a dinner party afterwards; the arrangements could be broken down into gorgeous centerpieces. Cici realized her musings were more than a little inappropriate under the circumstances, and she glanced guiltily at Bridget who sat next to her on the pew sniffling into her tissue.

"I'll never be able to look at another rose without thinking of her," Bridget whispered brokenly.

Cici patted her friend's knee sympathetically. "She did love roses," she whispered back.

Lindsay, who sat on the other side of Cici, leaned in close and murmured resignedly, "She's right, you know. I can forget about using roses at my wedding now."

Cici inclined her head in regretful agreement.

"It's just not right," Bridget said, blotting her face with the soggy tissue.

Cici looked at her reproachfully. "I'm sure she didn't do it just to ruin Lindsay's wedding. She couldn't have known everyone would send roses."

Bridget's wet, red-rimmed eyes looked at her friend as though she had never seen her before. "I meant," she said deliberately, "she was so young. Younger than I am."

Lindsay leaned across Cici and told her, "Actually, no. Farley said she was seventy-six." Farley was their handyman, and the second person they had met when they moved to this small Shenandoah Valley community. The first person was his sister-in-law, the subject under discussion.

"Oh." Bridget looked surprised, and cast a curious look across the aisle to Farley, who looked somber and distressed in a too-tight blue suit, his thinning hair slicked back, his fading ginger-colored beard combed but not trimmed. It was the first time since Easter they had seen him inside a church.

Bridget sat back, mollified. "She certainly looked a lot younger. Not," she added quickly, "that that makes it any better."

"No it doesn't," agreed Cici with a sigh. "Seventy-six still sounds young to me. And I can't believe I'm old enough to think that."

The other two women nodded glumly.

None of them was accustomed to thinking of themselves as old, and they all looked much younger than their driver's licenses would have them believe. Bridget was actually the oldest, but with her short stature, round face, and platinum bob, was often mistaken for the youngest. Cici was a tall, athletic woman with thick honey-colored hair and a penchant for the outdoors which had resulted in head-to-toe freckles, and a talent for carpentry and construction that left her, more often than not, concealing one or more scrapes behind a flesh-colored bandage. Although Lindsay's shoulder-length auburn hair might not be quite as naturally pigmented as it once had been, and though she had abandoned the fight against the few midlife pounds that had turned her willowy size-six figure into a slender size eight, she could still turn heads in a pair of skinny jeans and heels. Today, however, in their somber navy and dove suits, with their hair pinned up and their expressions muted with the shock of the circumstances, the lines on their faces and the years that registered in their eyes were not so easy to disguise. And no one cared.

Ida Mae Simpson, who sat next to Bridget in a black crepe dress, black tights, and a black felt hat with a veil and a rather scraggly looking black feather that had likely last seen the bird to which it belonged sometime in the 1940s, folded her arms across her chest and gave a curt nod. She was older than any of them by an indeterminate number of decades, and had known everyone in the community most of her life. By contrast, Lindsay, Bridget, and Cici had moved here only four years ago, when they had fallen in love with the fading brick Victorian mansion nestled in the lush Shenandoah Valley and had made the life-changing decision to leave the suburbs of Baltimore behind, pool their resources, and buy the place. Ida Mae, who had been taking care of the house almost as long as its new owners had been alive, was a bonus which, even on her best days, the ladies were not entirely sure was a good thing.

Maggie Woodall, the only real estate agent in town, had sold them the house. Now she rested, bedecked by roses, in the satin-lined casket at the front of the church while mourners murmured about how unfair life was and the organist played a medley of hymns that included "In the Sweet Bye and Bye" and "In the Garden."

"I thought she looked real natural," Ida Mae pronounced with satisfaction.

Several people, overhearing, nodded in agreement, and Bridget patted Ida Mae's arm with a weak smile.

Lindsay sat back, looking uncomfortable. "Why do people say that?" she muttered. "I hate it when people say that. The last thing I want to look when I die is 'natural.' I want to look dead."

"Sshh," Cici admonished, elbowing her as the organist switched chords and the soloist, resplendent in a ruby choir robe and gold stole, stepped to the podium.

It was, they all agreed later, a magnificent service, one of the finest funerals the little town of Blue Valley had seen since the untimely demise of its mayor half a decade previously, and a fitting tribute to a fallen pillar of the community. The hymns were heartfelt, if not always on key, the sermon was stirring, and the eulogies went on for forty-five minutes. Everyone, no matter how close or casual the acquaintance with the deceased, shed a tear. Afterwards, the congregation shuffled to its feet and stood in silent attention as the six pallbearers bore the rose-draped casket down the center aisle to the solemn strains of the organ. Farley took his place in the middle, and the shoulders of the blue suit jacket strained at the seams. Afterwards, the family attended a brief graveside service beneath the green funeral home canopy that had been erected in the cemetery, and friends gathered at the home of the deceased to deliver comfort, casseroles, and as many baskets of funeral roses as they could pile into their cars. Cici managed to transport six in the back of her SUV, along with a baked ham, a chicken and dressing casserole, and Bridget's famous coconut cake. All would freeze well.

The ladies were exhausted by the time they arrived back at Ladybug Farm shortly before sunset that evening. They climbed the wide front steps wearily, dropped their purses on the porch, and sank into the rocking chairs that were waiting for them. Cici glanced around to make sure no one was watching, and then stripped off her pantyhose and tucked them beneath a cushion before sitting down. Bridget brought out wine and glasses. Ida Mae said, "Y'all gonna want any supper?"

They all groaned a negative. They had stuffed themselves on the buffet that was the inevitable aftermath of any funeral.

"Good," declared Ida Mae, "because you could

get it for your own selves if you did." She was limping noticeably as she went into the house, and the three women shared a look of alarm and concern.

Bridget waited until she was out of earshot to say, softly, "She seems frailer to me. Does she to you?"

Cici poured the wine. "I worry about her going up and down those stairs."

"Have you thought about what we're going to do when she becomes, you know, too old to get around?"

Cici handed her a glass of wine. "What can we do? Someone tried putting her in a nursing home before, and that's how she ended up back here with us."

"Well, we need to at least have a conversation, ask her about her final wishes and everything. After all . . ."

"Oh, please, you two." Lindsay kicked off her shoes, tucked one leg beneath her, and held out her hand. Cici placed a glass of wine in it. "Ida Mae is going to outlive all of us, I thought we'd agreed on that. She's already outlived five popes and nine presidents, for God's sake. Can we talk about something else?"

Cici filled her own glass and sat down between Bridget and Lindsay. The early evening peace of Ladybug Farm settled in around them like the familiar folds of a well-worn shawl, and almost as one they released a soft breath of relief, sinking into the welcoming scents and sounds and sights of home.

The landscape had changed since the first time they had sat on this porch and opened a bottle of wine together. They hadn't even had furniture then, much less a plan, and they sat on the steps and watched the stars come out and wondered whether they were about to embark upon the biggest mistake of their lives, or the biggest adventure. Over the following years they had painstakingly restored the gardens, polished blackened statues, hacked away hidden paths. They had lost two trees and part of the sunroom. But after clawing away ivy and chasing away reptiles, they reclaimed a gorgeous stone dairy, and shored up a barn to house the unexpected gift of a flock of sheep. The barn subsequently burned to the ground, but from its ashes had risen the office of the brand new Ladybug Farm Winery, whose curving gravel drive now led to a hillside lush with vines. The dairy, also graveled with a separate parking area, had become The Tasting Table restaurant, opening in the spring for lunch and available any time for catered events, Chef Bridget Tyndale, proprietor.

Four years ago, they had been three women with a dream. Now they were an enterprise. In the interim, Lindsay had adopted a son, and that son was now wearing the uniform of the US Marine

Corps in Afghanistan. Cici's daughter Lori, who had been as pesky as a housefly and as enchanting as a butterfly around Ladybug Farm for the past three years, had graduated from college and moved to Italy. Bridget, who at the outset had been a new widow crippled by grief and intimidated by her grown children, now ran an Internet business and a restaurant. Lindsay was engaged to the manager of the Ladybug Farms Winery.

The purple hedge of mountains still cast long shadows across the lawn of Ladybug Farm. Fading pink and purple hydrangea blossoms still nodded in the breeze. A black-and-white border collie still leapt the fence every day at twilight to herd the placid flock of sheep into a corner of the meadow predetermined only by himself, and the sunset still painted an amazing Technicolor stillscape across the horizon of their lives. But everything had changed.

Cici said softly, "It seems like only yesterday that we walked through this house with Maggie for the first time, doesn't it? But look how much has happened since then."

Bridget shook her head sadly. "It's like the preacher said, in the blink of an eye everything can be gone."

"That's a cheery thought," Lindsay murmured, lifting her glass.

"Well, it *was* a funeral," Bridget pointed out reasonably.

Cici took a sip of her wine, and then paused, frowning as she held out her arm a foot or so in front of her face. "Does that look like a mole to you?"

"What?"

Cici held out her arm to Bridget. "There."

"It looks like another freckle to me."

"Not that. This."

Bridget patted her hair for her glasses, found them missing, and shrugged. "Could be."

Cici examined the blemish again. "Maybe I should have it checked out."

"Couldn't hurt."

Lindsay groaned. "How did we get so old? All we ever talk about any more is moles and menopause and the way things used to be."

"Wait until we start talking about ingrown toenails and cracked teeth," Bridget said, unconcerned.

Cici looked at Lindsay curiously. "What did we used to talk about?"

She shrugged, trying to remember. "I don't know. Stuff. Interesting stuff."

The three of them were thoughtful for a moment, trying to come up with something interesting to say. The result was silence.

Finally it was Lindsay who gave in with a sigh and said, "I just don't understand where the past four years went. Why does time seem to go by so much faster than it used to?"

"Because we're old, that's why," Cici said.

"Also, the earth is spinning faster, remember? We've been losing one-eighth millionth of a second a day since the Japan earthquake in 2011."

Lindsay stared at her. "How do you know that?"

"Bridget looked it up." And then she frowned a little. "Or maybe it was Lori. I remember it was someone who's always coming up with useless information."

"That is not useless information," Bridget protested indignantly. "I for one want to know if my day is getting shorter. It helps me plan. Besides, that's not why time seems to be speeding up—even though we *are* losing one-eighth millionth of a second every day." This was said a little defiantly to Lindsay, who simply shrugged. "The reason time goes faster as we age is because we're not making as many new neural pathways, and the reason for that is because we're not experiencing or learning as many new things for the first time as we did when we were younger."

"I don't know about that," Cici said. "I've learned more new things since we've been here than I have in the rest of my life combined."

"Amen to that," said Lindsay, and, as if on cue, Rodrigo the rooster, gathering his hens for the evening into the chicken coop behind the barn, gave a resounding crow of agreement.

"Speaking of which," Cici said, looking from one to the other of them, "did anyone remember to feed the chickens this morning before we left?"

Lindsay and Bridget exchanged a guilty look. "I meant to," Bridget said, "but I was running late getting the cake frosted."

"You know me," Lindsay admitted. "When my routine is thrown off my whole day goes to pot. If I don't write it down I forget it these days."

Cici said, frowning a little into her glass, "It sure does seem like there's a lot more to do lately, now that the kids are gone. Maybe they were more help than we realized."

"Anyway," said Lindsay, "it's good for them to eat bugs and worms."

Cici lifted her eyebrows. "The kids?"

"The chickens. That's why you pay three dollars a dozen more for free-range chicken eggs."

"The problem," Bridget pointed out, "is that there *is* a lot more to do these days. When we started out we didn't have chickens, or a goat . . ."

"Or a restaurant," added Cici.

"Or a winery," said Lindsay."

Bridget nodded. "I don't think this place can be run by three people anymore."

Cici smiled slowly, watching as the door to the barn office opened and Dominic emerged, lifting his hand to them before picking up a bucket and filling it with chicken feed. "Fortunately," she said, "it doesn't have to be. God bless him."

"I don't know how he does it," Bridget said, "taking care of his place and our place too. Not to mention running the winery."

Lindsay watched with undisguised affection as Dominic entered the chicken coop and scattered feed amongst the eager, clucking chickens that swarmed around his feet. "He is amazing," she agreed. "We were lucky to find him."

Cici grinned and lifted her glass to Lindsay. "Weren't we, though?"

"I meant to run the winery," Lindsay said, but a grin tugged at her lips too as she sipped her wine. "We were lucky to find him to run the winery." And she turned her gaze back toward her fiancé, her face softening as she watched him perform the simple evening chore.

Dominic was a wiry, work-weathered man with a deep tan, longish, slightly thinning hair that was salted with platinum, and a quick, warm smile that always went straight to his eyes. His father had created the original winery back when Ladybug Farm had been known as Blackwell Farms, and its wine had been known around the world. Dominic learned the business at his father's knee, and had virtually grown up on Ladybug Farm. After raising a family and spending twenty years teaching agriculture at Clemson University, he returned to the place of his youth as the county extension agent. When Cici, Bridget, and Lindsay had sought his advice about reopening the winery, it was a match made in heaven, and Dominic had come full circle back to Ladybug Farm.

"Has he decided what he's going to do with

his place after you're married?" Bridget asked.

Lindsay shook her head. "We've hardly had time to talk about it. There are so many decisions to make . . ."

"Not the least of which is a wedding date," Bridget pointed out. Lindsay had changed the date four times already, and she had only been engaged since summer.

"It's going to be too cold for an outdoor wedding before long," Cici added.

Lindsay made a brief rueful expression and lifted one shoulder. "Now that I can't use roses, what difference does it make?"

"I thought Dominic was set on having the ceremony in the vineyard."

Lindsay sighed. "Roses are my signature flower. I was going to have sprays of them at each row of seats, and winding through the grape arbor, and all along the reception table. And in the bouquet, of course."

"It's a little late in the year for roses anyway," Bridget said sympathetically.

"Unless you're planning to wait until summer," Cici said.

Lindsay brightened slightly. "That's a thought. The gardens are gorgeous in May."

Cici and Bridget exchanged a look. It was Cici who spoke. "You know, Lindsay—and don't take this the wrong way—but I was just wondering . . . are you *sure* about getting married?"

Lindsay looked both surprised and insulted. "What do you mean? Of course I am! It was my idea, remember? Why would you say that? Of course I am!"

"It's just," Bridget put in quickly, "you keep changing the date . . ."

"That's not all my fault," Lindsay protested. "Dominic had to go to that conference in California in August and we all agreed he couldn't afford to miss it . . ."

Cici and Bridget quickly murmured consent.

"And I couldn't get the dress altered in time for the next date, and the minister wasn't available on the next one, and my sister couldn't make it on the next one. And don't forget Paul and Derrick's grand opening pretty much took up all of last month, and since Paul is my wedding planner I could hardly do it without him, could I? Besides, most weddings take over a year to plan. We've barely been engaged three months!"

"Well," Cici pointed out a little less than tactfully, "most people aren't as old as you are when they start planning."

Lindsay gave her a sharp look.

"What I meant was," Cici corrected herself quickly, "you're the one who said why wait? It was your idea to have the wedding this year."

"There's a lot to consider," Lindsay said, only partially mollified. "It's not just the wedding, you know, but here we are about to bottle our first vintage, and Dominic is working overtime with the harvest coming up, which you might not know is a pretty big deal when you're running a winery."

"That's all true," Bridget agreed. "But you haven't even made some of the most important decisions, like where you're going to live . . ."

Lindsay frowned uncomfortably into her glass. "Well, it's not like we're college students, you know. We both have lives, and a lot of stuff to consolidate. It's complicated."

Cici nodded. "Just like it was when we all moved in here together."

"But this is a huge house," Bridget went on, "with more than enough room for a married couple, if that's what you're worried about. We can fence off a section of the pasture for the horses, and if the golden retriever is a house dog he won't even notice Rebel."

Cici shot Bridget a quick look. "Even though we've never had a house dog before."

"And Ida Mae would have a fit," Lindsay said. "She barely tolerates *us* in the house."

"And we can always use more barn cats," Bridget went on cheerfully.

"We already have a cat!" Cici exclaimed, and then looked around suspiciously. "Where is he, anyway?" The new kitten, whose name was still under debate, had an unnerving habit of springing out of what was apparently thin air to latch onto ankles, pants legs, shoulders, and sometimes scalps with needlelike claws, causing them all to mistrust the silence when they could not see him.

"This is a working farm," Bridget insisted firmly. "We need working cats."

"Which lets out that little monster of yours." Erring on the side of caution, Cici tucked both of her bare feet onto the top rung of the rocker, presumably out of harm's way.

"Maybe the four of us should all sit down and have a talk about how it's going to work," Bridget suggested, "just like we did when we decided to buy the house."

"Just like we did when we decided to go into partnership with Dominic on the winery," Cici clarified. "You're the one who's always saying that you can make anything work with a plan."

Lindsay nodded, and sipped her wine. "You're right. That's what we'll do. We'll all sit down and work things out. That will make everything so much easier."

"How about now?" Cici suggested. She lifted her arm to beckon Dominic to the porch. He latched the door to the chicken coop and waved back.

"Not tonight," Lindsay said. "I'm too tired. But soon."

"When?" Bridget said.

"Soon. Maybe next week. I'll see when Dominic has some free time."

"He has some free time now," Cici pointed out.

Dominic put away the feed bucket and started across the lawn toward them, but Lindsay was already shaking her head. "We'll get around to it. What's the rush, anyway?"

Cici glanced again at Bridget, who responded with a slight, almost imperceptible lift of her eyebrows that Lindsay chose to ignore. Cici said, "Look, Linds, we're on your side, you know that, whatever you want to do. It's just that we just went through this whole thing with Lori, remember, where she didn't want to pick a date, and she didn't want to try on dresses . . ."

"I have my dress!" Lindsay protested.

"Because Lori didn't need it," Bridget pointed out.

"Because the *reason* she didn't want to be pinned down about any of the plans was that she really didn't want to get married at all," Cici said. "So I'm just saying, maybe you should ask yourself if the reason you're having such a hard time making decisions is . . . well, you know."

Lindsay said patiently, "Look, we don't exactly have the best track record when it comes to weddings around here, you know. The first time we tried to have a wedding at Ladybug Farm a tornado came and the goat ate the cake."

"Not the whole cake," Bridget protested.

Lindsay overrode her. "And the second wedding we planned, the bride ended up running away to be with another man."

Cici objected, "I wouldn't say Lori ran away. Exactly." She frowned into her wine. "Besides, that had nothing to do with us."

"The point is," Lindsay said, "I've waited over twenty years to get married again, and you can believe me when I tell you it will be for the last time. All I'm trying to do is make sure everything is as perfect as it can be. And it will take as long as it takes."

Bridget sipped her wine, her expression thoughtful. "I don't know, Lindsay. After a certain age, it doesn't always pay to put things off. It's like the preacher said, we're not promised tomorrow."

Lindsay drew in a sharp breath to reply but let it out silently as Dominic came up the steps.

"Hello, my darlings," he greeted them. "How was the funeral?"

Lindsay made a face. "Why do people say that? It was a funeral. How good could it be?"

"It's a Southern thing," Bridget said. "We have this whole dark delight thing going on with funerals."

"Speak for yourself," Lindsay said. "I hate them."

"Actually," said Dominic, "I was just being polite."

"It was a lovely service," Lindsay replied dutifully. She extended one hand in welcome, but her smile seemed a little distracted.

"I'm sorry I missed it." He caught her fingers

and kissed them, then turned to pour himself a glass of wine. "I was fond of Maggie."

"You were at the visitation last night," Bridget reminded him. "I know the family appreciated that. Will you stay for supper?"

"Thank you, but I'll just have a sip with you, if I may, and then get along. The day is only half done." He lifted the wine bottle and examined the label before pouring, more out of habit than curiosity. In his world, the only wine that mattered was the wine from Ladybug Farm. All other vintages were just filling in the time until his own was ready to debut. "Good turnout, was there?"

"Everyone in the county," Cici replied. "If we hadn't gotten there early we never would have gotten a seat. Thanks for taking care of things while we were gone."

Dominic topped off Cici's glass, then Bridget's, then Lindsay's. He took his glass and sat next to Lindsay.

"You know, it makes you wonder," Bridget said thoughtfully. "How many people will come to our funerals when it's time?"

Lindsay groaned out loud again and Bridget insisted, "No, I'm serious. You see someone like that, who's been here so long and touched so many lives, and people are standing in line to pay their respects . . . but we've only been here a few years, and we don't know that many people. Really, who would come? And is there anything sadder than a funeral where nobody comes?"

"I'd come," Cici assured her, "and I'd make Lindsay come whether she wanted to or not."

"I'm sure your children would make the trip," Dominic added.

Bridget nodded, somewhat encouraged. "That's true, I suppose. And Katie would bring the grand-children."

"I'm not sure how I feel about little kids at a funeral," Lindsay objected.

"You can't protect children from everything in life," Dominic said. "It's important that they understand that what is today may not always be."

"Of course the girls have to be there," Bridget insisted, a little indignantly. "You always go to your grandmother's funeral."

"Paul and Derrick would come," Lindsay said. "Paul never misses a chance to give a speech."

"And I'm sure the garden club would send a representative," Cici asked. "You've done a lot of work for them."

"Not to mention the Ladies Aid Society at the church," Lindsay added.

"There, you see?" Dominic lifted his glass to her. "You've already gathered quite a crowd."

Bridget smiled contentedly. "I have, haven't I?"

Lindsay gave a small, disbelieving shake of her head. "And we're doing it again. Talking about funerals. Can't anyone think of anything less maudlin?"

Cici sipped her wine. "My grandma always said you should stop and take stock of your life every now and then by counting the number of people who would go to your funeral if you dropped dead today. If you can't find more than a dozen people who would make the effort, you're doing something wrong."

"I for one expect an impressive showing," Dominic said. "I'm very well liked, if I do say so myself."

"You've been here forever," Cici agreed. "Everyone knows who you are."

"Not to mention being in public service," added Bridget.

"I wrote a column for the paper for five years," Dominic pointed out.

"And every farmer in the county has probably had you to thank for his crops at one time or another."

Dominic inclined his head modestly. "Well."

"You ran the 4-H program and helped start the high school ag department," added Cici. "Now that's the kind of resume you need to have for a really good funeral."

"They'll be lined up in the street," Bridget decided.

"Perfect," said Dominic, "because I want the marching band to play 'American Pie' while everyone files past the casket."

Bridget and Cici laughed, but Lindsay pressed

her hands to her ears. "You people are ghouls," she said.

Dominic grinned. "Apologies, my love. But I do believe a well-done funeral is the reflection of a well-lived life."

"We should be planning a wedding," Lindsay grumbled, "not a funeral."

"That reminds me," Dominic said, "Cassie called this afternoon. She's put together a week of vacation days and is definitely committed to coming out for the wedding. So that gives us a Yes for all three of the kids. As soon as you set a date, of course."

Lindsay paused with her glass halfway to her lips, her attention sharpening. "Your daughter? She's coming?"

"She said she wouldn't miss it. Also," he admitted, "she thought the trip would give her a chance to meet with their east coast distributor, so it's a kill-two-birds-with-one-stone kind of thing."

Dominic had three children, but his daughter, who managed a winery in California, was the oldest, and the farthest away. Now that she had committed to coming all the way from California, the wedding had suddenly taken on new scope.

Lindsay realized she was looking a little non-plussed, so she forced a quick smile. "That's great. Your kids must really like you."

He laughed. "I like to think so."

"What I mean is, they're all coming such a long way, and it's a lot of trouble."

"I'd do the same for them."

"That's true, I guess."

"Besides . . ." He winked at her. "I think it's only natural to be a little curious about who your new stepmother is going to be."

Lindsay smiled, but it was a little weak.

"I think Katie would come from Chicago for my wedding," Bridget said thoughtfully, "if I decided to get married again. Of course, the twins would be flower girls."

"I'm sure Kevin could be talked into giving the bride away," Cici added.

Bridget made a wry face. "I think it's more likely he would refuse to give the bride away. Remember how hard he tried to talk me out of moving in here?"

"Up until the very minute we signed the papers," Cici agreed.

"He can be a little bossy," Bridget admitted. Then, "Don't you think Lori would come home from Italy for your wedding?"

"I'm not even sure she'd come home from Italy for my funeral." Cici's tone was glum, and she took another sip of her wine.

"And what do you hear from her?" Dominic asked.

Cici's daughter Lori, whose ambition was to be a winemaker, had apprenticed under Dominic during the summer, and he had more than a passing interest in her welfare. Though she reported she had secured another—paid, this time—apprenticeship at one of the most prestigious wineries in Italy, she was not as regular a correspondent as her mother would have liked.

"You probably hear more from her than I do," Cici admitted, her expression still dour. "She's still at Villa Laurentis, doing all sorts of obscure things with wine I can't even pronounce, and she seems very happy. She e-mails pictures every week or so. It looks like a beautiful place."

"Good for her," Dominic said. "I hope she's learning a lot and learning it fast, because we sure could use her help around here." "Here" began and ended for Dominic at the winery. "When is she coming home?"

Cici shrugged unhappily. "Who knows? If ever. I think," she confessed, "she's involved with that boy, that Sergio she'd been e-mailing with before she left. It's his father who owns the winery where she's working—and living, I might add."

Dominic chuckled. "I say again, good for her. Every young person should have two things in her life before she settles down: an adventure to remember, and an affair to regret."

Cici frowned. "You sound like Lindsay. She's the one who said every woman should be kissed by an Italian at least once."

Dominic glanced at Lindsay, his eyes twinkling. "Did you, now?"

"I think it's romantic," Bridget said with a sigh. "Lori's had a crush on this guy for over a year, she cancelled her wedding for him, flew across an ocean to meet him, and now she's living in his castle."

"Villa," corrected Cici, still frowning.

"Whatever. It's romantic."

"It's flighty and irresponsible."

Bridget gave her a dry look. "I'm starting to see why she doesn't call home more often."

"October twenty-fifth," Lindsay blurted.

Everyone stared at her.

Lindsay glanced around quickly, almost as though she was surprised to realize she had spoken out loud. But then she gave a decisive nod and repeated, "October twenty-fifth. That's our wedding day."

Dominic lifted an eyebrow. "Well, I don't know. I'll have to check my calendar." He, too, had learned to take Lindsay's constantly shifting dates in good humor.

Bridget smiled. "Sounds wonderful, Lindsay."

And Cici murmured, "Can't wait."

"No, I'm serious," Lindsay insisted. "This is it. October twenty-fifth."

"Okay."

"For sure this time. Really."

"We'll be there," Cici assured her.

Lindsay sat back in her chair and sipped her wine, looking satisfied. "You'll see. October twenty-fifth." She reached across and took Dominic's hand. He just smiled.

They sat for a time, sipping their wine, enjoying the gentle peace of the evening that floated down from the mountains and settled over the valley like a sigh. A bluebird landed on the feeder that Bridget had hung from the eaves of the porch, helped himself to a morsel or two, and darted away. Rebel the border collie raced across the lawn toward the house from the sheep pasture on a determined mission, then suddenly swerved in response to a call only he could hear and ran toward the woods; changed his mind and corrected course back toward the house. The chickens clucked and muttered as they found their roosts. A flock of barn swallows rose with a flutter of wings into the pale twilight sky.

Dominic said softly, "It seems only yesterday I was a boy sitting on this porch watching the day melt away. Where do the years go?"

Lindsay shared a quiet and private smile with him, and then with her two friends. "The more things change, the more they stay the same, I guess," she said.

Bridget added somberly, "There's nothing like a funeral to remind you how quickly the time passes."

Cici sipped her wine, watching a hummingbird

dart toward the feeder and then veer away. It all happened so quickly that the naked eye could not detect the pause the little bird had taken to drink from the feeder. "I feel bad," she said after a moment. "During the service, all I could think about was what a waste all those fresh flowers were. I know we weren't all that close to Maggie personally, but she did sell us this house and I realize now what I was trying *not* to think about was how she had changed our lives and how, now, everything is different. I know that doesn't make sense."

Bridget looked at her with an understanding, sympathetic smile, but Lindsay protested, "Things may be different, but they're better. Change doesn't always have to be a bad thing."

"I know." Cici blinked, surprised to feel the salty blur of tears. "But even good change is hard sometimes. We have Dominic and the winery and you're getting married and Paul and Derrick are living practically next door again and all of that is fabulous. But . . ." she cast an apologetic glance around the group, "as amazing as all that is, and it is amazing, I miss the way things used to be. My kid is having the time of her life in Italy, but I never hear from her and that makes me sad. And look at this place." A brief gesture encompassed the mountains, the lawns, the vines, the outbuild-ings. "It's more than we could have imagined when we started out. Remember how we almost froze to death that first winter? It's not that I ever want to go back there, or do the work that we did again to get here, but . . ." A brief, nostalgic smile touched her lips as she looked down into her glass, a little embarrassed. "I kind of miss the women we were then. And Maggie was a part of that."

Lindsay admitted uncomfortably, "I guess it was a little selfish of me to worry about not being able to use roses for the wedding. Without Maggie, there wouldn't even be a wedding."

The four of them were silent for a moment, contemplating the enormity of that truth. Then Dominic lifted his glass to the distant mountains, the sunset, the shadows sighing across the lawn. "To Maggie," he said. "You brought me my love . . ." he glanced at Lindsay, "my dear ladies . . ." the other two smiled as his gaze turned to them, "and you brought us all home. You will be remembered."

Cici, Lindsay, and Bridget lifted their glasses to his. "To Maggie," Bridget said, and added simply, "Thank you."

And when they drank, it was as much to themselves as to the one they had lost.

CHAPTER TWO
ಐಐ
There's Nothing Like a Good Plan

Late-summer mornings on Ladybug Farm began with the butter-yellow square of sunlight that crept across the age-worn brick floor of the kitchen from the east-facing window that opened onto the dining porch. A breeze might ruffle the blue tablecloth that draped the table there; a jewel of dew might glint from the lacy fabric of a spider web that spanned the petals of a fading hydrangea blossom in the garden below. The flutter of wings announced an early bird at the feeder while inside the kitchen a cupboard would open and close and utensils would rattle in the drawer as Ida Mae officially announced the beginning of a new day. In a moment the aroma of coffee would begin to waft its way throughout the house, perhaps to be joined in a few moments by the smell of cherry muffins baking or—if Ida Mae was feeling particularly contrary, because she knew the ladies were always watching their weight—bacon frying in the pan.

The rooster would crow lazily and the chickens would begin to cackle, the nanny goat would bleat a greeting, and Rebel the border collie would bark back. Before long the ladies would descend the grand staircase in their nightshirts and light summer robes, slippers scuffing and clattering on the polished mahogany treads. Coffee in hand, they would settle into the wicker chairs that were drawn up around the porch table and gaze out over the damp morning lawn with its colorful gardens and winding stone paths, listen to the birds chirping and rustling in the trees, and plan their day.

On most mornings.

On this morning, the first drops of coffee had barely begun to sizzle on the bottom of the automatic coffeemaker's carafe when Lindsay burst into Cici's room after the briefest of knocks and tugged the covers off her shoulders. "Family meeting," she said urgently, "Downstairs in ten minutes."

Cici bolted upright. "What happened? Is it Noah? Did Lori call?"

"No," Lindsay replied, "this is about me."

When Cici groaned and pulled the pillow over her head, Lindsay jerked it away and pummeled her lightly with it. "Hurry!" she called as she rushed from the room.

She crossed the wide, plantation-style hall and burst into Bridget's room in a similar fashion, her unbelted robe flowing behind her and bare feet slapping on the floor as she strode across the room. She swept open the heavy celadon damask drapes, then, for good measure, the embroidered ivory sheers. Bridget had done her room in an elegant Victorian style, which suited her personality, with floor-to-ceiling draperies, chandelier lamps, needlepoint footstools, and fringed throws. She was all but lost in the tall four-poster bed, squinting quizzically at Lindsay through the veil of her tousled bob as she pushed herself to a sitting position.

"What? What's wrong? Is it the kids? Have you heard from Noah? Is he okay?"

"No, they're fine," Lindsay assured her quickly, "but this is still important. Family meeting," she declared just before she sailed from the room, "ten minutes, in the kitchen."

"What is it?" demanded Bridget, flinging back the covers. "Is somebody in trouble?"

"Yes," Lindsay replied over her shoulder. "Me!"

Their faces barely washed and their hair barely brushed, Bridget and Cici met Lindsay in the big country kitchen slightly over ten minutes later. Ida Mae greeted them with a sour look. "Y'all're up with the chickens this morning," she said. "You gonna want eggs?"

"No, thank you, Ida Mae." Bridget opened the refrigerator door. "Just cereal and fruit for me."

"Good." Ida Mae started cracking eggs and separating the whites from the yolks into two bowls. "I'm gonna need them all for my angel food cake."

36

Cici smothered a yawn as she poured a cup of coffee. "You're making a cake? We still have half a pie left."

"Not for you. For poor old Mr. Farley. He's got nobody to cook for him now. You all can take it over to him after lunch."

Lindsay pushed the refrigerator door closed. "We'll eat later," she told Bridget. "This is an emergency."

"You know, Linds," Cici pointed out, "when you have one child serving in a war zone and another living halfway across the world with a complete stranger doing who-knows-what, 'emergency' is probably not a word you should bandy about at five forty-five in the morning."

Lindsay looked briefly chagrined. "I know. I'm sorry. But I was up half the night. I might not be thinking clearly."

Cici added to Ida Mae, "I'm sure Farley will appreciate the cake, but as far as I know, he never had anybody to cook for him but you and Bridget."

"Cici, focus, please?" Lindsay glanced frantically at the big Westminster kitchen clock on the wall. "Dominic will be here at seven and you know he always comes in for coffee. Ida Mae, this involves you, too. Everybody, sit down."

Lindsay took her place at the hickory table that was set in front of a now-empty fireplace, moving aside the vase of wildflowers to make room for the papers she had assembled during the long sleepless early morning hours. Bridget stirred sugar into her coffee, Cici raised a questioning eyebrow, and Ida Mae announced, "I'm not about to let my egg whites go flat listening to your folderol. I can hear you just fine from here."

Cici sat down, turning one of the papers toward her curiously. "What's this all about? What are you doing with our purchase agreement for the house?"

A sudden alarm shadowed Bridget's eyes as she came over to the table. "Lindsay, you're not going to sell your share, are you? You promised you wouldn't!"

Cici shot Bridget a quick warning look. "Not that we wouldn't understand if you did," she said. "That's why we have a contract. We just hope you won't."

Lindsay was shaking her head before Cici finished speaking. "No, that's not it. I told you, I'm not leaving Ladybug Farm. The thing is . . ." She drew in a deep breath, folded her hands in her lap, and announced, "I'm getting married."

Bridget eased into her chair, sighing in relief. Cici sipped her coffee.

"Seriously," Lindsay said. She looked expectantly from one to the other of them. "October twenty-fifth."

Ida Mae grunted skeptically and cracked another egg sharply against the side of the bowl.

Bridget said, "Ida Mae, save a couple of eggs and I'll make pancakes." She smiled. "That'll be a nice surprise for Dominic when he comes in."

Cici said, "I'll bet we have some strawberries in the freezer. I'll get them."

She started to get up, but Lindsay startled them both by slapping a manila folder down hard upon the center of the table. Cici sank back down into her chair. Bridget stared at her. Lindsay's expression was completely without mirth.

"October twenty-fifth," she repeated sternly. "That's barely six weeks away. This . . ." she took one paper out of the folder and shoved it toward Bridget, "is the guest list. You're in charge of the invitations. This . . ." another paper went to Cici, "is the diagram of the wedding ceremony and the reception. You're in charge of set up. This . . ." she presented another paper to Bridget, "is a sketch of my cake. White chocolate with raspberry filling *and* . . ." she tossed a triumphant look to both of them, "white chocolate roses with raspberry centers. Paul said you can order them online. Speaking of which—I mean whom—he'll be over for lunch to iron out the details. He's also bringing some shoes for me to try on with the gown."

"What about us?" Bridget put in hopefully. "Is he bringing bridesmaids gowns too?"

Paul Slater had been a syndicated style columnist and a widely acclaimed fashion guru before retiring with his partner Derrick only months ago to open the Hummingbird House B&B a few miles down the road from Ladybug Farm. He could still have his choice of designer gowns, shoes, and accessories delivered into his hands with nothing more than a phone call and the mention of a favor, which was how Lindsay came to be wearing Vera Wang at her wedding and her friends had hopes of doing the same.

"Don't be silly," Lindsay answered. "We can't order the gowns until we decide on the color scheme. Now."

She reached for another manila folder and began to sort through more papers. "These are the legal documents we have to talk about. I've been e-mailing back and forth with Delores, and she says we really need to modify our house-sharing contract if Dominic is going to move in here, even though my part of the deed will stay in my name—which I'm not changing, by the way. My name, I mean. After all, we'll be four now, and that changes everything."

Ida Mae said sharply, "What do you mean, you're not changing your name? You're getting married!"

"Women don't do that anymore, Ida Mae," said Cici, pulling one of the papers from the folder and glancing at it.

"Besides, at my age it's too much of a hassle," Lindsay explained. "Can you imagine all the places I'd have to notify after all these years?

Social Security, driver's license, pension fund, insurance, bank account . . . the paperwork alone would take the rest of my life."

"It's a crazy custom anyway," said Cici, who had resumed her maiden name after her divorce. "You'd think we would have done away with it by now. Why can't men change their names when they get married? Let them deal with the hassle."

Lindsay grinned. "I like it. Brand him like a cow so everyone will know who he belongs to."

"Why not? They've been doing it to us for centuries."

"That's not why it got started," Bridget said absently, turning a page on the guest list. "Having the women and children all take the man's surname was just a way of keeping up with family units."

"Even more ridiculous then," Cici said. "Anybody can claim to be a child's father, but there's never any doubt who the mother is. So children should take their mothers' last names. And so should husbands."

Ida Mae gave a disgusted sniff. "You women are an abomination unto the Lord. A woman takes her husband's name and that's that. You take your filthy mouths to somebody else's table."

"We didn't say anything dirty," Lindsay objected.

"Um, Lindsay." Bridget looked up from the guest list. "There are a hundred forty-eight people here. We don't even know that many people."

"I know," Lindsay admitted, looking worried, "but Dominic knows everyone in town, plus the people he worked with at Clemson, plus his family, who'll be coming in from all over the country—that reminds me, I've got to make reservations at the Hummingbird House—and I don't know where to start trimming it down. I've been working on it for weeks."

"Simple," said Cici, taking the list from Bridget and glancing at it over her coffee mug. "Family only. Twenty people, tops. Otherwise, if you start marking off people, somebody's bound to get their feelings hurt."

Lindsay's expression fell, but after a moment she gave a resigned sigh. "I really hate to do that. I mean, I'd hoped for something a little more . . . you know, festive, for Dominic. But I don't know how I can afford to feed a hundred fifty people, not to mention the wine."

"We'd have to take out a mortgage on the house." Cici returned the list to Bridget.

"Speaking of house," Lindsay said, her mind quickly jumping from one subject to another, "we're going to have to come up with a new way to divide the expenses once Dominic moves in. It's only fair."

Ida Mae gave a loud "Harrumph!" and clattered around in the cupboard for the hand whisk. "In my day, a woman got married, cleaved unto her husband, and moved into his house. That was it."

Lindsay craned her neck to look at her. "Ida Mae, don't you want Dominic to live here? That's why I wanted you at the meeting, so you could have a say."

"I am having my say, ain't I? It won't be no different than when he was a sprout, racing around here getting underfoot, always in one kind of trouble or another." She tucked the big glass bowl under her arm and began to whip the egg whites into a froth. "But it don't take a bunch of papers to make a home, that's what I'm saying."

"Oh, Ida Mae, why don't you use the electric mixer?" Bridget started to get up and find it for her. "You're going to wear yourself out, hand-beating those egg whites."

"You just sit there and meet," Ida Mae told her sternly. "I been beating my own egg whites going onto sixty years now and I don't reckon I'll be changing now."

Lindsay passed out papers to her friends, and put one at the empty place reserved for Ida Mae. "Here's the to-do list. Countdown, T-minus forty-five, which is how many days we have before the wedding."

"Wow, you made a spreadsheet," Bridget said, admiring it.

"There's a template on the Internet," Lindsay admitted.

"Shouldn't it be W-minus forty-five?" Cici suggested. "You know, W for wedding?"

"Where did they get T from anyway?" Bridget wondered. "What does it even mean?"

"I don't know. Who cares? T, W, whatever. The point is, we've only got forty-five days to get all of this done. Now, if you'll look in the first column . . ."

"You know," Cici felt compelled to point out, "it seems to me that whenever we got into trouble with planning a wedding, it was always because there was a short deadline."

"But we pulled it off," Bridget reminded her. "The first one was only a three-week notice. Forty-five days is practically forever."

"The point is," Lindsay said, "everything is all mapped out. Send out invitations, lock down menu, get license, get rings, order wine, order flowers, meet with officiator . . ."

"What about bridesmaids' dresses?" Bridget said, searching the spreadsheet. "Where do we come in?"

"It's on there, it's on there," Lindsay assured her impatiently. "Now, if you'll look on page two . . ."

Cici reached to the center of the table and thumbed through the papers there. "When did you have time to do all this? What got into you all of a sudden?"

"Dominic's *children* are coming," Lindsay said, and the way she widened her eyes at them made it seem as though the emergency should be perfectly self-explanatory. "And according to

44

Dominic, his daughter Cassie is the most organized, detail-oriented person in the western hemisphere, not to mention his favorite child—well, if parents are allowed to have favorites, which I'm not sure they are—and I'm not going to have her thinking her dad is marrying some kind of flake. Or worse, that I don't want to marry him at all! She's bound to be pestering him for updates, and I want him to be able to tell her everything is under control and right on schedule. And when she gets here I am going to be cool as a cucumber and she's going to find everything is shipshape, right on track, bright as a new penny, running like a Swiss clock!"

She paused for breath and Bridget added loyally, "She's also going to find that her dad has wonderful taste in fiancées."

Lindsay gave a decisive nod of her head. "Damn right."

Cici took a deep, thoughtful breath. "Well then. We'd better get busy painting the shutters."

"And the trim in the dining room," Bridget reminded her. "And we've got to do something about that hole in the carpet Rebel chewed when we brought him in during the ice storm last winter."

"You need to take down the drapes in the front room, too," Ida Mae said, whisking away, "and shake out all the dust mites."

"The chandelier needs to be taken apart and

washed in vinegar water," Lindsay added, scribbling on her spreadsheet.

"I'll tell you what you need," Ida Mae declared, whisking harder. "You need to ask that man of yours whether he even wants to move into a houseful of women. He might have a thing or two of his own to say about the whole thing, did you ever think of that?"

Cici and Bridget turned incredulous stares on Lindsay. "You mean you haven't even asked him what he wants to do?" Cici said.

Lindsay hesitated. "Well, not in so many words," she admitted. "Things have been a little up in the air, you know, but we always had an understanding we'd live here, of course we did." But even as she spoke a slight uncertainty came into her eyes and she looked from Cici to Bridget. "Didn't we?"

"We did," Bridget agreed, looking mildly distressed for her friend's sake. "But maybe he didn't."

Cici gave a small shake of her head. "A gentleman likes to be asked, Lindsay."

Lindsay looked momentarily taken aback, and she glanced distractedly over the papers that were spread across the table between them. "Well," she said in a moment, gathering confidence, "this is what this meeting is for. First we come up with a plan, then we get his approval. Right?"

Cici and Bridget nodded agreement, but Ida

Mae made an unintelligible sound as she slammed the bowl to the soapstone countertop with a clank. "Where's that dad-blasted mixer?" she muttered, and stomped off into the pantry.

Lindsay gave her departure only the mildest of curious glances, then turned back to the papers. "So," she said, picking up her pen. "What are we going to do with the dog?"

There was a thud, a crash, and an ear-piercing yowl from the pantry, followed by Ida Mae's declaration, "I'm gonna skin me a cat!"

Bridget leapt to her feet just as a blur of black and white fur exploded from the pantry. "Ida Mae, are you all right?"

Ida Mae appeared a second later, her iron curls quivering with righteous vengeance, a wooden spoon raised threateningly over her head. "That cat broke my best mixing bowl!"

"Well, thank goodness he didn't break your hip, is all I can say." Cici pushed back her chair as Bridget lunged after the kitten. "Bridget, you've got to do something about that cat. He's always pouncing on people and getting underfoot—somebody's going to trip over him and get hurt! I'll get a broom."

"Don't hit him with a broom!" cried Bridget, alarmed. She crouched down on the floor, trying to block the kitten as it skidded around a corner of the work island. She missed. "He's only a kitten! Here, kitty, here, Snowflake."

Cici gave her a sour look. "I meant I'll get a broom to clean up the mess. The mess *he* made."

Lindsay said, "Snowflake? Where did you get Snowflake?"

"I'm trying it out." Bridget scooped up the kitten, who responded with another angry squawk of protest, and cuddled it against her chest protectively. "You know, soft as a snowflake."

The first name Bridget had chosen for the new kitten was Ratatouille, which was cute until she realized the abbreviation was "Rat," or worse, "Ratty." Since then she had been through more kitten names than Lindsay had wedding dates, and none of them seemed to suit.

"Menace is more like it," Cici muttered, moving toward the broom closet.

"Hellfire is better," said Ida Mae, glowering as she tossed the spoon into the sink. "Whoever heard of animals in the house, anyway? Hair all over everything, shredding the furniture to ribbons . . . Miss Emily would have a fit."

"Well, good thing it's not Miss Emily's furniture," Bridget retorted. The kitten, as slippery as an eel, squirmed and wriggled to get down, but she held on tight. "He's too young to be left out at night. Besides, Rebel hates him."

"First good sense that dog has ever shown," Cici said, grabbing the broom and dustpan.

"Ladies, please," Lindsay said, "could we get back to the problem at hand?"

The clatter of broken pottery came from the pantry, and Ida Mae flung open a cabinet door, stretching for the flour canister. "Well, it ain't night now, and you can just get that creature out of my kitchen while I'm trying to make something fit to eat. Filthy animals. I never heard the like."

"This is a five thousand-square-foot house," Bridget went on, holding onto the kitten with both hands now. "Six bedrooms, six bathrooms, and at least three rooms we don't even have a name for! I think there's room for one little four-pound kitten."

"Not to mention a husband," responded Lindsay. "Ida Mae, be careful! Let me help you with that."

The flour canister threatened to tip over as Ida Mae dragged it toward the edge of the shelf and Lindsay bounded to her feet to help. Just then Cici pushed through the swinging door from the pantry with a dustpan filled with the shards of the broken mixing bowl. The door caught Lindsay's bare foot just as she walked into it and she squealed in pain, staggering back into Cici as she bent over to grab her injured limb. The broken pieces of the mixing bowl clattered to the floor and Cici cried, "Oh, Lindsay, I'm sorry! Are you okay?" Bridget reached out to steady Lindsay and the kitten launched itself from her arms and into the air, sailing across the countertop to land on Ida Mae's shoulder just as she was tilting the heavy flour canister off the shelf.

The flour canister exploded on the floor, spraying a volcano of flour into the air, covering countertops, faces, dishes, and clothing—not to mention the kitten—in a fine white ash. Ida Mae reached around and plucked the kitten off her shoulder. Bridget grabbed him before she could fling him across the room and snatched up a kitchen towel, trying to wipe the flour off his fur.

"*Now* he looks like a Snowflake," Cici observed, and then turned to Lindsay. "Lindsay, I didn't know you were there! Is it bad? Oh, be careful!" She grabbed Lindsay's arm just in time to prevent her from stepping back onto a shard of broken pottery.

"Look at this mess! Just look at it!" declared Ida Mae. "I told you what would come of having animals in the house! I told you! There goes my angel food cake. And what am I supposed to do with all these egg whites now? They won't whip up; they've got flour all in them."

"We'll put them back together with the yolks and make a nice quiche," replied Bridget distractedly. She gave up trying to clean the wriggling kitten and carried him to door. He sprang from her hands and across the yard as soon as she opened it. "Lindsay, are you okay? Should I get the first aid kit?"

"Do you see? All we have to do is talk about a

wedding and this is what happens!" Lindsay hobbled across the room and sank into her chair, bringing her injured foot to rest on her knee. "It's the curse of Ladybug Farm."

"There is no curse," Cici said, kneeling beside Lindsay. "Is it bleeding? Broken? Let me see."

Lindsay gingerly probed her bruised big toe, groaning out loud. "It's already starting to swell. I'm supposed to try on shoes today!"

"I'll get an ice pack," Bridget said quickly.

There was a light knock on the back door and Dominic came in. "Good morning, ladies." He paused, glanced around at the flour-covered kitchen, and remarked, "Doing some baking, I see."

Bridget, leaving a clean swath of skin across her face as she pushed back her hair, turned from the freezer with a quick smile. "Good morning, Dominic. I was going to make pancakes." She cast a swift glance around the disaster area and added, "It might take a minute."

"Thanks, but coffee is fine for now." He moved toward the coffee pot, dusted flour off a mug, and poured a cup.

Lindsay buried her face in her hands. Cici patted her knee reassuringly.

Dominic looked at Lindsay. "Everything okay, sweetheart?"

Lindsay mumbled something unintelligible into her hands, and Cici, with only a moment's hesitation, spoke up. "Family meeting," she said decisively, and stood. "You're invited."

Lindsay dropped her hands from her face, staring at her. Ida Mae made a satisfied sound in her throat, and Bridget hurried over with the ice pack. Dominic looked surprised, but then, with barely a hesitation, brought his coffee over to the table. Lindsay mumbled, "I think I broke my toe."

Bridget handed Lindsay the ice pack and sat down.

Dominic said with concern, "Do you want me to take you to the ER?"

"She's fine," Cici said, and Lindsay glared at her. "Have a seat."

He did, glancing at the papers. "What's all this?"

"It's our wedding plan," Bridget said.

Cici sat down, folded her hands atop the table, and leaned forward earnestly. "Dominic," she said, "I know Lindsay's been meaning to bring this up, but I think she's a little nervous so I say let's just get it out in the open."

Lindsay objected, "Cici!" and Dominic kept his expression guarded.

"This doesn't sound good so far," he said.

"But it is," Bridget assured him. "At least, we hope it will be."

Lindsay said, "Cici, really . . ."

Cici ignored her. "Dominic, we just want to say that we're really happy you're marrying us—I mean, Lindsay, of course—and want you to know that our house is your house. When we first decided to buy this place there was a lot of paperwork, but it's really not as complicated as it looks. We're a family now, and you're the best thing that ever happened to us—I mean, to Lindsay, of course—and we want you to be part of it. So we really hope that you'll consider moving in here when you and Lindsay are married, and making Ladybug Farm your home."

Bridget nodded in satisfied agreement. Lindsay sank back in her chair, her expression a mixture of astonishment, humiliation, and relief. Dominic's lips twitched with amusement as he looked from one to the other of them, and he said, "Why, I do believe that's the sweetest proposal I've ever heard."

Ida Mae clattered the broom and dustpan as she swept up the broken pottery. Bridget tossed over her shoulder, "Ida Mae, leave that. I'll get it in a minute."

Ida Mae clattered louder.

"We should have talked about this in private," Lindsay apologized.

"And a lot sooner," added Bridget.

"But now that we've got a countdown going," Cici said.

"To the wedding," Bridget clarified.

"There really isn't a lot of time to get these things settled," Cici finished. "No pressure, of course. But we want to make sure you know you're welcome here."

Dominic nodded, smiling. "Thank you."

He sipped his coffee. Lindsay looked at him questioningly. Bridget glanced at Cici, who seemed to have nothing more to offer. So Bridget said helpfully, "It's a really big house. You won't even know we're here. And there's plenty of room for your animals. We can fence off part of the pasture for the horses, and I've always wanted a house dog."

"That's very kind," Dominic said.

Lindsay looked a little uncomfortable. "Of course, you have your own things, with a lot of memories, and we never talked about what you'd want to do with your house . . . maybe you want to stay there, I can understand that. Of course, that might work too," she added, gaining confidence, "if we commuted back and forth. I mean, at this age, there's no such thing as a conventional marriage, is there? We can make our own rules. Whatever works, right?"

Cici added quickly, "We don't want to impose ourselves on your life—lives, I mean, yours and Lindsay's. We know it must seem like a lot of baggage to take on . . ."

"I would never refer to you lovely ladies as baggage," Dominic objected.

"Which is why, generally, when we have big decisions to make, we have a family meeting, like this one. And you're family now." Lindsay reached for his hand.

"Really," Bridget assured him. "So . . ." She practically held her breath. "What do you think?"

"Oh, for Pete's sake," Ida Mae declared impatiently, "will you tell them yes so they'll stop pestering? And somebody needs to drag out that vacuum from the storage room and clean up this mess."

Dominic's eyes twinkled. "Ladies," he said, "I'd be honored to join your household, and I'm even more honored that you'd want me." And just as their faces broke into smiles of relief, he added, "But there is one condition."

Lindsay looked at him cautiously. "What?"

He put his coffee cup on the table, stood, and reached into his pocket. "I couldn't help but notice," he said, opening the lid, "that your finger looked a little bare."

Lindsay barely had time to draw in a breath before he dropped to one knee. "You asked me the last time," he said. "I figured it was only fair that I should ask you back. Will you marry me?"

The ice pack that Lindsay had been holding to her foot smacked on the floor. She pressed her fingers to her lips and her eyes shone. "Oh, my," she said. "I mean, yes. Yes! Thank you!"

Laughing, she held out her hand and he slipped the ring on her finger. Cici and Bridget leapt to their feet, crowding around to see.

"Oh, Linds, it's gorgeous!"

"It's perfect!"

"Good job, Dominic!"

The ring was a silver twined vine pattern with a single round garnet surrounded by diamond chips. When Lindsay held out her hand, it caught the sunlight from the window and cast a brief spray of fractured pink light across the wall.

Dominic said, "I hope you like garnets. We didn't talk about it, but the color always makes me think of you."

"It's perfect," Lindsay said, and pressed both hands—the one with the ring on it prominently displayed—to her heart. She smiled into his eyes. He smiled into hers.

"Garnet!" exclaimed Bridget, clapping her hands together. "*That's* the color our dresses should be!"

"It's practically raspberry," agreed Cici. "Perfect with the cake."

"Lindsay! I have a pair of garnet drop earrings you have to wear! They can be your something borrowed."

Lindsay just kept smiling.

"Now all we have to do is decide on a flower in that color tone. Paul will have some ideas."

Dominic said, taking Lindsay's hand in his, "The wedding bands match. Do you want to see them?"

"I know!" Bridget exclaimed. "We'll use the ring pattern on the invitations! It looks like a grapevine, and that's the theme, right? Lindsay, take off the ring. Let me see it."

Just as Lindsay glanced at her in confusion, Ida Mae swatted Bridget across the rear with the broom, and then Cici. Both women yelped indignantly, and she commanded, "Get on out of their business, both of you! Can't you see the man wants to be alone with the woman he just proposed to? Now get! And bring me back that vacuum."

Bridget opened her mouth for an outraged objection, but Cici tilted her head meaningfully toward the couple and turned Bridget toward the door. Dominic pulled Lindsay onto her feet and into his arms. It was a truly beautiful moment until Lindsay, leaning in to kiss him, put weight on her injured foot and cried out, hopping on one foot while she tried to grab the other one to protect it. She knocked over a chair and almost fell, but Dominic caught her. Flailing for balance, she stepped back and onto a shard of broken glass that had escaped Ida Mae's broom . . . with her good foot.

Cici cringed and closed her eyes. "I can't watch anymore."

"I'll get the first aid kit."

Bridget and Cici hurried from the kitchen and closed the door behind them.

Five hours later a relative calm and order had been restored, which was to say that matters at Ladybug Farm were as orderly as they were likely to be for the next four weeks. Lindsay's feet, battered and bandaged but not permanently injured, were encased in soft open-toed slippers, which did not prevent her from trying on the wedding gown over her jeans and tee shirt while Bridget tried on the coordinating shoes and held her feet close to the hem of Lindsay's gown so that they could see the effect. Paul tried not to wince too notice-ably, but he couldn't prevent a sigh as he watched.

He was a tall, slender man with impeccably styled silver hair and a somewhat perpetually arch expression, exquisitely groomed and attired today in what he called his "rustic collection": tailored khakis and a windowpane-check shirt with the collar stiffened and turned up just so, the cuffs folded one and one-half turns, and the whole accented by a whimsical yellow kerchief tied with a half-Windsor simply because it brightened his mood. Although he had known Cici the longest, and adored Bridget with equal fervor, there was something special about his relation-ship with Lindsay. When she had asked Paul to walk her down the aisle, along with his partner Derrick, he'd actually felt the sting of tears in his eyes, and he hadn't wept over anything since the Gore-Bush election debacle. There was nothing he wouldn't do for her—for any of the girls, really—and he was determined that she was going to have the wedding of her dreams, even if it killed him. Or her.

"And to think," he murmured wistfully, watching Bridget balance on one foot as she tried to properly display each shoe against the hem of Lindsay's gown, "somewhere in this country at this very moment a bride is modeling gowns on a raised podium in a carpeted studio while her bridesmaids are sipping champagne on tufted velvet. Bizet is wafting through the speakers and the air is scented with just a hint of attar of roses. Two impeccably groomed attendants in dove-colored suits are pulling gowns while a dresser is taking measurements. Cici, please," he added, rushing forward quickly, "you know I love you, I do, but we simply cannot have cherry pie in the same room as white peau de soie!"

He took her fork in mid-bite and snatched away the plate. She gave him a sour look. "It *is* a dining room," she reminded him, and turned her attention back to the shoes Bridget was modeling—a different style on each foot—as he sailed through the door to the kitchen.

One of the best things about having Paul for lunch, aside from the fact that he brought with him a style portfolio, complete with samples, that was so heavy it required wheels, was the fact that Ida Mae considered company—any company—a grand occasion. While on an ordinary Wednesday the ladies would content themselves with a sandwich and a piece of fruit eaten at the kitchen counter for lunch, company required the dining room, the white tablecloth, a bacon and spinach quiche with hot rolls, salad and a freshly baked cherry pie. This worked out well because, once the dishes were cleared away, the big dining room table was perfect for spreading out samples. It did, however, limit the potential for seconds on dessert.

Lindsay, holding the strapless gown up at the bodice—it wouldn't quite zip over her jeans—peered down at Bridget's feet, which were as close as they could reasonably get to the hem of the dress. "I don't know," she said, craning her neck to see over the top of Bridget's head. "Which one do you think, Cici? The lace with the rose pattern or the satin with the buckle?"

"Neither one," Cici said. "The minute you step outside in those heels you're going to sink two inches into the mud. This is a vineyard wedding, remember?"

A flash of panic crossed Lindsay's eyes. "Oh, my goodness, you're right. How can I wear fabric shoes to an outdoor wedding?"

"By using an aisle runner," declared Paul, returning empty-handed from the kitchen. "And it's satin with the buckle, clearly."

Bridget held out the satin-clad foot skeptically. "A little young?"

"You can dress in the barn," supplied Cici with a nod, "I mean, winery. And if we set up right where the hill starts to crest, facing the vines, we'll only need about twenty feet of runner. That should keep your shoes clean."

Lindsay grinned. "I like that. It's a vineyard wedding, so I dress in the winery."

"Not too young at all," Paul told Bridget, holding out his hand for the shoe. "We're going to take off the buckle and replace it with a pearl cluster rosette."

Lindsay clapped her hands together. "Perfect!"

Bridget returned the shoes to Paul and Cici helped Lindsay shuffle out of the dress, folding it carefully at the waist to keep the hem off the floor. "The weather could be cold in October," she said. "You're going to need a jacket."

"And cover up this cleavage?" Lindsay looked horrified. "I don't think so."

Paul strode over to the garment bag he had spread out on the buffet and unzipped it, removing a long-sleeved lace jacket with a flourish. "It's a size four," he said, holding it up to Lindsay's chest, "but we can put in a few lace panels—no offense darling, you know you are the perfect size," he added quickly when Lindsay glared at him. "It's just that these vicious models with their disgusting binge-and-purge habits make life impossible for the rest of us. And look, it fastens here, just under the bust, so we have even more natural enhancement of the cleavage."

"Well . . ."

He swept the jacket away and whipped out two

hats from an oversized round box. "What do you think, ladies? Portrait hat or cloche?"

He set each hat on Lindsay's head and when Bridget and Cici agreed unanimously, "Portrait!" he rolled his eyes and put the big hat back into the box. "Cloche, obviously," he told them, and set the rolled satin hat slightly askew on Lindsay's head, twisting her hair into a rope over the opposite shoulder. He turned Lindsay toward the big gilt-framed mirror on the wall. "Fabulous, yes? And picture the half-collar of the jacket framing your face from the back . . . you will be a walking poem!"

"Yes," agreed Lindsay, eyes sparkling as she made a miniscule adjustment to the hat. "I will!"

Paul plucked the hat from her head and, ignoring Lindsay's protest, began to rewrap it in the blue tissue from which it had come. "No more time to play, girls. Moving on, moving on. We have decisions to make if we're going to keep this event on schedule."

Lindsay turned down a corner of her mouth and murmured, "And I thought *I* was going to get to be the Bridezilla."

"I heard that," replied Paul.

Ignoring them both, Bridget said, "Enough about her. What about our dresses?" She went to the table and began turning pages in the over-sized five-ring binder that was the style sample book. "Good heavens, Paul, you should go into the business. Look at all of this, Cici."

"Darling, if I were in the business, you couldn't begin to afford me." He spun the binder around, flipped to a new section, and turned it back toward Bridget. "Waltz length, bell skirt, three-quarter length sleeve cuffed at the elbow, braided gold belt four inches above the waist."

"Does it come in garnet?" Cici wanted to know, peering over Bridget's shoulder.

Paul reached into a plastic pocket on the design page and pulled out a swatch. "Also known as claret," he said, presenting it to her with a flourish. "The *only* color for autumn. And for you, my gorgeous blonde . . ." He took out another swatch for Bridget. "French rose, your signature color."

"I always wear pink," complained Bridget.

"That's because it's your signature color," Paul explained patiently. "And it does magical things for your skin."

"Well . . ." Bridget held up the swatch near her face and turned to the mirror.

"Nice," said Cici, rubbing the swatch of fabric between her fingers. "Shot silk." She looked at him hesitantly. "How much?"

"Designer label, off the rack prices," he assured her. "And I can get them both in two weeks. Now for the bouquets . . ."

"No roses," Lindsay warned, limping to the table.

He gave her a disdainful look. "Of course, roses. They're your signature flower. Garnet for Bridget, French rose for Cici, and a mixture of both, accented with ivory, for you."

"But the funeral . . ." Lindsay protested.

"Will be long forgotten by then. Roses, definitely."

"I don't know." Lindsay looked worried as she sank into the chair in front of the style book. "It might be bad luck. I don't want to take any chances."

Bridget leaned over her shoulder, turning pages of the book. "What do garnet roses look like anyway?"

"There is no such thing as bad luck when I'm in charge," Paul assured Lindsay airily. "Only expertise, precision, and execution. Speaking of which, we will of course be hosting your engagement party at the Hummingbird House, and it will be perfection personified. I'm thinking a champagne garden party, and we'll invite all our old friends from the city . . ."

"Oh, Paul! You'd do that for me?" Lindsay's face lit up and she clapped her hands in delight. "You're the best!"

She sprang up from the chair to hug him just as Bridget reached across her and lifted the heavy book off the table, saying, "Here they are! Cici, look."

She swung around with the book as Lindsay

lunged forward. Lindsay slammed into the book—
or the book slammed into her—so hard that it
knocked her back down into her chair. She just sat
there for a moment, clutching her cheek and
looking like a bird that had just flown into a
window, while her equally stunned friends
watched in horror as the flesh beneath her right
eye began to turn a purplish-red color.

"Well," Lindsay said after a moment, weakly,
"as long as there's no such thing as bad luck."

"Seriously, ladies." Paul gave Bridget a look of
mild reprimand as he replaced the dripping wet
washcloth that Cici had hastily procured from the
nearby washroom with a proper ice bag for
Lindsay's eye. "We are on a very short deadline
here and we have no hope whatsoever of meeting
it unless the bridesmaids stop beating up the
bride."

"It's not their fault." Lindsay scrunched down
in her chair so that her head was resting on the
back and applied the ice bag gingerly to her eye.
Cici and Bridget hovered helplessly. "It's mine.
What was I thinking? We should elope."

"Don't be absurd," Paul replied, "you can't go
anywhere looking like this."

"She thinks weddings at Ladybug Farm are
cursed," Cici told him.

"Well," Paul admitted, beginning to gather up
his samples, "she may have a point. Not . . ." he

raised a finger to ward off Cici's indignant protest, "that that has anything to do with the wedding at hand. After all," he pointed out to Lindsay, "you live here. This is your home. Everyone else was just visiting."

Lindsay slowly removed the ice pack from her eye and straightened up, looking slightly less miserable. "That's right," she agreed cautiously. "I suppose that could make a difference."

"Without a doubt," he assured her.

"Besides," Bridget added helpfully, "with only twenty people, how much could go wrong?"

Paul froze in place, staring at her. "Twenty people? You can't be serious. We can't possibly have a wedding for only twenty people. That's not a wedding, it's a dinner party! How does one even *do* that?"

"That's what I thought," Lindsay said, looking miserable again. "But . . ."

"But if we start trimming the guest list, someone's feelings are going to be hurt, and we can't afford a sit-down wedding and reception for a hundred fifty people," Cici explained. "So we're just inviting family and that's just the way it is."

"Besides," added Bridget, remembering that she was in charge of invitations, "we don't have time to send out that many invitations. Literally."

"Well, it's totally unacceptable." Paul gave a quick flick of his wrist, dismissing the possibility, and turned back to packing his samples. "Let's

66

make it happen, people, think outside the box. We are not having a mini-wedding in Vera Wang, we simply are not, and *that* . . .” he tossed a challenging look at Cici as he snapped a sample case closed, “. . . is the way it is.”

Cici opened her mouth for self-defense, glanced at Lindsay, who had shrunk back into her chair with the ice bag covering half her face, and changed her mind. She muttered, “We’ll figure something out.”

Paul air-kissed Lindsay’s cheek and Bridget and Cici helped him carry the samples to the car. “I mean it, ladies,” he told them sternly just before he left. “We are not going to let our bride down. After all, what are the chances of her ever finding another man at her age?” Then, glancing at his watch, “Must fly. We have two guests checking in this afternoon and I have to set up the sherry tray. They’re architects! Come for brunch Sunday, we’ll iron out a plan. Kisses!” And, waving to them from the window, he drove off.

Cici followed his departure with a sour look, but Bridget just sighed and sat down on the front steps. “He’s right, you know,” she said. “A wedding where no one comes is almost as bad as a funeral where no one comes. And to go from a hundred fifty people to twenty . . . it is kind of sad.”

Cici sat beside her. “The church was full at my wedding,” she admitted. “My parents spent a fortune, for all the good it did. If we'd had to pay for it ourselves we would have been in debt for years after we were divorced."

"But you got to be queen for a day," Bridget reminded her. "And you got to have your picture taken looking as beautiful as you've ever looked in your life . . ."

Cici smiled reminiscently. "Yeah, I did. Of course . . ." she slid a sideways glance at her friend. "I was up all night cutting Richard out of those pictures three years later."

"I know none of us are kids anymore, and no one wants to spend her life savings on a party," Bridget said. "But Lindsay's first wedding wasn't very memorable and I know she was hoping this one could be really special."

"Well then," said Cici, with resolve, "we're just going to have to make it special."

"All we need is a plan," Bridget said.

"Right," said Cici, leaning back on her elbows to contemplate the options. But her tone was a little flat as she added, "Because that's worked out so well so far."

Bridget glanced at her, searched for an argument, and found none. In the end she just folded her hands under her chin, leaned her elbows on her knees, and agreed glumly, "Right."

They sat there, searching for inspiration, for another ten minutes, but they never found it.

"The ring is precious," reported Paul, shaking out the wrinkles of a peacock blue silk throw and arranging it in a precise triangle at the foot of the bed. "Garnet, of course, but it's very on-trend to use semiprecious stones these days. And there *are* diamonds in the setting."

Derrick said, "Well he certainly took his time putting it on her finger, if you ask me."

"Custom designed," Paul pointed out.

"Well, in that case . . ." Derrick, looking slightly mollified, gave the silver candy dish on the nightstand a half turn, then frowned. "Purline!" he called.

Their ponytailed housekeeper entered the room with a stack of fluffy towels, cobalt blue to match the color of the door that opened onto the low-roofed porch that encircled the lodge. Each room had its own entrance from the porch, and each door was painted a different, vibrant color. At first Paul and Derrick had found that bizarre, but soon came to embrace the eccentricity. Color-coding the accessories to match each door also helped Purline, who was always complaining about their fussiness, keep up with what went where.

"What?" she demanded now, snapping her gum. "You find a smudge on the windowpane or something?"

"Fives and sevens, my dear," Derrick explained with an exaggerated air of forbearance. "Remember? We always display in odd numbers." He indicated the small silver tray which, as anyone could plainly see, contained only six wrapped Godiva chocolates.

Paul said quickly, "I'm afraid that's my fault. I ate one."

Purline rolled her eyes and took the towels to the bathroom, and Derrick gave Paul a disappointed look.

"At any rate," Paul went on, "the poor girl is a wreck." He fluffed the arrangement of autumn wildflowers that were displayed in a hammered copper bowl on the table in front of the window. "I honestly don't know what she'd do without me."

"All brides are nervous," Derrick said. "It's part of their charm." He examined the arrangement of blue and cream candles in the fireplace with a critical eye. "I don't know. Time to change the display to firewood?"

"Heavens no," said Paul. "That would only encourage the guests to light a fire."

"I don't know what you're worried about," said Purline, returning from the bathroom. "I'm the one that has to clean the ashes."

Derrick said, "Purline, please . . ."

"Candy, right." She paused to fold the throw at the foot of the bed into a neat rectangle, blew a bubble with her gum, and snapped it on the way out.

Paul immediately rearranged the throw into the perfect triangle in which he'd originally placed it. "Lindsay has bigger problems than pre-wedding jitters," he confided. "She's nothing but one accident after another, bumping into things, tripping over things, getting hit by things . . ."

"I knew a woman like that once," said Purline, returning with the box of candy. "Turned out she was blind in one eye and didn't even know it." She held up a gold wrapped chocolate between her thumb and forefinger, showing it to Derrick, and then placed it deliberately in the center of the candy tray.

Paul and Derrick shared a brief concerned look, then Paul said, "I'm sure that's not it. At any rate, Lindsay is completely convinced there's a curse on weddings held at Ladybug Farm."

"She may have a point," conceded Derrick. He nudged the chocolate that Purline had just placed a fraction to the left, then gave the dish another quarter turn. He stepped back to admire the effect. "If you think about it, every time they've tried to host a wedding, there have been problems."

"If you call a tornado a problem," agreed Paul.

"Or a runaway bride."

"I knew a fella that was hexed once," said Purline, punching up one of the down-filled cushions that lined the Queen Anne love seat in front of the fireplace. "Every one of his teeth fell out, then he lost his job down at the water plant—'course, that might've been because he was so ugly, without any teeth—then he cut off his pinky with a band saw, then his wife left him and his dog ran away. Got to where people'd cross the street when they saw him coming, for fear it was catching."

Paul and Derrick looked at each other with a mixture of skepticism and dismay. Purline began fluffing the pillows on the bed.

"If you ask me," Derrick said, discreetly returning the center crease to the cushion Purline had just fluffed, "it's too soon after Lori's broken engagement. Maybe there *is* a little lingering bad juju. It's practically the same date, for heaven's sake, and she's even wearing Lori's gown."

"Lori, the little heathen, hated the Vera Wang," Paul reminded him. "She wanted to cut it off at the knees and add a denim jacket!" His eyes darkened with recalled pain. "She said it was fussy! Right in front of me!"

Derrick winced sympathetically. "There, there."

"I couldn't snatch it off her fast enough," Paul said, his tone still disgruntled. He went behind Purline and rearranged the pillows on the bed. "And don't let me forget—we've got to find someone who can get the alterations done in a month."

"And that's another thing," Derrick said. "Who plans a wedding in a month?"

"Worse," Paul said, "we've got to plan an engagement party in twenty days."

Purline said, "My mama does sewing. She could get it done for you in half the time."

Paul gave her a smile that he hoped wasn't too condescending. "Thank you, Purline. But . . . well. It's *Vera Wang*."

Derrick said, aghast, "Twenty days?"

Purline shrugged. "Suit yourself. But she made twenty choir robes in two weeks last year. Everybody still says that's the best-dressed choir in the county." Then she frowned sharply, "You're not expecting me to cook for this party of yours, are you? I told you, I don't do parties."

"Of course not, dear." Paul gave her arm a reassuring pat. "We're having it catered."

"On twenty days' notice?" Derrick's eyebrows lifted. "Good luck with that. The only person we know who could do a turnaround like that is Bridget, and I suspect she'll be a tad busy with the wedding."

"What about that young fellow who did our grand opening? He turned out to be quite remarkable, despite the debacle with the hummingbirds which, to be perfectly fair, wasn't entirely his fault. And I'm sure he'd do us a favor. After all, we practically made his career."

"We *did* make his career," Derrick assured him, "not to mention his fortune—or at least his wife's. They're moving to Dallas to open their own restaurant, I'm sure I told you. They're calling it Annabelle's."

"Dallas," murmured Paul, disappointed. "That is rather far."

"We got a lovely note from them. Didn't you see it?"

"Actually," Paul said a little hesitantly, "we might not know a caterer, but we do know someone who knows every caterer on the east coast."

"Do you mean . . ." Derrick straightened up from refluffing the pillows and looked across at him, his eyes clouding with dread. "Harmony?"

Harmony Haven had become a more-or-less permanent guest at the Hummingbird House. To say she was eccentric would be to damn with faint praise, but she was eminently connected in the hospitality industry and, despite her many flaws, had a way of always coming through in a pinch.

"It's not," Derrick went on quickly, "that she didn't completely save us from certain doom the last time, and no one can deny that she's more than capable of getting the job done but . . . seriously? Must we?"

"You know we're not going to be able to keep her out of it," Paul explained practically. "We may as well put her to good use."

"Well, if that woman's involved," declared Purline with a decisive snap of her gum, "you can leave me out of it for sure." She took the throw off the bed before Paul could stop her, shook it out, and folded it into a square. She glanced toward the window at the sound of tires crunching on gravel. "Your folks're here. Fancy car. Look like big tippers." She started toward the door. "Guess y'all want me to set out the good wine."

"It's *all* good wine," Paul muttered under his breath, because it was hardly the first time he had told her so, while Derrick said, more pleasantly, "Thank you, Purline. That would be lovely."

Then, with one last critical look around the room, they went to greet their guests.

CHAPTER THREE
❧
Children and Other Disasters

TO: LadiLori27@locomail.net
FROM: Bridget@LadybugFarmLadies.net
SUBJECT: Wedding News

Lori,
You won't believe it! We have a real wedding date, with a spreadsheet and a countdown and a to-do list and everything. It's October 25, 4:00 p.m., on the hill over-looking the vineyard, with a reception to follow in The Tasting Table. We haven't quite ironed out all the details but this time it's really on! You'll be here, won't you? Because Lindsay and Dominic would be SO dis-appointed if you weren't! Dominic was just saying the other day how much he misses your help in the winery. I know you're doing important work and this is a once-in-a-lifetime chance for you, but we really miss you here. So even if you can't come home forever, please, please try to come home for the wedding.

I wish you could see the sunflowers in the garden. They're taller than you are! Lindsay wants to harvest them and toast the seeds, but I say leave them for the birds. The cardinals love them, and there is nothing prettier than those red birds when the ground is covered with snow. Except maybe the sunflowers.

I was going to send pictures of the new kitten but they all turned out blurry. I'm thinking of calling him Casper.

Write soon. We love you!—
Bridget

TO: LadiLori27@locomail.net
FROM: Cici@LadybugFarmLadies.net
SUBJECT: Wedding News

Hi Sweetie,

I guess you've heard from Aunt Lindsay by now that we have a new wedding date— Oct. 25—and this one appears to sticking. We're mailing twenty-five hand-designed invitations this week so it had better be! Yours will probably make it through the Italian postal system by Christmas. It would mean so much to both of them if you could be here. I know your dad would send you the ticket (even if it does have to be round-trip☹). Please let us know so we can kill the fatted calf. (Just kidding! No calves, and even if there were Bridget wouldn't let us kill it even if we were all starving and it was the last edible thing on earth.) I wish I heard from you more often. Do you need more minutes on your phone? I know you said the signal is really weak there, which I guess is why I'm never able to get through when I call, but maybe you could go to town once in a while and call your old mom? I love you, sweetie, and miss you like crazy—

Mom

TO: LadiLori27@locomail.net
FROM: Lindsay@LadybugFarmLadies.net
SUBJECT: Wedding News

Hi Lori!

You are cordially invited to attend the nuptials of Lindsay Sue Elizabeth Wright and Dominic Robert DuPoncier October 25 of this year at four p.m. at Ladybug Farm, Virginia. A reception will follow at The Tasting Table restaurant on the premises. The pleasure of your company will be most fervently appreciated!

RSVP the sooner the better. Dominic says we'll drink the first toast with Ladybug Farm wine, but how can we do that if the winemaker isn't here? We love you and miss you—

Lindsay & Dominic

Lori sat on the sagging brown sofa in the tiny lobby of her hostel and struggled to find a Wi-Fi signal on her phone, crushed between a sweaty fat man who was shouting either German or Portuguese—she had no clue which one—into his cell phone and a doe-eyed teenage boy who kept inching his leg closer to hers and smiling at her in an enraptured way. The sofa was covered in dog hair, although she'd never seen a dog inside, and smelled of garlic—although, come to think of it, that might have been the oversized gentleman to her left. The manager, a black-eyed, greasy-haired man with a perpetual two-day growth of beard, kept craning his neck to look at her from behind the desk, and whenever Lori happened to glance up he would wink and his leer would only grow wider, revealing teeth that were as yellow as the stains on his shirt. She had grown used to the creepiness factor by now and, for the most part, found him easy to ignore.

The sweaty German, on the other hand, was proving to be more of a challenge.

She knew she stood out in the small Italian village with her cascade of wild red curls, her porcelain white skin and blue eyes. She'd thought that would be an advantage, and she played it as much as she could, but the effort was getting old. Besides, standing out was not as much fun as it should have been in a culture that valued testosterone more than it did common sense. Or at least that's the way Lori saw it.

She typed: Mom, great to hear from u! She paused, shifted her weight a little to avoid the encroachment of the teenager's thigh—he had the body temperature of a blast furnace—and then shrank back as she felt a wedge of flabby skin press into her opposite side, leaving a damp patch on her sleeve. She thought about standing up and walking away but she knew from experience that the only Wi-Fi signal in the entire building began at one arm of the sofa and ended at the other.

She deleted the sentence and tried again. Congrats, Aunt Lindsay! Wish I could be there but

But what? She looked around the dingy little room and couldn't think of a single way to finish that sentence.

The hostel had once been a municipal building of some sort, and must have been magnificent in its day. Now the black and white terrazzo tiled floor was so covered with embedded grime that the difference between the black tiles and the white tiles was only a matter of degree. The wide marble staircase was stained yellow with half a century of cigarette smoke, and the scrolled marble banister was so encrusted with neglect that it was sticky to the touch. At first Lori had been horrified at the casual disregard with which the fine craftsmanship of these ancient buildings was treated, but after the first month she had begun to see the historic structures the way the natives did—not as treasures, but as just old.

The two arched windows that faced the street were boarded over, but the front door was open to admit a trickle of dingy light and the smell of dank sewer water from the street beyond. Lori's eight-by-eight cell of a room with its one narrow window was already so hot and stuffy at ten o'clock in the morning that she was grateful for any semblance of a breeze at all, even one that smelled like garbage and urine.

She erased the message and typed: Aunt Bridget, thanks for the great news! I hope this time is the charm. I wish I could see the sunflowers.

She stopped typing because the words in her head were coming too fast to keep up with her fingers. *I wish I could see the sunflowers and Aunt Lindsay's rose garden, especially the way it looks in late summer after a rainstorm with the petals scattered all over the grass like multi-colored confetti. I wish I could see the kitten chasing shadows on the porch, and I wish I could sit and watch the sun set over the mountains with you. I wish I could be in the kitchen when you're baking sticky buns for breakfast and the whole house smells like cinnamon, or when Ida Mae is roasting a chicken for Sunday dinner, and the way she puts those fresh herbs under the skin that get all buttery crisp, or even when it's canning season and tomato juice is everywhere and the humidity in there is like a steam bath and everything smells like vinegar . . . I wish I could wake up to Rodrigo the rooster crowing in the middle of the night, and watch Rebel chase the sheep across the meadow, and oh, what I wouldn't give for just one slice of your pecan pie. I wish I were there, I wish I were there, I wish I were there . . .*

She stared at the screen until her vision cleared and the hot moisture left her eyes. Then she erased the message and started over.

TO: Cici@ LadybugFarmLadies.net,
  Bridget @ LadybugFarmLadies.net,
  Lindsay @ LadybugFarmLadies.net
Cc: Dominic@LadybugFarmsWine.biz
FROM: LadiLori27@locomail.net
SUBJECT: Your Wedding News

Hi everyone!
Great news about the wedding date. So excited for you!! You totally should have the burning of the vines ceremony the same day, print up flyers, get it in the paper, send out a press release to the travel mags, put it on the website—great publicity for the winery! I would love love LOVE to be there and am going to do my very best. I promise. Things are really busy here this time of year so I must rush! More later. Love you all!
  Lori

PS. Here is a picture I took this morning of the view from my window at the villa. Am I the luckiest girl in the world or what? Send kitty pix!

Lori scrolled through her pictures folder for one of the hundreds of photographs of the Tuscan hillside she had taken when she first arrived, made sure it wasn't one she had already sent, and attached the file to the e-mail. She turned her phone this way and that, searching for the optimal number of bars on the Wi-Fi. The fat man shouted into his cell phone. She felt the teenager's arm slide down between their bodies, fingers rubbing up against the back of her jeaned thigh. She ignored both until she found the signal and pushed Send.

Lori dropped the phone into her jacket pocket and zipped it up. She'd learned to keep everything she valued in zippered pockets on her body shortly after she'd arrived. Then she turned to the teenage groper and seized an inch of his skinny bicep between her thumb and forefinger. She twisted until his eyes bulged out and he tried to jerk away. She leaned in and twisted harder. When he cried out and staggered to his feet, the man on the cell phone stopped shouting in her ear and stared at her.

Lori released the teenager and growled into his face, "You're lucky all I could reach was your arm."

She glared at the sweaty fat man and added fiercely, "You're next."

She strode out of the lobby and into the street, showing the desk clerk her middle finger as she went. He grinned in reply. It had become their routine, and he would miss it when she was gone.

The office of Ladybug Farm was a repurposed sewing room located on the back side of the house in a space underneath the grand staircase. Cici had built shelves and a nook for the desk, and Lindsay and Bridget had decorated it in bright yellows and reds. Here they accessed the Internet, paid bills, kept the household records, and coordinated all other aspects of Ladybug Farm not related to the winery. But the most important thing they did was video chat, all too infrequently and always too briefly, with Private Noah Wright of the United States Marine Corps.

Noah had first come into their lives as a fourteen-year-old runaway, the son of an alcoholic father and an absentee mother, who showed up one day to do odd jobs for them and was eventually found to be living in the abandoned folly on the edge of their property. Lindsay, the perennial teacher, had taken him under her wing and discovered that beneath that rough exterior there was not only an astonishingly acute mind, but an unexpected talent for art. After the death of both his parents two years later, Lindsay had officially adopted him, but he was in fact the child of everyone at Ladybug Farm.

Charcoal sketches of jeeps, guys in desert camo, bleak Middle Eastern landscapes and native children now adorned the walls of the Ladybug Farm office, edging out oil paintings of poppies and framed vacation photos. Noah confessed that he had become popular in his unit mostly because of his ability to send sketches home to wives and girlfriends, a skill he owed in great part to his teacher and his mother, Lindsay. And even though it had broken Lindsay's heart when he had chosen the military over college, not even she could deny a swell of pride to see the skinny, sullen teenage boy they once had known now transformed into the straight-shouldered, square-jawed young man with buzz cut dark hair whose face filled the computer screen.

"I don't know, Mom," he said a little ruefully, "I don't think they let you out of the Marines to go home for a wedding." And he frowned a little, looking more closely into the camera. "What happened to your eye?"

There was a slight time lag, and when Lindsay waved her hand in front of her face it appeared on camera as a series of jumpy staccato blurs. "Nothing," she said. "Bridget hit me with a book."

"Not on purpose!" Bridget piped up indignantly behind her.

Cici said, leaning in close to Lindsay's shoulder

to be seen, "We know you can't come home, Noah. We just want you to know how much we miss you."

"And you might get leave," Lindsay insisted. "Dominic and I would love it if you could stand up for us."

He said, "Me too. But you can send me pictures."

A flash of panic crossed Lindsay's face. "Photographer!" She looked at Cici. "How could I have forgotten the photographer?"

Bridget pushed in front of her for the camera. "How are you eating, Noah? Is the food okay?"

"Sure," he replied. "The chow is great." He wrinkled his nose a little and admitted, "Well, not great. Not as good as yours. Not very good at all, really. But there's plenty of it. I sure did like those cookies you sent."

"I'm mailing more today," she promised him. "And some cotton socks and paperback books."

He looked puzzled. "They give us socks, you know."

"I know, but I read on the Internet—"

"And I'm sending a new drawing pad," Lindsay said. "Portrait grade like you asked for. And two gum erasers and a charcoal pencil sharpener."

"Hey, cool. Thanks. I can't find them in the PX."

"Do you need anything else?" Cici asked. "Blankets or a warm coat or—"

"Come on, guys." His smile was both self-conscious and affectionate. "It's the desert. And I'm a Marine."

"Well, I'm sure I don't know what that's supposed to mean," Lindsay began tartly, but Dominic came up behind her just then and laid a hand on her shoulder.

"It means he can take care of himself," he reminded her. He leaned into the camera and said, "How's it going, Private?"

Noah grinned. "Hey. I hear they finally got a rope on you."

"That's what I hear too. I count myself a lucky man." His fingers massaged Lindsay's shoulder lightly.

"Yes, sir. I'd count you right."

Lindsay leaned her head back to smile up at Dominic.

Dominic said, "We sure miss your help around here, son. You get home safe, you hear?"

"Yes, sir."

Dominic added casually, "Say, who's guarding the gate over there, anyway?"

Noah returned forcefully, "The Marines are, sir!"

Dominic grinned, gave him a two-fingered salute, and straightened up. Cici took his place. "We're putting another prepaid phone card in the box, too," she said. "You'll call when you get it, won't you?"

"Yes, ma'am. As soon as I get to a phone tent."

He glanced over his shoulder. "Listen, my time is about up. How's that ol' dog? What do you hear from Jonesie? Do you see Amy much? How's she looking?"

They spent the next ten minutes catching him up on all the local news and goings-on around the farm, and when it was time for him to go the ladies all blew kisses, as they always did, and he looked embarrassed, as he always did, but also secretly pleased. When the screen went dark. Lindsay sat back in the chair and everyone was quiet, feeling empty.

"He looks good," Dominic said.

"Did you see those shoulders?" Bridget added.

"He said he was lifting weights," Cici reminded her.

"He's changed," said Lindsay, sadly.

"But in a good way," Bridget insisted.

Lindsay said, "He doesn't need us anymore." She shifted her gaze upward to Dominic and added, "You were right. I was afraid the Marines would turn him into one of those mean-eyed, robot-brained brutes you see on TV, but you were right. He's different, but better. Grown up."

"The military can ruin some boys," Dominic admitted, "but others know what to do with it, how to take advantage of what it offers. That kid never had anybody before you ladies who cared enough about him to make him challenge himself. He's going to be fine. Now." He caught

Lindsay's fingers and pulled her to her feet. "How about coming down to the office and helping me with some of this bookkeeping? I need to check the irrigation pump, and start netting the vines before the birds eat our crop."

Cici said, "Do you need any help?"

"Yeah." He looked wry. "How about giving that daughter of yours a call and see if she can be here by lunchtime? What this winery needs right about now is another winemaker."

Bridget took Lindsay's place at the computer as she and Dominic left the room and opened up a search page. "Do you suppose there even *is* a wedding photographer around here?"

"Try Staunton."

"We don't need anything fancy—none of those sepia still-lives with the bride's veil floating against a sunset sky—but it would be nice to have a couple of good portraits, especially since who knows when we'll ever get a chance to wear those dresses again. And of course," she added, "Lindsay and Dominic will want one to frame."

Cici gazed thoughtfully at the door through which the couple had left. "Have you thought about what we're going to give them for a wedding present?"

"Well," said Bridget, typing, "we're giving them a wedding."

"I know, but Lindsay's paying for it, and if we can't figure out a way to trim that guest list without having half the county mad at us—not to mention Dominic—"

"And Paul."

"—it won't be much of a wedding." Cici tapped a finger against her lips thoughtfully. "It should be something they both can enjoy. And it should be nice."

Bridget stopped typing and glanced up at her. "What do you have in mind?"

"I'm not sure yet," Cici said, her tone still thoughtful as she left the room. "But I might have an idea. I'll let you know."

Cici found Ida Mae sweeping off the back porch, which she liked to do every morning. The porch didn't really need sweeping, and it took Ida Mae four times as long to do it as it would have taken any one of the younger women, but it was her routine and they had all learned not to argue with Ida Mae's routine. Cici came out from the kitchen, careful to cushion the screen door with her hand so that it wouldn't slam behind her. Ida Mae hated it when they let the screen door slam.

"Ida Mae," she said, "didn't you say that that room next to Lori's old room, the one we're using as a guest room—didn't you say that used to be Miss Emily Blackwell's old room?"

Ida Mae grunted in reply, not bothering to look up from her work.

"Because I couldn't help noticing it's a lot

smaller than the other rooms on that side of the hall, and so is Lori's. It seems to me that the owner of the house would have had a bigger room. Is that where she slept when she was married, too?"

Ida Mae looked at her, scowling. "Now how in blazes would I know that? How old do you think I am, anyhow?"

Cici tactfully refrained from answering that. Ida Mae's exact age was a mystery on par with how the pyramids were built. She said instead, "What I mean is that you said there was a lot of remodeling done during the sixties, and I wondered why they didn't make that room bigger."

"Because they just got done making it smaller, I reckon." Ida Mae swept a speck of imaginary dust over the edge of the porch and into the bushes with an expression of satisfaction, and started on the steps.

"I knew it!" Cici's eyes lit with triumph. "Lori's room and the guest room used to be one big room, didn't they? That's why there's a fireplace in the guest room and none in Lori's room, and why there's only one bathroom between them."

She lifted one shoulder expressively. "Could be. All I know is they changed a lot of rooms around during the war, when all them women lived here."

The house, built at the turn of the nineteenth century as a grand mansion with all of the latest

91

amenities—electrical wiring, indoor plumbing, dumbwaiters, marble floors, and imported chandeliers—had undergone many incarnations in its life, one of which was as a rooming house for war brides during the nineteen forties. It made sense that some of the large rooms might have been subdivided to accommodate more people.

"Perfect," Cici murmured, eyes shining. "Thanks, Ida Mae!"

She hurried down the steps, practically skipping as she crossed the yard to the tool shed. There was absolutely nothing that made Cici happier than a project.

Twenty minutes later the grind of a saw and the clatter of falling wood sent Bridget rushing up the stairs. She found Cici in the guest room, power saw in hand, smiling proudly at the six-inch hole she had just cut in the wall. The floor was covered in a plastic drop cloth and the furniture had all been moved to the other side of the room. Crowbars, sledgehammers, and an assortment of power tools were scattered at her feet, and a forty-gallon trashcan awaited filling. She pushed back her safety glasses and grinned at Bridget. "Look!" she invited.

Bridget looked, her expression a cross between astonishment and horror. "There's a hole in our wall!"

"It's just a pilot hole," Cici explained, "so that I

could make sure there were no electrical wires or pipes in the way."

"But . . ." Bridget stepped carefully into the room, her dismay growing as she looked around. "We're having a wedding! This is our guest room!"

"Wrong," replied Cici with a grin. "This is our wedding present to Dominic and Lindsay."

Bridget stared at her. "A hole in the wall?"

Cici spread her hands expansively. "A master suite."

Cici put down the saw and knocked her fist against the wall with the hole in it. "I always suspected this was a dummy wall," she said. "The way these two rooms at the end of the hall are so oddly shaped, with the big windows and the little doors. That's because they used to be one great big room—and they will be again as soon as we knock down this wall." Bridget's eyes went big and Cici corrected quickly, "I. *I* knock down the wall. It's going to be fabulous," she went on before Bridget could speak. "A master retreat away from everyone else, two closets, that marvelous big bathroom, the view, plenty of room for a king-sized bed and any furniture Dominic might want to bring . . . I figured I could do the construction work and you could do the painting and decorating. It'll be just like one of those makeover shows on TV! Don't you see?" she insisted. "Telling Dominic he's welcome here is one thing, but showing him—and Lindsay—is another." She gave a final, decisive nod of satisfaction. "It's the perfect wedding gift."

Bridget's expression went from alarmed to thoughtful as Cici spoke. She gazed around the room. She went into the hallway and to the room next door, looking through the hole in the wall. She returned to Cici. "You know," she said, "you're right."

Cici grinned.

"I'd put a nice big overstuffed chair there in front of the fireplace, and that darling little secretaire from Lindsay's room underneath the window. And . . ." Her eyes lit up. "That tea table in the attic that I've been dying to find a use for! A few bookshelves . . ."

"I don't know if I'll have time for bookshelves," Cici objected.

"That oriental rug of Lindsay's we've been using in the sunroom, a few candles, some art . . ." And then she looked at Cici sharply. "If you're *sure* that wall will come down—without bringing the roof with it."

Cici gave her a patient look. "Of course I'm sure. Do you think I would have cut the hole if I wasn't? We can take it down with a sledge-hammer in an afternoon."

"There you go with 'we' again."

"I might have to get Farley to help me take down the frame," she admitted. "But two days tops."

"It's not going to be easy to keep a secret like

that from Lindsay for two days," Bridget pointed out.

Cici frowned. "Oh, I don't think we can keep it a secret from Lindsay. Maybe from Dominic. But we should at least ask Lindsay what color she wants the walls painted."

Bridget looked around the room dubiously. "That means all this wallpaper will have to come off."

"Not all of it," Cici pointed out. "Just three walls."

"Six. There are two rooms, six walls."

"It's as crisp as parchment," said Cici, peeling back a strip near the hole she had cut. "It should come off like wrapping paper."

Bridget's expression grew speculative as she peeled back a longer strip. "You know," she said, "I might be able to use this in the invitations. Or the place cards. It's too pretty to waste."

"It's not garnet or rose," Cici pointed out.

"Maybe I'll leave one wall as a feature wall."

"Or two. Then you only have to paint four walls."

They had been dimly aware of the border collie's attack-mode barking for some time now, but they had become so accustomed to the unpredictable nature of his moods that they barely noticed anymore. It wasn't until they heard Ida Mae shouting up the stairs, "Comp'ny!" that they registered their surprise.

"What in the world?" Bridget went to the window, and let out an exclamation of delight. "It's Kevin!" she cried.

"Kevin?" Cici went to the window to see for herself. Bridget's son, though he only lived a few hours away, wasn't in the habit of dropping in unannounced. "Were you expecting him?"

Bridget shook her head, looking both puzzled and pleased as she turned toward the door. "It's not like him to be impulsive, is it?" She hesitated, her expression slowly settling into suspicion as she added, "Something must be wrong."

There was a list that every young man carried around in his head of things he never wanted to tell his mom, and not as many of them had to do with sex as the average mother might think. At the top of that list, no matter who you were or what you had done, were two simple words: *I failed.* Conversely, there was no time in a man's life that he needed his mother more than in the midst of a devastating failure.

Kevin Tyndale had no intention of telling his mother the truth. He just really, really needed to see her.

Kevin had been skeptical—maybe more than skeptical—when his mother had announced her plan to sell everything she owned and buy an old mansion in the middle of nowhere with her two best friends. It wasn't that he had anything against

Lindsay and Cici; they were practically family, after all, and there was no one to whom he would have trusted his mother's welfare more than the two of them. But the whole scheme had sounded crazy—still sounded crazy, if he were perfectly honest—and he had to admit that a large portion of his disapproval centered around the fact that she had made such a major decision without consulting him. But all that was before he had seen the life the three women had created here, and how happy it made his mother. Now he envied them all.

Kevin was a good-looking young man with wavy chestnut hair and a square jawline, complemented by black-framed designer glasses that made him look both intellectual and disarmingly rakish. He had been in the highly competitive world of a top DC law firm, with its eighty-hour work weeks, cutthroat colleagues, and ever-increasing demands for billable hours for six years last January. An unrelenting dedication to his job and a willingness to cross any line had earned him a six-figure salary, a stock portfolio, and a condo overlooking the river that he hardly ever saw because most nights he worked so late it didn't make sense to go home. When he had time off, he did the clubs or one of those glamour trips to Telluride or Belize, usually with people he didn't know and didn't much like. He had been raised better than that.

He drove a red Maserati—for a few more weeks, anyway—and the minute he pulled up, that crazy border collie came charging from somewhere in back of the house, tail whirling, teeth bared, snarling and barking like it planned to take down the car and driver single-handedly. Kevin wasn't afraid of the dog, exactly, but the last time he had been here it had taken a chunk out of his favorite pair of Dockers. He'd discovered the best course of action was to stay put until someone with more control over the beast than he had appeared to take charge.

He didn't have to wait long. Just as the dog launched an attack upon his tires, the screen door burst open and the old woman, Ida Mae, appeared with a broom in her hand. He never knew quite what to make of her and it seemed to Kevin that she always regarded him with an air of suspicion, but she was hell on wheels with that broom.

"Hey, you filthy animal! Get on outta here!"

Kevin assumed she was talking to the dog, so he kept his place behind the wheel.

"Scat!" For a woman her age, she had a voice that could raise thunder. "Scat, I tell you!" She stomped down the steps in a faded print dress and army boots, swinging the broom like a machete, and the dog finally took notice. With one last resentful bark and a warning stare at the tires, he spun on two legs and took off in the direction from which he'd come, leaving nothing but a blur in his wake.

Ida Mae, shouldering the broom, glared at Kevin through the windshield. "Well?" she demanded. "You getting out, or not?"

And before he could respond or even reach for the door handle, she turned and boomed over her shoulder, *"Comp'ny!"*

Kevin reached for the bouquet of flowers he had brought—which was rather like taking coals to Newcastle considering the riotous bloom of late-summer color that filled the flower gardens around the house—and opened the door. In another moment his mother pushed open the screen door, followed closely by Cici. "Kevin!" Bridget cried, running down the steps with arms open. "Sweetie, what are you doing here?"

"Kevin, what a treat!" added Cici, following. "We didn't know you were coming!"

There was the usual jubilation of hugs and greetings. Lindsay came up from the winery with Dominic and all the excitement and questions started over again. Bridget put the flowers in a vase and Cici brought a pitcher of iced tea and a plate of cookies out to the round wicker table on the porch. There were always cookies at Ladybug Farm. Kevin supposed that was why, whenever he came there, it felt so much like home.

"Not that we're not wild about seeing you," Bridget said, fussing over him as she poured the tea and made sure he had a napkin and urged the cookie platter on him, "but what on earth brings you all the way out here in the middle of the week? Why didn't you tell us you were coming?"

Before she stepped away from his chair to fill the other glasses, she paused to smooth back a lock of his hair in an unconscious motherly gesture, and it made him smile. "I just thought I'd surprise you," he said. "Can't a guy visit his mother every now and then?"

"More than every now and then would be even better," Bridget replied. She pulled out a chair and sat next to him, her expression pleasant but curious. Lindsay and Cici looked at him in the same way—welcoming, but puzzled.

Dominic took a couple of cookies and saluted Kevin with them. "Well, it's nice seeing you, Kevin, but I need to get back to the vines. Come out to the winery later and I'll give you a tour."

"Sounds great. I'd like that."

Kevin lived in DC, which was an easy enough drive for any occasion, but it embarrassed him to realize he had not been to visit his mother more than half a dozen times in the four years she had been here. There was no excuse for it. He always planned to visit more, and every time he left, the good country cooking and quiet shadowed evenings would linger in his memory, making him promise to return the following weekend. But when the weekend came he usually had to work, or there was a party he wanted to go to, or a client invited him on his boat, or he had a date. He tried to get down to visit sometime during the Christ-mas season, and for his mom's birthday, and once he'd even made it for Mother's Day, but usually he just sent flowers. He had not, he realized, been a very good son.

"Congratulations," he told Lindsay, hoping to take their focus off himself. "Mom e-mailed you've set the date."

"Thanks," she said, smiling. "You'll be getting your invitation next week."

"But only if you promise to come," Bridget pointed out. "Otherwise we're taking you off the guest list."

He hesitated. "Actually, I have news."

Bridget's eyes lit up. "Kevin! Are you getting married? But who? How? *That's* why you drove out here in the middle of the week!"

"Wait, no!" He held up a hand in self-defense, looking mildly horrified. "That's not it."

Cici said, "You'll have to forgive her. We're wedding-obsessed around here."

"Well, all I can say is thank goodness," Lindsay said, while Bridget looked a little disappointed. "I don't think we could stand another wedding in the works. What's your news, Kevin?"

He glanced around the table, picked up his glass, and took a sip of sweet tea. The pause might have appeared to be for dramatic effect, but in fact he needed the time to find just the right words to introduce the subject, just the right tone to make it sound like a good thing. "I've been thinking about changing jobs," he said. "I have an opportunity. In Rome."

"Rome!" Cici exclaimed.

And Lindsay echoed, "Rome, Italy?"

Kevin said, "Well, actually . . ."

"But," Bridget said, looking stunned, "you have a job!"

She had been so proud when he decided to go into law, and even prouder when he landed a job at the big Washington firm. So proud.

Lindsay elbowed Bridget in the arm. "For heaven's sake, Bridge, this one is in *Rome!*"

"But," Cici said, "don't you have to have a special license to practice law overseas?"

He said, floundering, "Um, it's more corporate."

Bridget sank back in her chair, the astonished expression in her eyes giving way to wonder. "Oh, my goodness," she breathed, "my little boy, working in the international marketplace." She pressed her hands to her cheeks, and abruptly her eyes flashed bright with tears. "Oh, Kevin, your dad would be so proud!"

He looked around desperately, feeling trapped. "Really, Mom, it's not that big a deal. I might not even get it."

"Of course you will!" Bridget said it as though

to think otherwise was blasphemy. "Why wouldn't you?"

And Lindsay said, "When will you leave?"

"It's not a sure thing," he reiterated, trying not to panic. "I'm not even meeting with them until next week."

That much was true at least. He was, in fact, one of over two hundred people who had managed to wrangle his way into an interview with what amounted to the assistant director of human resources, and that was only thanks to some very creative writing on his resume. It had seemed like something to hope for at the time. Now . . . not so much.

Lindsay said, "Do you speak enough Italian to work in Italy?"

"I might not take it," he assured her quickly, wishing for all he was worth—which wasn't very much at the moment—that he could rewrite the past five minutes. "In fact, I probably won't. I just thought I'd mention it, just in case, you know . . ." he summoned up a coaxing smile, the kind his mother never could resist, "they make me an offer I can't refuse."

Cici said, "Lori's in Italy."

He looked at her, more grateful than he could say for the change of subject. "That's right, Mom mentioned that." He couldn't believe he'd forgotten. "What's she doing there, again?"

"She's got a boyfriend," said Lindsay.

Cici gave her a cool look. "She's apprenticing at a winery." She sipped her tea. "And she has a boyfriend."

"Where is she?" he inquired, to be polite, and to keep the focus off of himself.

"Siena," Cici said.

Bridget's eyes lit up. "Oh, Kevin, you've got to look her up while you're there. I'll get you her address before you leave. We're dying for some real news from her and . . ." She glanced at Cici. "I know her mother would appreciate knowing what you think of this fellow of hers."

Cici must have sensed his discomfort because she said quickly, "Bridget, I don't think Siena is anywhere near Rome, and—"

"There's a train," Lindsay said helpfully, "and it's a gorgeous trip from Rome. I know Lori would love to see a familiar face. She must be so home-sick!"

"How can you go to Italy without seeing Lori?" Bridget demanded. "Or Tuscany, for that matter!"

Cici looked hopeful. "If you do go," she said, "I have a few things I'd like to send to her. Nothing that would take up too much room in your bag," she promised. "Just some of her favorite bath salts and some English magazines she can't get over there, things like that."

"And cookies," declared Bridget. "We'll have to send her cookies."

Kevin understood then how a mountain climber

must feel at the moment the avalanche finally overtakes him; at that instant when panic turns to horror and finally gives way to inevitability, acceptance, and yes, even relief. That was it then. There was no way he could backtrack now. His mother was baking cookies. Cici was depending on him. Everyone was proud of him. He was going to Italy.

And what the hell? One last hurrah. There were certainly worse ways to end a career.

So he sat back, smiled, and picked up his tea glass. "Sure," he said, "it'll be fun to see her. And I've never been to an Italian winery. I'll send you a case of wine."

"You're staying overnight, right?" Lindsay said, rising. "I'll get the guest room ready."

Cici said, "Um, about that . . ."

"No," Kevin said quickly, "no, I can't stay." He wanted to, he longed to. Nothing would make him happier than to sink into the oasis that was Ladybug Farm, to listen to the crickets at night and watch the birds in the morning and be fawned and fussed over by people who thought he was a rare and wonderful creature whose very presence on this earth was cause for celebration. But he knew he couldn't bear the pretense for another twenty-four hours. He wasn't that good a liar.

"But I was going to make fried chicken for supper," Bridget said, disappointed, "and my caramel apple pie that you like so much." Then she cheered. "I could make it for lunch. You can stay that long, can't you?"

He smiled. "Oh, I think I could probably be talked into that."

And so he lingered. He admired the winery and walked the vines with Dominic; he laughed and talked with his mom and her friends and stored up all the gossip to share with Lori. He ate fried chicken and apple pie until his stomach was swollen. He drank deep of the sweet country air and looked long into the gold-etched mountains, and there was an ache in his chest when he hugged his mother good-bye.

He left Ladybug Farm with a bag full of gifts for Lori and the smiles and good wishes of everyone he left behind, and he made reservations for his flight to Italy without ever once mentioning that the job—the one he probably wouldn't get anyway—was, in fact, in Rome, Georgia.

Lindsay stared in dismay at the hole in the guest room wall, which was now almost as big as a barn door. "Oh no!" she said, bringing her fingers to her lips. "Cici, what happened? Can you fix it?"

Cici, who was tearing at another square of lathing with her crowbar, looked up and pushed back her glasses, looking both surprised and disappointed. "I thought you were cutting back the tomato vines."

The visit from Kevin had been a fun diversion from the routine and the ladies had enjoyed it, but the dust of his departure had barely settled on the drive before they were all back at their chores. With the schedule they had to keep, there was no time for idleness.

"I was." Lindsay took a hesitant step into the room, looking around at the rubble. Broken strips of lath and chunks of plaster littered the plastic-covered floor, wallpaper hung in huge sagging strips from all the walls, and a fine coat of white dust covered everything, including Cici. "I heard the noise and came to see what was wrong."

"Oh. Well, it can't be helped now I guess." Cici gave an apologetic shrug, and then grinned. "I wanted to get more done before I showed you, but what do you think?"

Lindsay's consternation grew as she looked from the floor to the wall to Cici. "Think?"

"It's going to be your new suite," Cici explained. "Yours and Dominic's. You see, these two rooms used to be one great big room—Miss Emily's room when she was married—with the two windows overlooking the garden and the marble fireplace . . . didn't you ever wonder why it was off-center? Look, the floorboards are even flowing the same way, and if I'm careful all I'll have to do is touch up the finish underneath this frame. The bathroom is twice as big as the one in your room, and it even has a shower!

You're always having to use the guest bath to wash your hair. All we have to do is knock down this wall and the room will be just like it used to be, and big enough for two people. It's our wedding gift to you," she added, a little breathlessly. "Mine and Bridget's."

Lindsay's lips parted but for a moment she didn't seem to know what to say. She turned in a half circle. She looked at Cici. "But . . . we have a wedding in a matter of weeks! And trim to paint and chandeliers to wash and—and a wedding to plan!"

"We'll have this done long before the wedding," Cici assured her. "Seriously, a matter of days."

"But . . ." It was almost possible to see the thoughts flickering and wrestling for attention behind Lindsay's eyes. "Give up my room? I like my room. I worked hard on it."

"But it's your room," Cici replied patiently. "Don't you think you should have a room that's yours *and* Dominic's? You know, to start your new life together?"

"Wow." Lindsay let this sink in for a moment. "A new life." She brought herself back to the problem at hand with a visible effort. "But—all this work! Cici, I can't let you and Bridget do this! You're doing so much already!"

Cici waved it away. "Look what you did for Bridget when you turned your art studio into The

Tasting Table. Look what you did for me when I broke my collarbone. Look what Dominic did for all of us. This is nothing."

Hesitantly, Lindsay bent down and peered through the opening into the other room. "It sure looks like a lot."

"It's simple. I've done all this just since Kevin left. Here." She handed the crowbar to Lindsay. "You try. It's kind of fun."

Lindsay took the tool, glanced at Cici dubiously, and took a halfhearted swing at the wall. The plaster gave a satisfying crack and a few pieces crumbled to the floor.

"Like this." Cici corrected her grip and suggested, "Try pulling instead of hitting. And stand back if you don't want to get hit by falling plaster." She hesitated, remembering Lindsay's recent mishaps, and added, "Maybe you should wear a helmet."

Lindsay returned a grimace and said, "Maybe you should just do it."

She offered the crowbar back to Cici but they both turned at the sound of Bridget's voice.

"Cici! Did you see this e-mail?" She appeared at the door and stopped short at the sight of Lindsay. "Oh," she said, and then smiled. "How do you like it?" She gestured with the paper in her hand. "Great idea, right?"

"Actually," Lindsay agreed, "it is. Thank you both. But it's an awful lot of work."

"Don't be silly. You deserve it, both of you, and we want to do this."

Cici said, "What e-mail?"

Bridget passed her the printout. "It's from Lori," she said excitedly, "and it solves everything!" She turned to Lindsay. "How about this? Instead of a formal run-of-the-mill wedding reception like everyone has, we'll open up the vineyard for the burning of the vines! Just like we did for the blessing of the vines last spring. We'll publicize it all over town, put it on the website, make it a great big open house! We'll have a wine tasting and sell tickets! We'll have cheese pairings, of course, and heavy hors d'oeuvres instead of a sitdown meal, and nobody gets left out!"

Cici looked up from the paper with a light in her eyes. "It's tax deductible," she said. "And it's entirely possible we could actually *make* money on your wedding reception!"

Lindsay scanned the e-mail. "What does Dominic say?"

"He says Lori is a marketing genius and when is she coming home?" Bridget watched Lindsay, her eyes sparkling. "What do you say?"

Lindsay looked up from the paper. "We could have that band from town, you know the bluegrass one that Dominic likes so much. And we'll light the bonfire as soon as it gets dark and everyone will gather around and we'll have toasts and wedding cake . . ."

"So much more romantic than a sit-down dinner," Cici agreed. "I've got to admit, sometimes that kid of mine is pretty smart."

"Now you see?" Bridget beamed at Lindsay. "Sometimes things *do* work out."

"Yeah," Lindsay said happily, grinning back. "Sometimes they do."

With a laugh of delight, she swung the crowbar against the wall as Cici had shown her and pulled hard. There was a clang, a clatter, and the sound of rending metal. Lindsay stumbled backward and sat down hard as a geyser of water shot from the wall.

Bridget squealed and ran for the door, but Cici just stared at Lindsay in disbelief, oblivious to the torrent that was quickly soaking them both. "And sometimes," she said, "they don't."

At the Hummingbird House

ᑐᘉᒧ

Cocktail hour in the wildflower garden was one of the unadvertised delights of the Hummingbird House, for both the owners and the guests. At the end of a long day of hiking, antiquing, sightseeing, or simply rocking on the porch, the guests would drift out onto the stone terrace to sample the sherry and the cheeses their hosts had selected for them, to chat and share their days while the hummingbirds buzzed and darted around the feeders and the yellow daisies and purple columbine nodded in the breeze of a setting sun. As the days grew shorter and cooler, their hosts would light the torches that meandered along the stone paths and guests might linger around the dancing flames of the outdoor fire-place for one last glass before departing to keep their dinner reservations. It was also, for the busy proprietors of the B&B, often their first opportunity of the day to catch up.

"So *then,*" Derrick reported importantly, setting a tray of sherry and glasses on the patio bistro table, "they had to turn off the water to the entire second floor, but not before the carpets in two rooms were soaked through. Cici doesn't think there's any damage to the underlying structure, thank heavens, but it's going to take days to repair. Lindsay is in an absolute panic that it won't be finished before the wedding."

Paul followed closely with the cheese board and a selection of beautifully arranged sliced fruit and water crackers. "It's not that I don't have perfect confidence in our girl Cici," he confided, "but honestly—who takes on a job like that mere weeks before hosting a wedding?"

Derrick sighed. "She and Bridget wanted to make the bridegroom feel welcome."

Paul placed the cheese board beside the sherry tray and began to arrange the Hummingbird House logo cocktail napkins in a fan shape between them. "Poor Lindsay. She's letting this wedding turn her into a complete wreck. She's usually so competent and composed, but I've seen twenty-year-olds with more sangfroid about their big day than this. When she was over here the other day to drop off the dress for alterations, she backed her car into the oak tree trying to park—no damage to either one, thank goodness, tree or car—and then tripped on the bottom step and almost dropped the gown in the mud before she even got to the front door. Then . . ." he looked mildly abashed. "I'm afraid I might have stabbed her with a pin a couple of times during the fitting, which was *completely* not my fault because you know she's utterly incapable of standing still for more than ten seconds at a time. But the odd thing was, as soon as the dress was boxed up and ready to be shipped to the seamstress, she was perfectly fine again. We had a lovely tea, and she even helped me cut flowers for the dining table—using real gardening sheers—with absolutely no incidents whatever. I just don't know what to make of it."

"It's perfectly clear to me," announced Harmony, sailing across the patio with her empty wine glass extended. "The poor girl has an attached spirit or two. A quick exorcism and she'll be as good as new."

Harmony Haven was a large woman some-where on the far side of fifty with a headful of riotous blonde curls and a bosom that had been compared once too often to the jutting prow of a ship. She had a tendency to dress in flowing colorful garments and outrageous jewelry combinations, and she promoted herself as an expert on all things spiritual, esoteric, and arcane. She had moved into the fuchsia room almost before the B&B was even open, and had shown no signs of ever leaving. Fortunately, they had managed to convince her—ever-so-diplomatically —to pay in advance.

Paul looked alarmed, although whether that was from her words or from the fact that she clearly intended to pour sherry into a glass that had only moments ago contained red wine was not clear. "Whatever you do, don't tell Lindsay that." He took her glass and passed it to Derrick, who quickly filled a proper sherry glass for her. "She already has one foot on the slippery slope of no return as it is."

"What, exactly, is an attached spirit?" Derrick inquired, passing the sherry glass to her. He had the look of one who both dreads and anticipates the answer.

Harmony waved a casual hand and cut herself a slice of cheese. "The easiest thing in the world to manage. Far easier than exorcising a whole house. I could take care of it in half an hour."

Paul met Derrick's eyes and then they dismissed the notion with a quick and mutual shake of their heads. Paul said, "Seriously, I read an article only the other day in *O Magazine* about how people define their futures and I'm starting to get a bit concerned."

"Nonsense." Derrick filled his own glass. "We make our own happiness and Lindsay is just being silly. The only thing we have to worry about now is an engagement party that will make her feel like the princess she is."

He turned a meaningful look on Paul, who swallowed his pride with a visible effort. "Harmony," he said. "About that . . ."

CHAPTER FOUR

༚

Surprise

Lori knew she was not very good at her job. She wouldn't have been very good at it even if everyone spoke English, or if she spoke more than a mangled version of Google-translator Italian. She wouldn't have been good at it even if she had liked her job, which she did not. She was not put on this earth to serve grappa and cappuccino to sweaty Italians for ten hours a day, and that was not simply a conceit. In the first place, she didn't like grappa; in the second place, she didn't like Italians—both of which were significant handicaps for someone who worked in one of the busiest cafés in Siena. As far as she could tell, the only reason the owner had hired her at all was because he liked to pinch her ass.

Of course, the charm of that had worn off for Lori fairly quickly, and had become meager compensation for her boss after the first day of spilled drinks, misplaced orders, and angry customers. Now they coexisted in a state of wary dislike that occasionally flared into active animosity, if not outright violence, and Lori was quite sure that if she could understand even half of what her employer was saying when he got all red in the face and shook his fist at her she would have quit weeks ago. As it was, she found him fairly easy to ignore amidst all the rest of the high-decibel chatter and clutter that characterized the afternoon cappuccino rush.

The café was something of a cross between a Starbucks and a corner bar, with wine, grappa, and hard liquor served any time of the day, along with a confusing variety of coffee drinks and even pastries. It would have been hard enough to keep up with the orders even if she could understand what they were ordering. Already she had sloshed hot coffee on one customer, given the wrong change to another, and dropped a tray of drinks on the floor. They were standing six-deep at the bar, and the boss was at it again, yelling something in her ear with many grand gesticulations, while she tried to remember which button was espresso and which one added the milk on the giant, brass-coated octopus that resembled a time-travel machine more than a coffee maker. That was when she heard an American voice shout from the back of the crowd. "Hey! What does a man have to do to get some service around here?"

There was a time when the sound of an American accent would have made her heart soar, but now it just annoyed her. All the Americans ever wanted to do when they came in here was take up her time gushing about how authentic the place was, and how did she like living here and what was she doing here and did she know any good places for dinner, and then they'd leave her a fifty cent euro for a tip—like they actually thought the big 50 on the coin meant something other than fifty cents—or sometimes they'd walk off with nothing but a friendly wave. They were big, they were loud, they were pushy, and most of the time they made her embarrassed to be from the same country. She had even less patience for the Americans than she did the Italians.

So she shouted back, without even bothering to turn around, "McDonald's is down the street!"

That usually got rid of them, but this one was determined to be a pain in the ass. He returned, "Is that the way you talk to a customer, dollface?"

Dollface? She abandoned her struggle with the stubborn machine and turned around to give him the death stare. She saw a chestnut-haired young man in a yellow Polo shirt making his way toward the bar. He pushed his sunglasses into his hair and smiled at her.

"Kevin!"

Lori scrambled over the bar, pushing cups and canisters and outraged customers out of her way, and launched herself into his arms. He caught her up, laughing and staggering backwards, and she wrapped her legs around his waist and her arms around his neck and covered his face with kisses. "Kevin! Kevin, it's you, it's you, it's really you! What are you doing here? How did you find me? I can't believe it's you!"

Then she jumped onto the floor again and gave him a hard punch on the arm, staring at him suspiciously. "What are you doing here?" she demanded again. "Did my mother send you to check up on me?"

"Hey!" he rubbed his bruised arm, scowling. "Give a fellow a chance, will you?"

The owner of the café shoved his way through the crowd, and he did not look as though he was in the mood to give anyone a chance. His jowls were swinging and his beet-red face was sweating and he was yelling at Lori at the top of his considerable lungs. Lori, who had had enough for one day, shot back every Italian curse she knew. He looked momentarily startled, but when the customers nearest him started to grin and even chuckle, he gave a roar of rage that made even Lori shrink back. Kevin let forth a stream of Italian that ended with the belligerent chin-flipping gesture that, until she moved to Italy, Lori thought had been invented by the Sopranos. Then, not waiting for a reply or a reaction, Kevin gripped her arm hard and dragged her out of the café.

"Wow," said Lori, when they were far enough down the street that the café owner's furious threats were only background noise, "I didn't know you spoke Italian."

Kevin dropped her arm, gazed at her for a

moment, and then deliberately lowered his sunglasses down over his eyes. He started walking again. "I hope you didn't like your job."

"Hated it. Why?"

"Because you're fired."

"Fired?" She looked outraged. "Just for a little argument? What did you say to him?"

"Me? You're the one who called him a penis-face and invited him to go make love to a pig."

Lori slowed down, grinning. "I did?"

"God, Lori, you're living and working in Italy and you can't even be bothered to learn the language?"

"It's not that I can't be bothered!" She frowned a little, shoving her hands into her pockets as she walked beside him. "I'm trying. I'm just not very good at it. Turns out I'm not very good at a lot of things," she added, so lowly it was almost inaudible.

She could feel Kevin's glance, but she did not look up. They walked in silence for a while, strolling with tourists who gawked at the crumbling architecture and colorful storefronts, dodging the purposeful strides of the natives with their cell phones and intense expressions. In a moment Lori said, "So? Did my mother send you?"

"Not exactly," he said, then admitted, "My mother did. Of course . . ." He slid a glance at her. "You're not exactly where they thought you were, are you?"

Lori chose not to reply to that.

Kevin said, "Mom also sent cookies."

Lori's eyes lit up. "Really? What kind?"

"Chocolate chip, with nuts. I ate most of them on the way over, though."

And when her expression grew stormy again he grinned, and nodded toward a kiosk just ahead. "Come on, I'll buy you a gelato. And maybe you can tell me how you went from living in a castle at one of the most prestigious wineries in the region to serving coffee for tips with a penis-face for your boss."

Lori said glumly, "For that you'll have to buy me dinner."

He draped a companionable arm around her shoulders. "Let's start with gelato and see how it goes."

She smiled and leaned into him, just a little. She had never imagined how good it would be to see a face from home.

"At least you're being a good sport about it." Bridget set a platter piled high with sandwiches on the table while Cici replaced the vase of yellow daisies and purple asters with a pitcher of iced tea.

"I am not being a good sport," Lindsay said grimly, bending her head over the papers that were spread out in front of her. "I am soldiering through."

"Anyway, what has she got to be a good sport

about?" Cici demanded. "I'm the one who had to spend two days without water in my bathroom."

"It would have only been one day if you'd called a plumber in the first place," Bridget pointed out.

Cici rolled her eyes, grabbed a sandwich, and sank into her chair.

The work on the soon-to-be master suite had been stalled for over a week, thanks not only to the broken water pipe but to the myriad of other wedding-prep details that were constantly pulling their focus. The gazebo had to be repainted, along with the shutters, the front door, and the trim. The vegetable garden, now that the last of its produce had been harvested, had to be plowed under and mulched, and Lindsay thought the fence surrounding it could use a fresh coat of paint, just for appearances' sake. Even Cici was beginning to wonder whether tackling a major remodeling project this close to the wedding might have been a mistake.

But it was, of course, too late now.

Hand-lettered invitations fashioned on thick vellum paper supplied by Paul had gone out to family members and closest friends. Paul had shown them how to singe the edges of the paper for a weathered look, and Lindsay had sketched a stylized grapevine in gold ink on each one. Flyers advertising the burning of the vines and the wedding celebration had been printed up and left in shops and businesses all over town, pinned to bulletin boards and posted on the Ladybug Farm website. Bridget had had the idea to add "reservations suggested" and so far had taken almost fifty calls. And that was in addition to the usual business of running the farm: the fruit that had to be turned into jam before it spoiled, the dozens upon dozens of bags of corn and beans and squash that were sliced, blanched, and packed into their two freezers; the lawn that had to be mowed and the shrubs that had to be pruned and the flower beds that had to be raked clean of early falling leaves.

In the past ten days, Lindsay had stabbed herself with a fruit knife while helping Bridget prepare pears for the compote she wanted to serve at the reception, stepped on a rake and almost knocked herself out, and slammed the car door on her fingers. But her black eye was almost completely gone, and most of the time she walked without a limp.

She was using the lunch table—which, until cool weather drove them inside, would always be the round wicker table on the side porch that overlooked the flower gardens—to do her daily audit of the pre-wedding checklist. Dominic stopped by to grab a sandwich and a glass of sweet tea to take back to his office, and lingered just long enough to assure his fiancée that he had no intention of wearing the poet's shirt and brocade vest Paul had decided on for groom's attire. Lindsay nodded, marked it off her list, kissed him absently, and sent him on his way.

"Okay, we got the marriage license and delivered it to Reverend Holland," Lindsay said, checking off a box. "It's good for sixty days. Dominic asked his oldest son to be his best man. We've got the rings. The wedding bands are gorgeous, by the way; mine fits rights into the engagement ring like a single vine. Oh, and Paul sent out seventy-five save the date cards for the engagement party." She had a sandwich in one hand and a pen in the other, and she glanced over the top of her reading glasses to check a notation on one of the papers as she spoke. "He said it's great advertising for the B&B even if only half of them come."

"It was sweet of them to go to so much trouble."

"It sure was. At least I know one thing about this wedding is guaranteed to go right."

"Hey," Cici objected, "we give great parties."

Lindsay glanced at her apologetically. "I know. And it's not as though I don't appreciate all you're doing. It's just that I only get one shot at this. I want it to be perfect. Or at least as perfect as I can afford."

Cici nodded. "I totally get that. I wanted the same thing for Lori."

Lindsay held out her glass, checking a box on one of the papers with her other hand. "More tea. Have you heard from her, by the way? Or Kevin?"

Cici leaned over the table to refill Lindsay's glass. "Just the usual. 'No time to write, must run.' "

"Kevin landed safely though," Bridget said. "And he e-mailed to double-check the name of the place where Lori's staying, so I'm sure he'll let us know when he sees her."

"I don't know why you didn't just tell Lori he was coming," Lindsay said.

"He wanted to surprise her," Cici said with a shrug. "Who knows why?"

"I know why," Bridget said. "In case he got too busy to look her up. You know kids. They hate to be tied to a schedule."

Cici finished her sandwich and sat back for a moment, sipping her tea. The day was one of a string of exceptionally warm ones for this time of year, and already the temperature on the porch was almost too high to be comfortable. The lawn looked crisp, the flower beds wilted, and even the mountains in the distance looked hot and dusty. The sky was the color of acid-washed denim, bleached and tired looking. "Indian summer," she said, pressing the chilled glass briefly against her cheek. "How can it be hotter than real summer?"

"It's not Indian summer," Bridget said, beginning to gather up the dishes. "It can't be Indian summer until after the first frost."

"Terrific," muttered Lindsay, "something else to worry about. I just ordered a custom-altered jacket to cover up my custom-altered strapless gown and with my luck it will be too hot to wear it."

Cici shrugged. "So you'll sweat."

"Or I'll have a hot flash while standing in ninety-degree sun and pass out and you'll have to call the paramedics." She frowned. "All things considered, it might not be a bad idea to have them standing by anyway, just in case." She made a note on her list.

Bridget began to clear the table, and stacked Lindsay's plate atop the others. "You know, there is such a thing as over-managing."

Lindsay frowned without looking up. "I'm not over-managing. I'm just being careful."

Cici's eyebrows arched. "Which is why you have bandages on every finger and a big bruise on your forehead."

Lindsay pulled self-consciously at the swath of hair that was supposed to be covering the bruise. "Those were accidents."

"Because you're making yourself so crazy about the wedding you've completely lost your ability to concentrate on anything else," said Bridget. "Why don't you just relax and try to enjoy it before you end up in a body cast?"

"Ha. Easy for you to say. *You* try planning the biggest day of your life while swimming through a menopausal brain fog and trying to fit into a dress that's already two sizes too small, not to mention . . ."

She cut herself off so abruptly that both her friends stared at her. Lindsay focused intently on her spreadsheet.

"What?" prompted Bridget. "Not to mention what?"

"I just want everything to be perfect." Lindsay glanced at them uncertainly. "I don't want Dominic's kids to think he's making a mistake. I don't want *Dominic* to think he's making a mistake."

"Ah," said Bridget with soft understanding. "So that's it."

"What?" demanded Cici, looking confused. "What's it?"

"The children," explained Bridget patiently. She put the plates back on the table and sat down. "It's always the children. It's not the wedding she's worried about, it's that Dominic's family will think she's not good enough for him."

"Well, that doesn't make any sense at all," Cici said. "His children are scattered all over the country. You'll see them for a few days at the wedding and send cards at Christmas. What do you care what they think?"

"Well, of *course* she cares what they think," Bridget said. "They're his children. And she'll be . . . well, their stepmother."

Lindsay smothered a groan. "Cassie is only ten years younger than I am."

Bridget hastened to add, "Not literally, of

course, because they're all grown up and living away from home, but still . . . it's family."

Cici looked at Lindsay thoughtfully. "And a step-grandmother," she pointed out.

Lindsay looked at her.

"Doesn't Dominic's oldest son have children?" she said.

Lindsay nodded mutely.

"What do you know about that?" Cici grinned. "You'll be a grandmother before I am. Whoever would have thought?"

Lindsay sank down in her chair. "Oh, God."

Bridget said sternly to Cici, "You are not helping."

Lindsay blew out a soft breath. "I know I've been a maniac. And I'm not like this, really I'm not. You *know* that." She looked at them with a note of pleading in her eyes and they nodded encouragement. "It's just that . . . you remember in the spring, when we sat on this very porch and I knew I was falling in love with Dominic and it terrified me because I'd already found what I wanted. Here. With you guys. And I didn't want anything to change. Well, now it's changed. And there's no going back. And I'm still terrified."

Bridget smiled. So did Cici.

"Ah, Lindsay," Bridget said, "we know that. I mean, seriously, look at what you've done to yourself. Every accident you've had has been because

128

of us. You've literally been beating yourself up over us."

"After all," Cici went on, "Bridget gave you the black eye and I'm the reason you stubbed your toe, and if it hadn't been for Ida Mae dropping the flour you wouldn't have cut your foot."

"And I did ask you to peel the pears," Bridget said a little apologetically.

"And I'm the one who gave you the crowbar," Cici said, but couldn't help adding under her breath, "A mistake I'll never make again."

"You left the rake in the garden too," Lindsay pointed out suspiciously.

"But you slammed your own fingers in the car door," Bridget added.

Lindsay turned an accusing look on her. "While running errands for you."

"Which were all related to your wedding," Bridget said quickly.

"The point being," Cici said, "that it's pretty clear that what your subconscious is trying to tell you is that you're afraid of losing us."

Lindsay lifted an eyebrow. "Or maybe you're afraid of losing me. After all, you're the ones who are doing all the beating up."

"Not on purpose," Cici reminded her firmly.

"Lindsay," Bridget said, reaching for her hand, "we're family. Nothing can change that. Noah is family. Lori is family. When they moved in, everything changed, but we were still family, right?

Now Dominic is family, and his children are family, and his children's children are family. But here," she placed her hand firmly over her heart, "nothing has changed. Because the only rule about families is that there's always room for more."

Lindsay blinked, and her nose reddened. "You're going to make me cry."

"Well, good." Bridget released her hand and sat back. "Because I've got to tell you, you've made me want to cry more than once these past few days."

The three of them laughed, and Cici got to her feet. "I've got to get back to work. Farley's coming this afternoon to help me take down the rest of the wall."

"Do you need any help?" Lindsay offered.

"No," Cici said quickly, and when Lindsay looked insulted she added, managing a smile, "My wedding gift, remember?"

"I said I was sorry about the pipe," Lindsay told her, looking something less than mollified.

"I know. Only . . . we just got the plumbing fixed and there are sharp instruments involved, so . . ." Cici put on her most persuasive face. "Menopausal brain fog, remember? So let's not take any chances."

Lindsay just frowned and turned back to her spreadsheet.

At the Hummingbird House

∽∾∽

"Belly dancers!" declared Harmony. She burst into the office of the Hummingbird House with a flutter of scarves and a sound like tinkling bells, which, upon close examination, was produced by the pyramid of tiny discs she wore dripping from each ear and both wrists. Silk scarves were draped in layers around her shoulders and tied around her ample middle, and she had even arranged a bright pink scarf in a gypsy cap, tied with more jingling discs over one ear. Her feet were bare except for silver rings encircling each surprisingly slender toe. "We'll have belly dancers and a drum ceremony! What could be more perfect? And . . ." She clasped her hands over her chest with a gasp of delight, "A fire-walking ceremony! Can you just imagine how glorious that will be by the light of the full moon? I know where we can get a dozen with practically no notice at all!"

Paul looked up from the computer and blinked, as he often did when seeing Harmony, and Derrick, on the opposite side of the antique partners desk, gazed over the top of his reading glasses in bemusement. "Belly dancers?" he repeated, trying to look open-minded. "Walking on fire?"

Purline, in skintight jeans and a cropped tank top with beaded fringe, squeezed past Harmony.

The two women gave each other a single head-to-toe look that left no doubt about what each one thought of the other's outfit, then Purline turned to Paul. "The folks in the red room want to know could we fix them a picnic lunch to take out to the falls."

Paul managed to tear his gaze away from Harmony to Purline, but his dismay only grew as he took in her attire. It wasn't her mostly bare torso that offended him so much as the sheer tastelessness of the fringe, but he resisted the urge to cover her with his jacket. He and Derrick had already discussed the fact that they could hardly criticize Purline's taste when they tolerated Harmony's and they furthermore, quite frankly, couldn't afford to lose either one of them this close to the party. He replied instead, distractedly, "Ruby room, Purline. It's the *ruby* room. And I've told you before, whatever our guests want, it's theirs without question. I'm sure you can find some cold chicken and potato salad."

"They *want*," replied Purline pointedly, "a bottle of that fancy wine you charge eight dollars a glass for."

Derrick lifted an eyebrow. "Well, of course that would be extra."

"And do you want me to send out your nice glasses with it, or plastic cups?"

Paul said, "Real glasses, of course!"

Derrick's lip curled slightly in distaste. "Do we even *have* plastic cups?"

Harmony spread her hands wide, her eyes shining with passion. "We'll dig the pit behind the butterfly garden, and fill it with green laurel. We'll light the fire at sunrise and let it burn all day."

Purline looked at her skeptically. "You planning a barbeque?"

"No," Paul said quickly. "No barbeque. No pit, no belly dancers."

Purline said, "Well, that's good, because laurel wood is about worthless for smoking meat. Unless you're planning on roasting a goat, maybe."

"But it's the laurel smoke that calls down the favor of the spirits," Harmony explained patiently. "That's the whole point."

Paul turned back to Purline. "Be sure to fold up a stadium blanket in the picnic basket. You can use that to cushion the glasses."

"I was going to use the one you keep on the back of the rocking chair."

"That's cashmere!" Paul and Derrick objected at once.

"And belly dancers," Harmony went on, smiling benignly, "have been a symbol of fertility and feminine power since ancient times. Of course you want to celebrate your friends' marital union with the gift of belly dancers!"

Purline rolled her eyes and muttered, "I *told*

you that woman was going to turn your party into a circus."

And before either Paul or Derrick could admonish her, Purline threw up her hands and turned to the door. "Got it. No cashmere, no plastic, charge 'em for the wine."

"But for heaven's sake, don't put a bill in the picnic basket!" Derrick called after her, and she waved him away over her shoulder.

Paul turned to Harmony with a breath. "Harmony, we appreciate your help, but all we really need is a caterer who doesn't mind driving out here and who can do the event on short notice. We've already taken care of the entertainment."

"Not a problem," Harmony assured them with a flick of her wrist. "I just booked Ahmed Bianca out of Richmond. He specializes in Moroccan."

"Moroccan." Paul and Derrick looked at each other thoughtfully.

"That's an interesting idea," Paul allowed.

"I had a lamb tajine in London that I still dream about," Derrick recalled.

"And what about the spareribs mechoui that we had in that little place in Georgetown?"

"To die for," admitted Derrick.

"No one else would think of doing a Moroccan garden party." Paul's excitement was growing. "But it's perfect for this time of year. We'll get wrought iron braziers and light them all around the patio and the garden paths, and cover the tables with paisley . . ."

"Blue clay pots with herbs for centerpieces," put in Derrick.

"Surrounding a single sunflower," added Paul with an approving nod.

"And Moroccan tiles as chargers."

"Perfect!"

"And," declared Harmony, beaming, "the belly dancers will go on just as the sun reaches the crest of the mountain—"

"No belly dancers!" declared Paul and Derrick as one, and Harmony turned a very stern look on them. They held steady.

"Fellows," she said after a moment, "I really can't help but feel you're not properly exploiting my talents. I have so much to offer, and your vision is so limited."

Derrick looked as though he wanted to take offense, but Paul spoke up quickly. "Limited vision," he agreed. "Completely limited."

She regarded him for a moment as though debating whether or not to pursue the issue, then seemed to concede. "I'll speak with Ahmed about the menu," she said.

"Mention the tajine," suggested Derrick.

"We could serve it in white ceramic bowls with a wedge of pita," suggested Paul.

"With a single edible flower on top," added Derrick.

"Divine," declared Paul.

Harmony folded her hands at her waist and smiled at them beatifically. "Now," she inquired, "where shall we dig the fire pit?"

Kevin and Lori took their gelato across the street and sat at the base of a fountain to people-watch. If there was one thing Siena had plenty of, it was fountains. This particular one featured three giant horses with their hooves raised in battle while sheets of water cascaded over their greenish-bronze forms. Lori used to be impressed by things like that. Now she barely noticed.

"So," Kevin said, digging the wooden spoon into his cup, "Sergio seemed nice."

Lori groaned out loud. "You met him."

"Also his lovely wife."

She muttered, "Crap."

"And his mother, and his father . . ."

"All right, already. Jeez." Lori scowled as she applied herself to the gelato.

Kevin gazed mildly ahead, his expression all but obscured by the sunglasses. "So I'm guessing this Sergio dude is the one you're supposed to be madly in love with, and his dad is who you're supposed to be working for."

"I never said madly in love," Lori protested quickly. "I never said that." And then she sighed, licking the back of her spoon. "It's not as bad as it sounds."

"Couldn't possibly be."

She gave him a dark look. "How'd you find me, anyway?"

"It didn't require a private detective, if that's what you mean. You told your folks you were working at the Villa Laurentis. The Marcellos were nice enough to tell me where you were really working. You're just lucky it was me, and not your dad, who decided to fly over and surprise you. Seriously, how long were you planning to keep this up?"

Lori stretched her legs out in front of her and crumpled up her empty paper cup, her expression glum. "I don't know. As long as I could, I guess."

"I don't see the point."

"Well, you wouldn't."

"What's that supposed to mean?"

"Seriously? Kevin the Wonder Boy, who never made a mistake in his life. What do you know about anything except the view from your ivory tower?"

He seemed to tense a little beside her, and Lori thought she might have hurt his feelings. She was so wrapped up in her own misery that she didn't much care.

She said after a time, "Are you going to tell my mother?"

He finished his gelato. "That depends."

"On what?"

"What the story is."

137

He held out his hand for her empty cup, and crossed the street to dispose of it. He returned after a moment with two bottles of water, and handed one to her. He opened his bottle and took a sip, but didn't say anything else. He just waited while the fountain splashed behind them and the tourists paused to aim their cell-phone cameras, and a group of men in white shirts strolled by, talking loudly in Italian.

Lori said, "I got to know Sergio—kind of—in college, when I was researching internships. He helped me line up a summer job at the winery, but he never told me it was his family's business. Of course I figured it out later, but by then it didn't matter because I broke my leg and couldn't go, and then I met Mark . . ." She glanced at him. "You know about Mark? I was engaged to him. And when that blew up . . . I mean, when I screwed that up . . ." She shrugged. "It seemed like a good idea to try to pick up where I'd left off. I always had this fantasy that something great was waiting for me in Italy, like my destiny, you know? And okay, so for a while maybe I thought it was Sergio. But, you know, while I was engaged to Mark of course I knew Sergio was seeing some-one else. Why shouldn't he? I just didn't know he had married her. Not until I was here, anyway."

She lifted the water bottle and took a long drink, eyes straight ahead. "Still, his dad wanted to honor his commitment and offered me an apprentice-ship and a place to stay, which was nice. But after a few days I could tell that wasn't going over so well with certain other members of the house-hold."

Kevin murmured, "I can imagine."

She looked at him sharply. "What's that supposed to mean?"

"You're kidding, right? No woman wants her husband's old flame moving into the house, especially when she looks like you."

Lori wrestled for a moment between insult and flattery, then let it go with an unhappy shrug. "Anyway, it wasn't his wife. It was his mother." She took another drink of water. "Italian women are strange."

Kevin laughed softly, but stopped when he saw the look on her face. "So you moved into town and told them to forward your mail so your folks wouldn't know what had happened," he guessed.

"More or less."

"I still don't know why you didn't just go home."

"Like I said, you wouldn't." And when he drew a breath for a sharp retort, she held up a staying hand. "People like you don't have any idea what it's like to be me. I changed my major three times in college. I had an affair with a married professor. I flunked two courses. I left UCLA because I couldn't keep up and I barely made it into UVA.

I got engaged to the most wonderful guy in the world and walked out on him three months before the wedding. All I've ever done my whole pathetic life is screw up and waste chances and I just couldn't face that look in my mother's eyes one more time. You're good at everything, Kevin, you always were. You were team captain, you were class president, you made law review, you didn't just pass the bar, you practically sailed over it, and the next thing we know you're pulling down a half mil a year and dating the boss's daughter. You're in the top freakin' one percent, what can you know about what it's like for the rest of us who are barely squeaking by?"

"Not the top one percent," Kevin said. He took a drink of his water and replaced the cap. He glanced at her, trying to coax a smile. "Maybe the top ten."

But Lori just stared miserably at her feet. "Don't you get it, Kev? I've never been good at anything. Not one single thing. I had one chance to do one thing right, and—surprise! I blew it again. I can't go home. Not ever."

Kevin said, "Well then, you'd better start learning Italian, baby, because the only job lower than the one you just walked out on starts on a street corner about three blocks from my hotel."

She lunged angrily to her feet but he caught her arm. "Forgive me, princess, but I have a hard time feeling sorry for anybody who could solve all her problems with one phone call to her rich daddy back in the States. You're not the only person in the world with troubles, you know, and most of them are a lot worse than yours."

She jerked her arm away and for a moment they glared at each other, her nostrils flared, his lips set tight. The silence grew a little awkward, both of them realizing that they did not want to spend whatever time they had together fighting, but neither one of them knowing quite how to end it.

Lori muttered, "You always were a prick."

He replied, "And you always were a brat. Now it seems to me you've got two choices. You can stalk away in righteous indignation, or you can let me buy you that dinner. What's it going to be?"

In another moment she sank back down beside him, her hands clasped loosely between her knees, still scowling. "It had better be expensive."

He grinned a little, and nudged her gently with his elbow, and this time, after only a slight hesitation, she smiled back.

"Yes'm, it was a blow, a real blow," said Farley solemnly. "She was a fine woman. I appreciate all them cakes and casseroles you left, though."

Lindsay patted his arm sympathetically, and Cici added her own murmurs of sympathy. This was the first time they had seen Farley since his sister-in-law's funeral.

Bridget's eyes were brimming with compassion.

"It's never easy to lose a family member. You just let us know if there's anything we can do, you hear? And I wrapped up a cherry pie for you this morning. Don't leave without it."

"Yes, ma'am, Miss Bridget." He touched the brim of his camo cap respectfully, his ginger-bearded face softening as he looked at her. "That's right kind of you."

He was a gruff mountain man with a limited vocabulary and a rather unpleasant chewing tobacco habit, but in all the years the ladies had lived in the old house he had never failed to show up when they needed him, whether it was with tiles to repair the roof or a sheep dog to gather escaped livestock or a tractor to clear their snowed-in driveway, and he never charged them more than ten dollars. Not ten dollars an hour; just ten dollars. It was no secret that he had a tiny crush on Bridget, which was hardly discouraged by the fact that she was always sending him home with pies and cakes and plates of cold chicken—which was only fair, she insisted, considering all the cheap labor he gave them.

He turned to Lindsay. "I hear you're getting married, Miss Lindsay."

Lindsay beamed at him. "That's right. Next month. We're going to have a big party here afterwards. You're invited, of course."

He replied by spitting a stream of tobacco juice into the soda can he carried for that purpose.

"You need anybody to say the words over you, you let me know."

Lindsay looked briefly horrified, but disguised it quickly with a smile. Farley, as it turned out, was a mail-order cleric who had saved their spring blessing of the vines ceremony when he stepped up to the occasion. Weddings were, of course, another matter entirely.

"Thank you, Farley," Lindsay said, "but I've already spoken to Reverend Holland."

"Well," he agreed, shifting the tobacco wad to the other cheek, "wouldn't want to cut into his business none."

Cici came to Lindsay's rescue, even though she was barely able to keep a straight face herself. "Farley, we'd better get started before it gets too hot."

For the next two hours the house rocked with the clatter and crunch of demolition and disposal. Nails screeched and posts fell. Farley lowered four-by-sixes through the window and into the waiting bed of his pickup truck with a thunderous clatter while Cici filled barrels with smaller pieces of debris. Lindsay decided this would be a perfect time to drive over to the Hummingbird House to consult with Paul on some wedding details, and Bridget locked herself in the workroom with six dozen gift bags to fill. Ida Mae turned up the radio, opened the kitchen windows, and started a batch of apple-cheese bread that could be frozen until it was time to turn it into finger sandwiches for the wedding.

Farley left with a truck full of scrap lumber, ten dollars in his pocket, and a cherry pie on his front seat. Bridget tied back her hair, grabbed a broom and dustpan, and went upstairs to help Cici. The space was still covered with plaster dust and plastic drop cloths, the furniture from both rooms had been piled in the hall, and the wallpaper still clung to the grayish, bedraggled walls in a few stubborn patchy spots. But for the first time, with the dividing wall gone, the room was revealed for what it must have been in its prime and soon would be again: a light open space with high whitewashed ceilings, dark wide plank floors and soft sunshine filtering through the two big, wavy-paned windows. When they first moved in, Cici had built a closet for each room and had spaced them against the far walls, so that a nook was now opened up on either side of the big room. The fire-place with its painted mantel was now perfectly centered, rather than crowded against the door as it once had been, and already Bridget could envision two wing chairs drawn up before it, maybe with a comfortable ottoman between them holding a tray and two wine glasses, and a pretty shawl casually tossed across the arm of one chair. She had already purchased five gallons of Wedge-wood blue paint, because Lindsay said that was one of Dominic's favorite colors, and bright white for the trim and the paneled wainscoting that defined two walls and was now a rather non-descript eggshell color. There was an Oriental carpet in the attic done in shades of blue and gold, and Lindsay had some gorgeous cobalt pieces that would look stunning on the bookshelves Bridget intended to persuade Cici to build. She couldn't wait to get started.

"Wow, Cici, this room is going to be gorgeous. What a difference! You know what we should do? We should put up a curtain and keep this place off-limits to Lindsay until it's finished, then do a big reveal just like they do on those television shows. Oh! We could put a bow across the door, and bring Dominic and Lindsay up to see it at the same time!"

Cici looked around the room in satisfaction, leaning on the snow shovel she had used to scoop up the demolition debris from the floor. "It's a little more work than I thought," she admitted, "but it'll be worth it when it's done." She looked at Bridget a little anxiously. "It *will* be done on time, right? Because it won't be much of a wedding gift if all we have is a big empty room with dusty floors and stripped-down walls."

"Oh, sure," Bridget said. "All we have to do is paint and bring in some furniture."

"All I had to do was take down a wall," Cici reminded her, "and that took two weeks."

"But we also got the wallpaper down and all the

stuff moved out. The floors are mostly covered already so we don't have to worry about drop cloths. I'll start taping off the trim tonight, and once that's done everything else goes pretty fast."

"Well, I guess we've done this enough times by now to be experts. Will you have time to make curtains?"

Bridget turned a mildly challenging look on her. "Will you have time to build bookshelves?"

Cici considered that for a moment, then gave a resigned, lopsided grin. "Deal," she said. "But I don't know how you're going to be able to do all this, plus bake a wedding cake, plus make all the food for the reception—I mean, vine-burning party—if I'm going to be too busy building shelves to help."

"You'll have those shelves done in no time," Bridget assured her. "You'll have plenty of time to help."

"That's a relief," Cici murmured with a small roll of her eyes.

Bridget ignored her sarcasm and looked around the room, her expression a little wistful. "Did you ever think when we bought this place that one day we'd be making room for a man to move in?"

"We made room for Noah," Cici reminded her.

"That's different. He was a child."

Cici nodded. "I know what you mean. It is a little strange. This has always been a woman's place. Our place. And now . . ." Her smile held a trace of nostalgia. "Well, everything is different, isn't it?"

Bridget nodded. "And it's about to get a lot more different. You know, I really can sympathize with Lindsay letting herself get so crazy about the wedding. It's a lot easier to focus on the things you can control, like musicians and photographers, than things you can't, like how your life will never be the same once a man moves into your bedroom."

Cici nodded, sighing. "Isn't that the truth?" Then, "Fortunately, she has friends to make sure he has a bedroom to move in *to*. Come on, let's get the rest of this dust swept up and I'll help you tape the trim."

They were late gathering on the porch. Dominic had joined them for supper, then returned to his office to finish up paperwork, as he often did. The lights still burned in the barn. Bridget had wanted to finish prepping the walls and taping off the trim, and Cici had gathered a bushel basket of apples which seemed to have fallen to the ground overnight. She threatened to send them all home with Dominic for his horses, but knew that the thriftiness within all of them would have them peeling, blanching, canning, freezing, and drying apples for most of the day tomorrow. Still, she secretly looked forward to the day when

Dominic's horses would move in and save them all the bother.

The dove gray sky brought with it a pale, chill breath that tasted of snowy winters and wind-stiffened days yet unborn. A lone star twinkled in the distance, and faintly, on the hillside, there was a dull patch of washed-out color, courtesy of early turning leaves.

Bridget pulled her cardigan around her shoulders. "Fall will be here before you know it."

Lindsay smothered a groan. "You don't have to tell me. Twenty-five days left."

They didn't have to ask what she meant. The only calendar that mattered to anyone on Ladybug Farm these days was the calendar that counted the days to the wedding.

"What if it snows?" Lindsay worried out loud now. "Remember we had three inches on Halloween last year. I should have thought of that. How could I not think of that?"

By now her friends had come to accept the uselessness of trying to convince Lindsay of the absurdity of her catastrophizing. Instead, Cici sipped her wine and observed, "I can't think of anything more romantic than an outdoor wedding in the snow."

And Bridget added, "I have a gorgeous fur-trimmed white cape you could wear, with a hood."

Lindsay said excitedly, "I love that cape!" Then

she settled back and took a sip of her own wine. "I hope it snows."

The kitten, who was currently called Rumplestilskin, strolled nonchalantly across the porch. All three women watched him warily, protecting their glasses. But he surprised them by leaping lightly into Bridget's lap and curling up contentedly on her knee. Bridget looked smug.

"We need to start gathering up those walnuts before the squirrels do," Cici observed, rocking easily in her chair now that she knew where the cat was. "And Ida Mae says if we don't cut back the blackberry bushes they're going to take over the raspberries. She's probably right."

"Noah always does that," Lindsay said. And then she corrected herself firmly, "Did that."

Bridget sighed. "I don't want to alarm anyone, but we may be getting too old for this."

"Bite your tongue," said Cici. She cast a glance over her shoulder and added in a lower tone, "Especially around Ida Mae. I have this ongoing nightmare that if she ever does realize how old she is, that will be the end of her."

"I don't have time for blackberry bushes. I only have twenty-five days before the wedding."

"And I have four hundred sixty miniature fondant grape leaves to make next week," Bridget sighed.

"We'll help," Lindsay and Cici volunteered quickly.

She smiled. "Thanks. But you're going to be busy making the miniature grapes."

Lindsay let out a sigh and sank down in her chair, resting her head against the back and cradling her wine glass against her chest. "You know what we're too old for, don't you? Weddings."

The other two raised an objection but she insisted, "I'm serious. There's a reason people get married in their twenties."

Cici, after a moment, gave a reluctant nod of agreement. "Their parents are still alive to take charge of everything."

"And if you think about it," Lindsay went on, "this really was Lori's party. Everything from the dress to the vineyard theme to the colors to the decorations, I completely stole from her."

"That's not true," Bridget objected. "Lori's colors were cabernet and rose. Yours are—"

"Garnet and rose," replied Lindsay placidly. "I defy you to tell the difference."

The other two considered that for a moment. "Well," said Bridget at last. "That may be true, but you have better bridesmaids."

The three of them lifted their glasses to one another in a salute.

"Besides," Cici said, taking a sip of her chardonnay, "if you think about it, none of those choices were really Lori's. We kind of pushed her into all of them. So it really was our wedding from the beginning."

"Well, maybe," Lindsay agreed. "But I still think the world would be a happier place if there was a rule that everyone over forty had to be married at the courthouse in front of a justice of the peace and two witnesses."

Bridget and Cici exchanged a look. "Well, this is a change," observed Bridget. "It was your idea to have a formal wedding. You wanted everything to be perfect, remember?"

Lindsay lifted one shoulder in a small shrug. "It's entirely possible," she admitted, "that perfect is overrated." She looked at Bridget. "How many miniature grapes do we have to make?"

"Six hundred thirty," replied Bridget, and both Cici and Lindsay stifled a groan.

"You know," said Cici, glancing at the empty chair next to Lindsay, "this is going to sound strange, and no offense to you guys—but I really miss Dominic when he's not here. He always has something interesting to say."

"Well, I am offended," objected Lindsay, though she did not look it.

"I know what she means," Bridget insisted. She stroked the sleeping kitten absently. "It's nice to have something to talk about besides weddings and menopause and sagging breasts."

Lindsay raised her eyebrows high. "I hardly ever talk about my sagging breasts."

"Then you're the only one," said Cici.

They rocked and sipped their wine while the

shadows deepened along the porch. "The days are getting shorter," observed Cici.

Lindsay glanced at the chardonnay left in her glass. "We should switch to merlot soon."

"Chardonnay in the summer, merlot in the autumn, cabernet in the winter," agreed Bridget.

The lights went out in the barn, and they all smiled, each to herself, as they watched Dominic cross the yard. "Good evening, my ladies," he said, mounting the steps. He dropped a kiss on Lindsay's head. "The days are getting shorter. Always bad news to a farmer."

"We were just saying that," Cici said.

"Although I'm not sure about the bad news part," said Bridget. "Even farmers need to rest some time."

He smiled and picked up the bottle of wine. "What are we drinking tonight?" He examined the label in the light from the open window, and poured himself a glass. "It will be merlot season soon. Chardonnay in the summer, merlot in the autumn, cabernet in the winter."

He lifted his glass to them, and took his chair. Another Ladybug Farm evening had begun.

CHAPTER FIVE
ฌ
Friends and Lovers

Lori wanted to change for dinner, even though it meant having Kevin wait in the filthy lobby of her building. She would have invited him up, but with two people in the room there wouldn't have been room enough to change her mind, much less her clothes. When she came down, he was brushing suspiciously at his own clothes and glaring at the desk clerk. "Jesus, Lori, I think this place has fleas."

"I think so too," she agreed gamely. "Funny though, I've never seen any dogs in here."

He glanced around in undisguised distaste. "This was the best you could do? Don't you have a credit card?"

"It's my dad's. And if he starts seeing things like rent and groceries on it, he'll be over here in a heartbeat."

Kevin noticed her dress, a cute little boat-striped jersey with a cut-out over the chest that hugged her figure like a glove, and the red patent shoes that set it off. He lifted an eyebrow. "Well, I'm glad to see poverty hasn't affected your fashion sense. What is that, Prada?"

She grinned and did a little twirl, copper curls

bouncing in the dusty light. "Now *this* is the kind of thing my dad expects to see on his credit card. I didn't want to disappoint him."

Kevin drew a breath for an exasperated reprimand, caught himself, and settled for, "You look nice."

The smile she returned told him he'd made the right choice. "Thanks. And if it makes you feel any better, I got it in a consignment shop. The shoes are new, though." She stretched out her foot to show him.

The desk clerk leaned forward to better appreciate the view, leering at her. Kevin locked down his gaze and said something sharp in Italian. The other man straightened up when Kevin put a protective hand on Lori's back. "Let's get out of here before we catch a disease."

"He's a perv. Just ignore him." Lori glanced up at Kevin, a corner of her lips turned up with a speculative smile. "What did you say to him, anyway?"

"I told him to keep his eyes to himself and his hands off my sister."

"Oh yeah? It sounded like you said something else."

"How would you know?"

"It sounded like you said 'lover.' My lover."

"That much Italian you know. I should have figured."

She laughed as they stepped out into the filtered

154

golden sunlight of an early Italian evening. The streets were not so crowded now, the pace was a little slower. Voices called from open windows and laughter spilled out of open doors. The air was scented with garlic and yeasty bread, overlying base notes of rich dark earth and damp stone and ripe, sun-baked fruit that was the very essence of the Italian hill country. Kevin leaned back his head and took a deep breath.

"Well, I guess this is worth it, even if you have to live in a place like that," he said. "Just look at that sky. It's like a Renaissance painting. If I were you I wouldn't want to leave either."

Lori said, "Yeah, I felt like that when I first got here, too. But after a while, it's just a place." She glanced at him suspiciously. "What is this, some kind of reverse psychology? Aren't you supposed to be talking me into going home?"

He laughed softly. "Honey, I'm the last person in the world to be telling you what to do. I promised to look you up and deliver some presents, that's all. Maybe I'll take a few selfies of us in front of some ruins and send them back to your mom, but then I'm done."

Lori said expectantly, "Presents?"

"Your mom sent you some stuff. Bath salts, I think."

"Jasmine?" she said hopefully.

"I don't know. I didn't open it."

"Well, you ate my cookies."

He said, "Don't pout."

"Did you bring them?"

"What?"

"My presents."

"Do you mean now? Tonight?" He shook his head. "They're back at the hotel."

"Can we go get them?"

He gave her an incredulous look. "No. I'm hungry. You really *are* a brat, aren't you?"

She looked annoyed for a moment, and then she sighed. "No," she said, "just homesick."

Kevin dropped a hand on her shoulder, giving it a brief, sympathetic squeeze. And then, because she didn't seem to mind, he left it there throughout the walk to dinner.

They were seated on a walled terrace next to yet another fountain, this one set into a hanging garden of riotous red and purple blooms. A warm breeze tossed the candlelight around while the sky slowly faded into that gentle lavender color that seems to last all night in the hill country. Lori grew animated as Kevin brought her up to date on the news from Ladybug Farm, and she asked a dozen questions in between enthusiastic bites of mushroom ravioli and stewed calamari, occasionally answering them herself and waving her wine glass for emphasis. Had he tasted the first crush? What did he think? Of course it was young yet, but had he noticed that whisper of elderberry in the top notes? That was going to mature into a complex flavor layer that, when blended with the syrah they were growing now, would be worth putting up for an award, or at least that was what Dominic said. And speaking of syrah, had they started harvesting yet? Because the plan was to harvest at least half a ton this year from the old vines, which wasn't a lot but it was enough to tell whether or not it was worth bottling on its own, or whether it would be better to wait until the new vines starting bearing next year. And speaking of that, what did he think of the label? Because a label could make or break a wine when they started distributing, especially if they expected to get into the better retailers.

By the time the main course was served, she was educating him on the politics of the wine industry in the US—California, according to her, practically ran its own wine mafia—which was nothing compared to Italy or, even worse, France. For his part, Kevin was pleasantly surprised by how much fun she could be when she talked about something other than herself, and by what an interesting young woman she had become. He ordered another bottle of wine. He sat back and sipped it while she finished a story. He said, "You know, kiddo, I think you were wrong."

"About what?" She mopped up a bit of sauce with a crust of bread and popped it into her mouth.

"About not being good at anything. Dominic said you were a hell of a winemaker."

A slow delight spread over her face like a blush. "He said that?"

"He did. And he seemed really anxious for you to get home." He shrugged. "Of course, I didn't get a chance to spend a lot of time with him, but I couldn't help noticing there doesn't seem to be any real plan in place for sales. You don't have to major in business—which I believe you did—to know you can't succeed in business without sales."

She frowned a little and picked up her glass. "Dominic has a sales plan. It just can't be a priority right now. After all, he's only one person."

"He mentioned that."

"Ha." She finished off her wine and set it down with a flourish. "So I was right. You were sent here on a secret mission to talk me into going home."

"Nope." He refilled her glass. "I don't care what you do. I was just pointing out that you're not as dumb as you like to pretend, and I don't feel sorry for you anymore."

She glared at him. "I never asked you to feel sorry for me."

"Good. Because I don't."

They stared each other down for a long moment. Lori was the first to blink. She shrugged uncomfortably and took a sip of her wine. "I'll go home," she said. "Just as soon as I figure out what to tell everyone."

"I take it the truth is not an option."

She gave him a sour look. "I meant something that doesn't make me look like a total loser."

"I see your problem." But he said it with the kind of smile that made her resist the urge to toss the contents of her glass at him.

The waiter came over to clear their plates and said something to Kevin, whose response in easy Italian seemed to please him. When he was gone, Lori said, "How did you learn to speak Italian, anyway?"

He looked at her for a moment as though he was debating whether to answer, and then he lifted his own glass. "I spent some time here right after I landed my first big client. There was a girl, and I thought I had a lot to say to her. But she didn't speak English."

Her eyes took on a teasing spark. "And this was before or after the boss's daughter?"

"After." He took a thoughtful sip of his wine. "I think."

"Well, that explains how you knew my dress was Prada. Were you in love?"

He smiled and tilted his glass to her in a brief salute. "Everyone falls in love in Italy."

"What happened to her?"

"No clue."

"You're a pig."

"Oh, I remember now." He pretended thoughtfulness. "That's what she said too, right before she broke up with me."

Lori laughed, and he smiled back. They drank more wine, and the silence between them rested easy. She glanced down at her glass, and then at him, almost shyly. "Can I tell you something?"

He inclined his head curiously.

"I used to have a giant crush on you," she admitted.

"Oh yeah?" He looked mildly surprised, and hugely pleased. "When?"

"I don't know. When I was a little kid." She gave a small awkward shrug. "I thought that whole Clark Kent thing you had going on was crazy sexy."

He grinned and pushed at the bridge of his glasses. "Is that right?"

"Clark Kent," she told him sternly, "not Superman. You *do* know the difference, don't you?"

"Yep." He took off his glasses and began to polish them importantly. "Spandex."

That made her giggle, and her eyes danced in the candlelight. He replaced his glasses and came around to her chair. "Hold that smile," he said. He took out his cell phone, bent low so that his head was close to hers, and stretched out his arm to snap a photo with the fountain in the background. "There," he said, typing out a message as he returned to his chair. " 'Lori says hi.' " He sent the photo to his mom.

She took a sip of her wine and set down her glass, looking at him speculatively. "So what's the deal, Kevin? I know you didn't fly all the way over here just to take me to dinner. Which was delicious, by the way. Thanks."

He returned his phone to his pocket. "I told Mom I was going to Rome for a job interview. She figured since Tuscany was practically across the street, I should stop by."

Another girl would have let that slide right by. Lori caught it like a Venus fly trap. "Did you? Have a job interview, I mean."

He picked up his wine glass, leaned back in his chair, and regarded her with absolutely no expression for a time. Then he said, "No."

Her brows quirked together curiously. "Anyway, what happened to your job at the law firm?"

There was a moment of debate, but not too long. For some reason, while lying to his mother had been difficult but not impossible, lying to Lori just seemed pointless. He sipped his wine, watching her. "I managed a couple of big trust funds for the firm," he said. "One of them, I happened to know, was plumped up mostly by money that was obtained in questionable ways . . . mostly by taking little old ladies' life savings and investing in bad bonds. Not anything that was provable, you understand, but it irked me just the same, especially when one of the little old ladies in question came to me for help with an IRS problem. She was about to lose everything—her house, her bakery business, her car, and even her future income—for a $75,000 debt. She'd worked all her life, was barely getting by as it was, and wouldn't you know she'd invested over a hundred grand with this dude and his bad bonds five years ago. If she hadn't she would have been able to pay her tax bill before it got that high. Usually I can negotiate these things out, but she'd had some bad legal advice before she even got to me, piling up a ton of debt in attorney's fees, and everything I tried fell through. Finally it came down to the wire one Friday afternoon. Her assets were frozen, my hands were tied, and she was going to jail unless she paid that bill in full by five o'clock. So I transferred the funds from the other client's trust fund account to pay the IRS."

Lori's eyes were big. "God, Kevin."

He toyed with the stem of his glass, his eyes falling briefly. "It was stupid. I don't know what got into me." He frowned abruptly and said, "Actually I do."

He looked at her. "When I first got into law I was just like every other bright-eyed kid, ready to go out and defend the downtrodden, fight for the right, all that crap. What I found out is that practicing law is mostly about trying to figure out how to get around it, or to figure out how people who are rich enough to pay you can get away with breaking it. And that most of the time what's right and what's legal don't have a lot to do with each other. It doesn't take long for the lines to blur. And it's not just that, you know." The frown deepened. "I think that after all those years, doing the *right* thing for a change, instead of the legal one, actually felt like vindication. Like it was restoring the balance, somehow."

He shrugged and took a sip of his wine. "Anyway, like I said, it was stupid. Of course, first thing Monday morning I cashed in some stocks and replaced the money in the client's account. I went to my boss and told him what I'd done."

She looked horrified. "You *told* him?"

"I had to. This is serious business. Besides . . ." He shrugged. "It would have been picked up on the next internal audit anyway."

Lori shook her head. "You make a terrible criminal." And she thought about that for a minute. "But I guess if you have to be bad at only one thing in your whole life, that would be the one to pick. So the client was mad?"

"Don't know. I was escorted out by security within the hour."

"They fired you?"

"And disbarred me."

"What?" Her eyes went wide. *"Disbarred?* But—but that means you're not even a lawyer anymore! How can they do that?"

"They had no choice. What I did was criminal, and that's frowned upon in the law profession." The faint imitation of a smile that touched his lips did not reach his eyes. "Kevin the Wonder Boy, huh?"

"But . . ." Lori cast around for the words, her eyes filled with disbelief. "But you put the money back!"

"Which is why I'm not in jail."

"And then you confessed, and your client, the little old lady—you saved her! Doesn't that count for anything? Most people would say you're a hero!"

This time his smile seemed a bit more genuine. "I am also unemployable. It turns out 'embezzlement' is one of those red flags they look for on a resume."

Lori sagged back against her chair, staring at him, her hand resting on her chest. "Kevin," she said. "I am so sorry."

The genuine distress in her eyes touched him, embarrassed him, and pulled at him in some indefinable way. He couldn't face it for very long, and he dropped his gaze, lifting his wine glass again. "Anyway, that was nine months ago. Since then I've had a lot of time on my hands, so I thought . . ." He forced a brief light note into his tone. "Why not go see what Lori is up to?"

Her tone was quiet, still filled with shock and disbelief. "What are you going to do?"

"I've been living on savings," he said. "Cashed in my investments, rented out the condo, sold all the furniture . . . turned in the car before I left. I'm going to have to leave DC anyway; too expensive. And I don't have as many friends there as I thought I did."

"Wow," she said softly. "Wow."

He leaned across the table and refilled her wine glass. "My mom doesn't know. I'll have to tell her eventually, but I was hoping to frame it in a happy ending before I did. You know, one of those 'but it all worked out for the best' things. So far, happy endings have been a little hard to come by. Like jobs."

Lori regarded him solemnly for a long moment. "We are a couple of hot messes, aren't we?"

He lifted his glass to her. "Here's looking at you, babe."

She raised her glass back. "And you."

They drank.

The waiter left the check and Kevin reached for his wallet.

"Kevin . . ." Lori looked worried. "Can you afford this? Not just dinner, but this trip, the hotel . . . Do you need a place to stay?"

Her concern was so genuine, and he was so touched, that for a moment he didn't know what to say. And then he took out a credit card and held it up between his thumb and forefinger before placing it on the table. "I may not have much left," he assured her, "but my credit is excellent."

"Well, in that case . . ." She pursed her lips

thoughtfully, then raised her glass again. "Let's order dessert."

He gave her a single small, incredulous shake of his head, then turned and signaled for the waiter.

Kevin and Lori joined the crush of people on the street for the traditional after-dinner passeggiata, when the locals left their homes for the relatively cool outdoors to stroll and be seen, to catch up on gossip, perhaps to go for gelato or to window shop. It was a time of gaiety and easy social discourse, friendly, noisy, busy. The two Americans blended in easily, taking their time, smiling at the locals, peering into shop windows. They walked with their fingers linked unself-consciously, absorbed in the sights and sounds of a culture that was not their own.

"What would you be doing if you were home right now?" Lori asked.

Kevin glanced at his watch. "Let's see. It's four in the afternoon there . . . probably sitting in my underwear with a bottle of beer watching *Ellen*."

She punched him playfully. "You would not."

"Woman, you know nothing about me. What about you?"

Lori's expression softened, her eyes focusing on a place he could not see. "I don't know. Getting all sweaty cleaning the chicken coop, maybe, or walking the vines. Only a few weeks before harvest so you want to be really careful about bugs and disease. Or maybe working down in the winery with Dominic, or . . ." A smile lit the corners of her lips. "I'll tell you what I'd really like to be doing—taking orders in the office! And some-times, if Ida Mae and Aunt Bridget are starting supper and the windows are open, you can smell bread baking and maybe pork chops with that spicy applesauce . . ."

He groaned out loud. "Seriously? You're talking about food after the meal we just had?" And then he looked at her curiously. "So that's home for you? Ladybug Farm?"

She seemed surprised at the question, and even more surprised by the answer. "You know something? I think it is."

The thoughtful frown on her brow evaporated as she was distracted by something in the distance. "Look," she said, pointing. "The chocolate shop is open. Can you smell it? They make the most incredible dark chocolate cherry nougat thing, you've got to try it." She tugged at his hand. "Come on!"

They bought a bag of chocolate and shared it as they strolled around the city. She told him about the time she had decided that Ladybug Farm should go into the wool-production business, but had sheered the sheep a month too early and ended up having to buy sweaters and coats for the whole flock when a late freeze came. He told her about the time he had defended a sheep for trespassing in a mock trial in law school, and they both laughed until they staggered and the locals thought they were drunk. They reminisced about growing up together on Huntington Lane. They talked about their parents, and their school friends, and about the dreams that hadn't come true and the few that had. They eventually left the crowds behind, lost in their own conversation as they took a winding cobbled path that climbed above the city. They sat on the remnants of a stone wall that dated back to the Romans, and speculated about how it must have been here then while they watched the lights of the city below. They talked about art and architecture, and when Kevin discovered Lori had not yet been to Florence, he decided they should take the train the very next day and see it all. Kevin noted with some surprise that midnight had come and gone hours ago, and they started back down the path.

The little street was lined with houses that were decorated with painted doors and bright shutters, and pots of fragrant herbs and flowers climbed the stone steps that led to them. There was darkness behind most of those windows as families slept the peaceful sleep of those who worked and played hard. Streetlights were few and far between, but the sky still held the remnants of a Tuscan day that was so saturated with light darkness never really fell, and the air smelled like lavender. Kevin kept his hand on her waist, because it was late and the street was uneven and it seemed like a gentle-manly thing to do, but also because he liked the way it felt. And Lori leaned close to him, simply because it was good to be close to him. It almost seemed, in fact, as though there had never been a time when she was not close to him, and there never would be.

Her voice was drowsy and comfortable as she said, "Thanks for coming all this way to rescue me, Kevin, even if I didn't need rescuing. You always were a perfect big brother."

One of her curls tickled the back of his hand, and he caught it with his forefinger, twirling it absently. It felt like silk. "I never thought of myself as your big brother."

"Well . . ." She glanced up at him coyly, a flash of starlight in a midnight sky. "To tell the truth, neither did I. But you would have made a great one."

Kevin smiled at her. Her skin was like porcelain in the shadowy purple light. "Now can I tell you something?"

"Sure."

He said, "I used to have a crush on you, too."

She stopped and turned to face him, her face alight with astonished delight. "You did not!"

"The summer I came home from my junior year in college," he admitted, "and you had just turned sixteen, you about drove me wild."

She laughed out loud, her eyes bubbling with

pleasure. "What do you know about that?"

"Yeah," he agreed. "What do you know?"

She looped her arm through his and started walking again. After a moment she said thoughtfully, "Why do you suppose we never got together, Kev?"

"Aside from the fact that you were a brat?"

"And you were a prick."

"And for most of my life you were jailbait . . ."

"Well," she admitted, "there's that."

"Not to mention the fact that every time I saw you, you were dating some football player twice my size."

She said in a voice that was oddly soft, almost shy, "I would have dropped them all in a heartbeat for you."

He stopped walking. She turned to him, placing her hands lightly on his chest, looking up at him. "I'm not jailbait any more, Kevin," she said.

"No," he replied huskily. He was surprised to note that he could hardly hear his own voice over the thunder of his heart. He put his hands on her waist; he drew her close. "You're not."

She wrapped her arms around his neck. He bent his head to hers. They sank into the kiss like sea creatures too long out of the water, like birds first discovering the joy of flight, like wandering orbs suddenly and gratefully pulled into each other's gravitational path. And afterward neither would be able to explain why they had waited so long.

CHAPTER SIX

ဢ

Folly

Long before there had been a Ladybug Farm Winery, Blackwell Farms had been shipping its award-winning wine all over the country. And long before that, at least according to Ida Mae, whose degree of reliability about such things varied widely, the cellar beneath the barn had been a speakeasy and a moonshine distillery. Even now, on particularly damp days, an imaginative person might catch a whiff of corn whiskey seeping up through the stone floor, its faintly pungent aroma wafting like a ghost beneath the rich fruity smell of fermenting grapes.

None of the farm's current owners had even known there was a cellar beneath the barn until the original building burned down. There, beneath an almost-buried trapdoor, they had discovered the old Blackwell Farms winery, all of its equipment from the sixties still intact and, for the most part, still functioning. Even though it had taken over a year to crystallize, the dream of Ladybug Farm Winery had been born that day when the three of them descended that narrow set of stairs and explored the dusty old winery by flashlight.

That cellar was now a brightly lit, clean and

sanitized space whose walls were lined with casks of wine, stainless steel sinks, cupboards, and bottling equipment. There was a raised oak table in the center and a rack of glasses overhead, although the only tasting that went on in this room was done by the owners. The public tasting room, when it opened next spring, would be in The Tasting Table restaurant a few dozen steps away. Twin steel doors opened at the far end of the room directly onto the vineyard, so that wagons filled with grapes—and trucks filled with crush —could back up to the doors and empty their cargo directly into the winery. The big room was alive with the breath of fluorescent lights and the heart-beat of pumps.

The barn had been rebuilt over the winery and sectioned off, with part of it for domestic use and another part for the winery office. Although they could no longer keep animals there—except for Rebel, who could always find a way to be wherever he was not wanted, and the kitten, who seemed convinced there were mice to be found and who was no doubt right—they still used the big space for storage and workshop projects. They had wanted to move the winery office to the restaurant, which was much nicer, but Dominic insisted on staying close to the wine. So they built walls, added electrical outlets, a telephone, and Internet connections, and turned one corner of the barn into the operations office for Ladybug Farm Winery.

Lindsay could not, of course, be satisfied with a utilitarian space filled with file cabinets and steel shelves, so she had given it her own decorative flare by whitewashing the plank walls and hanging an oversized painting of a cluster of grapes over the desk, adding framed photos of Dominic's father and Judge Blackwell during the days of the original winery to the shelves, and bringing down a patterned carpet from the house for the floor. There was a sturdy oak table in the center of the room, just big enough to accommodate five or six chairs, and it was here that the partners in the winery gathered to have their meetings.

When the ladies had established the Ladybug Farm Winery a mere nine months earlier and taken on Dominic as a partner and operations manager, he had insisted that the company be run like an actual company. Board meetings were scheduled once a month, reports were given, proposals approved, and votes were taken on matters small, like where to order bottles, and large, like how to price those bottles. While Lori had been a part of the operation during the summer, those meetings had been filled with lively debate and a multitude of questions. These days three of the four board members were more than a little distracted by deadlines that were much more pressing than the spring launch of their first vintage.

"There's a definite advantage to a ten-dollar

bottle of wine," Dominic explained to them at the October meeting—the last one before the wedding. "But there's a real downside too. If we decide further down the line to ship out of state, the taxes and licensing fees will eat us alive . . ." He cast a puzzled glance around the table, but no one would quite meet his eyes. "Ladies, do I have your attention? Is everything all right?"

"Oh, yes," Bridget said with a quick smile, but her foot was tapping impatiently under the table.

"Fine," Lindsay assured him. "Green bottles."

"Ten dollars," added Cici, checking her watch. "Perfect."

Dominic hesitated, then said, "I propose a retail price of $12.95 per 750 milliliter bottle."

Cici looked at her watch again. Bridget drummed her pen absently against her steno pad. Lindsay maintained an absent smile and a gaze that seemed focused somewhere on outer space until the silence became palpable and she abruptly came back to earth. "Second," she said, a little too loudly.

Dominic swept the others with a studious look. "In favor?"

"Aye," the three of them chorused on cue.

Dominic lifted an eyebrow toward Bridget. "Madame Secretary?"

"Right." She scribbled a note on her pad.

He fixed his gaze on her. "Further business?"

"Oh," she said, looking confused. Then, "Oh!

Yes, burning of the vines party. The website has presold fifty tickets already! At five dollars apiece, I know it wasn't designed to make money, but I think we can offset costs. And that's not even counting the people from town who will pay at the door. I'm thinking we might have as many as a hundred fifty people! And I was remembering last year when Lori found those monogrammed wine glasses at a dollar twenty-five each . . ." She looked cautiously hopeful. "I know it's last minute and we might not be able to pull it off, but if I could find her source and we could get the glasses monogrammed with the name of the winery and the date, people could take them home as souvenirs and, while it wouldn't exactly be like having 'Dominic and Lindsay' engraved in a heart, it *would* be an advertising expense and we wouldn't have to wash the glasses."

Dominic grinned. "I vote aye. Ladies?"

Everyone murmured an enthusiastic agreement, and even Lindsay seemed to relax. "That's a great idea, Bridge," she said. "Thanks."

When Ladybug Farm Winery was first established, their board meetings had been held at the kitchen table around a pot of coffee and a plate of cinnamon rolls. Even though prosperity, in the form of a semi-anonymous investor, had enabled them to move out of the kitchen, morning meetings still included coffee and a plate of Ida Mae's homemade cinnamon rolls. Dominic reached for one now, endeavoring with the gesture to take the meeting to a less formal level.

"Ladies," he said, "I know your heads are filled with orange blossoms and lace, and don't think I don't appreciate that. After all, I'm getting married too." A glance around the table elicited smiles that were slightly less distracted than they had been before. "But . . ." There was only a slight sobering of his tone. "We're still running a business here and, for better or worse—to coin a phrase—the wedding date also happens to be our busy time. We'll start bottling the crush next week and let it lie until spring—well, except for the bottles we'll be sampling at the wedding party. I'm holding half in reserve to blend with the new crush that should be ready by early summer. Now, as we discussed before, we're leaving the grapes on the vines longer than normal to concentrate the flavor, but that's risky. Bad weather—drought, an early frost, even a bad rainstorm—could put us out of business for this harvest. We might have to put some money into hiring extra workers, and if we do that we'll have to cut back somewhere else. If you'll all take a look at your budget sheets, you'll see that we're going to be running slightly in the red for the winter as it is, so . . ."

A glance around assured him that no one was looking at her budget sheets. Bridget scribbled on her pad, Lindsay leaned over and whispered something in her ear, and Cici, stretching to read what Bridget was writing, pointed at one of her notes. Dominic said, "I don't suppose there's any chance that those are minutes of this meeting."

Bridget looked up guiltily and the other two sat back. "Oh, Dominic, I'm sorry," she said. "I have been taking minutes, they're right here . . ." She flipped a couple of pages on the pad, looked a little flustered, and said, "Well, they're mostly in my head. It's just that there's an awful lot to do before the wedding, and I have to write things down as I think of them."

Cici said quickly, "I did look at the budget, but we all knew we'd be running negative revenue longer than we expected when we decided to wait until spring to ship, right? And we all agreed not to sell an unfinished wine, right?" She looked to the other women for support, then back to Dominic. "Is that the right term? Unfinished?"

Dominic looked grave. "Cici," he said, "I don't mean to push into family matters, and I know I was the one who encouraged Lori to stick with this apprenticeship in Italy, but you need to know we can only go so far as a one-man operation. If there's any way you can convince Lori to come back here and work—even for a stipend—you need to do it. I know she'll probably be getting offers from all over the country once she finishes her year in Italy, but you've got pull, right? After all, this is her wine. And it's really very, very important that someone other than myself understands the business if we're going to survive. So would you ask her?"

Reading the temperature of the room, he found it a bit less warm than he would have liked, so he added, "Once the wedding is over, of course."

Cici seemed relieved that his request was no more complicated than that, and she smiled. "Sure. I'll ask her."

There was a beat of awkward silence, and then Bridget said cheerfully, "I got a cute e-mail from Kevin. He had dinner with Lori. I'll send you the picture."

Dominic said, "Thanks."

Lindsay said abruptly, "Okay, that's it, then. I move we adjourn."

Before Dominic could reply, Cici said, "Second," and pushed back her chair.

"Aye," said Bridget, and quickly gathered her pen and notebook.

Dominic said, "Ladies, I know you've got a lot on your plates, but before you go we really need to talk about—"

"Whatever you decide, Dominic," Cici said, moving toward the door. "We trust your judgment."

"After all, you're the manager," Bridget added brightly, following Cici. "Great meeting, though. Thanks."

The door opened on a bright square of morning light and closed again quickly, leaving only

Lindsay behind. "Honey, I don't mean to complain," Dominic said with a small frown, "especially when I know the reason everyone is so distracted is because you're all working so hard on the wedding. But this first year is crucial for the winery, and I need you all to know what's going on. Someone has to be able to take over for me when I'm not here, and if I'm traveling around the country selling the wine I'm not going to be able to be here every day running the winery, now am I?"

"I know, I know, I really do," Lindsay said, placing her hands on his chest in a quick, reassuring gesture. "You probably think you've gone into business with a bunch of pinheads, but we're really not. Not usually, I mean. It's just that—well of course, we all want the winery to succeed, but you're the expert and, well, if we're not giving you the kind of support you need it's all my fault, so don't blame Bridget and Cici. I just . . ." She cast her gaze around the small room helplessly, as though looking for words. "This is such a big step for us, Dominic. For all of us. I just want this wedding to be magical. And maybe . . . I don't know. Maybe I'm trying too hard. I know I'm driving the girls crazy, and you too, and I'm really nothing but a walking disaster area, but it's all because I want this so much. I want us all to be a family. I want your family to be happy. I want you to be happy with us, with living here. I want it all to be perfect. I want . . ." Her eyes were suddenly hot and wet as she looked up at him, and she could feel her nose go red. "*Everything* for you."

The shadow of frustration that had been building in Dominic's eyes slowly faded into a gentle, thoughtful regard, and then he extended his hand. "Walk with me, cherie."

Lindsay dashed a hand across her eyes impatiently and sniffed. "Oh, Dominic I know you're busy and so am I. Just ignore me. I cry about everything these days. Really, you don't have to . . ."

"Walk," he repeated sternly, and wrapped his fingers firmly around hers as he pushed open the door and stepped into the sunlight.

The morning sun had crested the mountains, and the dew evaporating off the vines gave off a fine golden mist. The goat bleated a greeting from behind its sturdy wire fence a few dozen yards away and Rodrigo the rooster flapped his colorful wings atop the hen house and crowed importantly as they passed.

A well mulched path led around the cultivated vines and behind the barn, wandering into the woods. A hundred years ago those woods had been formal gardens lined with hedges and accented by topiaries, complete with reflecting pools and statues and artificial waterfalls that tumbled into artificial meandering streams, all of it fashioned after the overdesigned gardens of European aristocrats. It hadn't been called The Gilded Age for nothing, and no excess was too grand for those with the means to afford it. And no European garden—or imitation of one—would have been complete without a folly in the center of it.

The follies of the grand European estates of the time were often open-sided pavilions shaped like pyramids or the Grecian Coliseum or even cathedrals. They served absolutely no purpose except as an architectural indulgence, but were usually elaborately designed and constructed. The folly that the Blackwells had built to accent their garden had been a bit more practical, with a door and windows, marble floors, a wraparound porch and a fireplace with carved cherubs. It looked like a little fairy house with its pointed tin ceiling, octagonal shape, and excessive ginger-bread trim. Garden parties once had been held there, along with ladies' afternoon teas and even a wedding or two. It had fallen into disrepair over the years, and the woods had grown up to hide it so completely that the ladies might never have known it was there had not Lindsay happened to stumble on it during an afternoon walk. It had quickly become Lindsay's favorite place on the entire property, and earlier that year Dominic and Noah had restored it back to its former glory, replacing the broken windows, shoring up the sagging porch, painting it the same deep green it once had been, with white trim and a bright yellow door. Lindsay used it as her art studio now, and sometimes she and Dominic would have lunch here, or a picnic supper with wine and candles. It had become their place.

Dominic slipped his arm around her waist as they walked down the path toward the folly. He said, "In the first place, we already are a family— you, me, Noah, and Bridget and Cici and Lori, too. A piece of paper and some vows won't make that any more true, and you of all people should know that."

She ducked her head a little, embarrassed. "I do know that. Of course I do."

"And in the second place," said Dominic, holding aside a low-hanging branch that had encroached partway across the path, "I'm really not sure how much more magic you think this wedding of ours needs, because it seems to me like we've already gotten more than our share. At least I know I have."

She smiled. "That's sweet of you to say."

"I'm serious." His fingers caressed her back in silence for a few steps, and when he spoke again his tone was somber. "When Carol died, it was a dark time for me. We'd been married almost thirty years, and with the kids gone . . . it wasn't easy to get used to, not any of it. Eventually, of course, I left South Carolina, moved back here, settled in, started over, because that's what you do. You go on. I'd had a good life, better than most men, better than I deserved. I'd loved a good woman, raised great kids, done interesting work. But it was over, or at least that's the way it seemed, and all that was left for me now was just to go through the motions and wait for time to spin out. And then that young Lori came bouncing into my office one day talking about opening up a winery, and then I met you ladies, and next thing I know I'm back home again, working the same vines I grew up with, watching a dream come true that I'd given up on forty years earlier. And if that wasn't enough, there was you, and you snatched my heart right out of my chest the first time I laid eyes on you. It would have been more than I could ask for just to be here, and get to look at you every day, just to feel the way you made me feel. But you loved me back. You actually wanted to marry me. I thought my life was over . . . and then it started up again, better than ever. Honey . . ." He stopped as they reached the folly, and turned her in his arms, looked down at her quietly. "If that's not magic, I don't know what it is."

Lindsay circled her arms around his neck and tilted her head back to look up at him. What she saw filled her eyes with gentle wonder, as it so often did. "You," she said softly, "are the most incredible man. I don't know what I did to deserve you, but I'm so glad I did it."

"Then, my darling girl . . ." he stroked her cheek with his knuckles, his eyes quiet with gentle question as he studied hers. "What are you so afraid of?"

She searched his eyes. "Dominic . . . what if your children don't like me?"

He looked puzzled by the question. "Of course they'll like you, cherie. Everyone likes you."

"But," she insisted, "what if they don't? Or . . . or what if I don't like them? It's different with you," she rushed on. "You've already met everyone I love, and they love you back. But . . . these are your children, and they will always be your children, and . . . what if they don't like me?"

He nodded thoughtfully, understanding. "Well then," he decided after a moment, "I'll simply have to disown them, won't I? Take them out of the will, turn their pictures against the wall, strike their names from the family Bible."

She gave a nervous, self-deprecating laugh, and started to turn away. He clasped her hands and brought her back to him, his expression serious. "Lindsay, love, I'm proud of my children and I'll always love them. But do you remember that life I told you about, the one before you? That's where I raised them to be strong and independent, and now they're off living their own lives, being exactly what I taught them to be, and they've been doing that for a good many years now. They have no part in the life you and I are building together,

184

and they know that. Although," he added, coaxing a smile, "they're always welcome to visit, I hope."

"Of course!" she said swiftly, and she looked both embarrassed and relieved. Her shoulders even sagged a little, as though having suddenly released an invisible burden. "I know that. I know everything you said is true, but . . ." She pressed her face against his shoulder, hiding it. "Do you remember the first time you brought me here?"

"I do."

"You told me you loved me, and I . . . wouldn't say it back."

"I noticed."

"I wanted to," she assured him with another quick, apologetic glance. "But I couldn't. Because you said something else that day, do you remember?"

"No." He cupped his hand against the back of her head, twining his fingers lightly through her hair. "But if it made you hold your tongue, I'm sure it was very foolish."

"Actually, it was pretty smart. You said we'd both seen too many summers to make mistakes." She stepped back a little so that she could look up at him, trailing her hands down his arms until she entwined her fingers with his. "Everything is so perfect, Dominic. You are so perfect, and I waited so long to find you, and I only get one chance to do this right. I don't want to make a mistake. Not with the wedding, not with the reception, not with you, not with anything or anyone that's important to you. But it seems that the harder I try to make everything perfect, the more mistakes I make. I don't want to disappoint you."

His eyes crinkled with a smile. "Well, let me ease your mind on that score. You will disappoint me someday, just like I'll disappoint you. That's half the fun of growing old together, learning about the parts that fit together and the parts that don't and deciding that both those things are okay. As for the wedding—I hope it's not perfect. I hope it rains, or the dog runs away with the ham, or someone drops the ring in the mud, because that's what memories are made of, now aren't they?"

Her eyes went wide and dark with anxiety. "The dog! I didn't even think about the dog!"

He threw back his head and laughed. "You see, cherie, why I love you so?" He dropped a kiss on her nose, and then on her lips, tenderly. "Thank you for not being perfect."

He stepped away and tugged at her hand. "But I didn't bring you here to fritter away the day with kisses, as sweet as they are. I have a wedding gift for you."

"A wedding gift? Oh Dominic, I didn't think we were going to . . ."

He covered her eyes with his hand and encircled her waist with his other arm, guiding her around the small building. "Step lightly, now," he cautioned. "Lean on me."

"Dominic, what . . ."

He stopped and turned her forty-five degrees, and then removed his hand from her eyes. Lindsay blinked and looked around, unsure at first about what she was seeing.

On the east side of the folly, just where the creek bank curved into a small noisy waterfall, an area of about twenty square feet had been mowed flat and staked off with contractor's tape. The path down which they had just walked from the barn widened and circled around almost like a driveway. Lindsay looked up at him, puzzled.

"I have a contract on my house," he told her. "We close in thirty days."

She squealed out loud with delight and hugged him hard. "Dominic, that's wonderful! I'm so excited for you! Oh my goodness." She stepped back on a breath, her hands clasped together against her lips, her eyes shining with wonder and no small amount of trepidation. "This is really happening. We're really getting married."

"I certainly hope so," he confessed, eyes twinkling, "otherwise I'm going to be homeless."

She laughed and threw her arms around his neck again. "I'll start helping you pack tomorrow. The girls can help too. Oh my." She sank back again, arms still looped around his neck, only this time she looked uneasy. "There's an awful lot to do."

"Not as much as you think. The couple is buying

it furnished. All I need to pack are my clothes and tools. But that's not why I brought you here."

He turned her again to face the taped-off square of ground and explained, "I thought we could use the profit from the sale to build our own place. Here."

She blinked and stared at him.

"The structure is sound," he went on, "and there's plenty of room for a small kitchen. We'll enclose the west side of the porch for your studio. You said the light is best there, anyway. And this . . ." he strode around the taped area gesturing, "is the master suite, with a small screen porch overlooking the creek and big windows on either side. The spring is plenty deep enough for a gravity fed water system, and it's only a hundred feet or so to run utilities from the main power pole at the street. This is good flat bottom land, fine for gardening, and if we thin out a few of those saplings to let the sun in, your roses will thrive here. Look . . ." He extended his hand to her. "I've already started your garden."

Wordlessly, she followed him around the side of the building, to where a trellis had been built adjacent to the eastern column of the little porch. In the center of a freshly mulched circle of earth was a new rose cutting.

"A rose," she said, kneeling to look at it.

"Not just any rose," he corrected, smiling as he watched her. "Your rose. The Lindsay rose."

For their first Valentine's Day together, Dominic had given her a rose bush that he had cultivated specifically and named for her because, he said, the color of its bloom reminded him of the color of her hair. If she were perfectly honest with herself, Lindsay would have to admit that it was at that moment that she had known somewhere deep inside that he was the man she wanted to marry. They had planted the original bush in the formal rose garden beside the house, but he must have kept a cutting and rooted it for an occasion just such as this.

"I ran an irrigation hose from the stream," he explained, "to keep it watered for the next couple of weeks. But it gets plenty of sun here, and by the time we're settled in here next spring, it should be blooming like crazy. And every time it does, it will remind you of our union, and the life we're making together."

Lindsay stood and walked to him, took his face between her hands, and kissed him hard on the mouth, and then, melting into his embrace, more tenderly. "You," she said softly, "sure know how to brighten my day. In fact, you brighten my whole life. Thank you for the rose."

He smiled into her eyes. "You're more than welcome, my love. We'll put up a picket fence to keep the deer out, and paint it white. This place will be a little paradise in the glen."

"But Dominic . . ." She hardly knew where to

start, or what to say. She looked around, and all she saw was love. She looked at him, and she knew she was exactly where she wanted to be. So all she said was, "I've never transplanted a rose this late in the season before. Not in this zone, anyway. Shouldn't we have waited until spring?"

"Not at all. Roses do best when exposed to a little stress. It makes them stronger." He smiled and tweaked her nose. "Just like people."

She turned and leaned back against him, looking at the folly and the beginning of the little garden he had started, relaxing in the circle of his arms. "Wouldn't it be something to bring the old gardens back the way they used to be? We could plant the whole place with Lindsay roses."

"We could do that," he agreed thoughtfully. "But it would be more practical to clear the land for vines."

She cast an amused glanced toward him. "Well, that's a relief. I was afraid you might be getting too sentimental."

His eyes twinkled. "You see? I told you I would disappoint you one day. And now it's out of the way. But if it makes you feel any better, I'll make a point of saving room for your rose garden."

"I appreciate that."

Lindsay couldn't help smiling as she turned back to look at the folly with its gingerbread trim and fairy-tale columns, the imaginary white picket fence upon which roses would climb and nod their heads in the breeze. The bright gurgling stream, the cottage kitchen with herbs in the window boxes, the screen porch where they would sit in the swing and have morning coffee. The winter evenings when they would sit beside the cherub-etched fireplace and watch snow fall silently in the woods. The life that would unfold in quiet contentment before them here, in this enchanted place.

And it broke her heart to turn back to him and say, "Dominic, it all sounds beautiful, and I love you so much for thinking of it, and it's not that I wouldn't love living here, but . . . we already have a place to live."

He smiled. "I know, love, and the ladies are very generous to want to share the big house. But every married couple should have a home of their own, and this is ours. If we start building now and the weather holds, we should be in by Christmas," he added.

Lindsay's eyes clouded with uncertainty. "Not have Christmas at Ladybug Farm?"

He laughed softly. "Sweetheart, this *is* Ladybug Farm. You're a hundred steps away from the front door. Of course we'll have Christmas there. Easter too, and most Sundays, and wine on the porch every evening. Nothing will change."

"Everything will change," she whispered. And it was as though, once she said it, the very hills and valleys and woods and streams, every blade of grass and spark of sun and random breeze took the words into themselves and echoed them back to her: *everything will change.*

She gave herself a little shake, as though if she refused to listen to the words they would cease to be true. She turned back to Dominic, pleading for his understanding. "It's just that . . . oh, I wasn't supposed to tell you, it was supposed to be a surprise, but . . . Cici and Bridget have gone to so much trouble fixing up a place for you, for us, remodeling the entire second floor, practically . . . it was their wedding gift to us. They wanted us to have a room of our own. In the house. They made a whole suite, tore down walls, repainted . . . They wanted you to feel welcome."

"Ah," he said, and nodded slowly. "So that's what all the construction noise was about. I should have known Cici was up to something."

"It's just that . . ." She looked at him helplessly. "How can I hurt their feelings? They've worked so hard."

He said nothing for a moment. Then he smiled and kissed her nose. "Well then. I'll try to act surprised."

She searched his eyes. "You're not disappointed? Because if this is what you really want . . ."

"Sweet girl," he said simply, "all I want is for you to be happy. That's all this was about. Making you happy."

He squeezed her waist and kissed her hair, and

they walked back to the house. Lindsay tried hard not to admit that she had never felt less happy in her life.

Kevin's pillow smelled like jasmine. He smiled even before he opened his eyes, letting the moment linger. He turned over in bed and found his glasses. Lori was sitting in a patch of buttery sunlight on the faded upholstered bench of the window embrasure that overlooked the courtyard below, sipping cappuccino from a paper cup and turning the pages of an Italian newspaper. She was wearing a loose white tank top and a long printed skirt, and her hair, spilling wild and curly over her shoulders, reminded him of bright new pennies tumbled in a stream. He wanted to tell her that she looked like a Botticelli painting. He wanted to tell her that he would conquer the world for her and ask nothing, not even a smile, in return. He wanted to tell her that he loved her beyond all reason or possible understanding. Instead, he propped himself up with a pillow behind his head and said, "Whatcha doing?"

She turned a page of the paper. "Looking for a job. I figure if you're going to be able to continue to support me in the style to which I've become accustomed, at least one of us needs to be working."

Kevin's hotel, while a far cry from the hovel in which Lori had been living, was not exactly the

Ritz Carlton. But the air-conditioning worked most of the time and there was daily maid service, and it was on a quiet street less than a block from the shopping district. There was a coffee shop downstairs and some excellent restaurants within walking distance. For the past two weeks they had lived like tourists, dining out for every meal, sharing a bottle of wine in the courtyard in the evening, taking the train to nearby attractions, walking the vineyards, touring the wineries. Kevin wanted to show her everything, give her everything, make her eyes light up at every possible moment. Of course he knew they couldn't keep that up forever, but forever was not something either of them talked much about.

But he thought about it. A lot.

He said, "Since when did you learn to read Italian?"

"I didn't." She got up and came over to him, two cups of cappuccino and the newspaper in hand. "That's why you should probably be the one with the job."

He took the newspaper from her and set it aside. "As it happens," he said, "I know a place where there's an opening for a barista."

He took the coffees from her and put them on the nightstand. He pulled her into his arms and lost himself in her dancing eyes and the smell of jasmine. She tasted like cappuccino and every dream he had ever had, and when finally, reluctantly, they parted, he could tell she kept her expression stern with an effort.

"I'm serious," she said.

"So am I." He pushed her hair away from her face with a single tender stroke and added softly, surprising himself, "Oddly enough."

She looked a question at him, but before he could answer it, or even think of an answer, she lowered her lashes, which were pale and coppery without makeup, and turned in his arms. She rested her head against his shoulder and gazed at the ceiling. "There's something you should know about me, Kevin," she said.

"Do you mean the part about you having terrible luck with men?"

She cast a quick sideways look at him. "Yeah. That part." Her fingers, like the delicate treble notes of a haunting melody, slid down his arm and entwined with his own. He actually heard music in his head when she did that. She said, "You need to know this. I loved them all, I really did. Jeff, he was a fantasy. A daddy fantasy, if I were to be completely honest. And Sergio . . . well, he was the mystery, wasn't he? And there's always some-thing so irresistible about a mystery. Mark . . . I think he was what my mother wanted for me. Safe, practical, steady."

She was aware of his attention, which was piercing and true, a physical thing. She said, choosing her words carefully, "But I think every girl has a picture in her head of her ideal man, her Prince Charming. Any guy who comes into her life has to meet those minimum Prince Charming requirements or it's a no-go, a complete non starter." She glanced at him quickly, a little shyly. "My Prince Charming wore Clark Kent glasses and quoted Daniel Webster and was a total ass about getting the details right. He'd drive an ordinary girl crazy in two minutes. But somehow, in the back of my mind, that's the standard I was holding everyone else up to and . . . that's why, in the end, everything fell apart."

He was silent for a long time, just holding her. Then he nodded somberly. "Well, I guess there's something you should know about me, too."

"You mean the part about you being a criminal?"

"A not-very-good criminal," he reminded her.

She smiled. "Right."

He said softly, "Guys have a picture in the back of their minds too, you know. And all this time . . . I think it was you."

Her smile slowly faded and she sighed, her fingertips stroking the back of his arm, her eyes upon the ceiling. "Did you ever think you'd have to travel halfway around the world just to find what was in your backyard all the time?"

He kissed her hair. "Never," he replied, "in a million years."

Now she turned to him, her eyes dark and

serious. "Everyone falls in love in Italy, Kevin."

"Oh, thank God." He stroked her eyebrow, the curve of her cheek, and let his fingertip brush the fluttery silk of one coppery eyelash. His throat was so full he could hardly speak, and his voice was husky. "Because I am quite desperately, hopelessly, madly in love with you."

The breath of her sigh whispered across his lips. "That's good. Because I'm pretty crazy about you, too."

He kissed her nose, her ear, the curve of her neck. She whispered, "Oh, Kevin, what are we going to do?"

He settled back against the pillow, drawing her again into the curve of his shoulder. "Baby, you ask me that every day." His tone was gently indulgent. "Do you want me to make something up?"

She turned her eyes up to him, fingers curled upon his bare chest. "Yes, please."

He was thoughtful for a moment, and as he thought, his face grew sad. "Okay," he said. "Summer will end. It always does, even in Italy. The winter winds will come, blowing the roofs off houses and freezing the water in the fountains. You'll hate it here. You'll go back to California, get your master's degree in wine-making, go on to run a famous winery in the States. Marry some lucky investment banker, have three kids and a nanny. I'll hop a freighter to the South Seas, grow a long beard, end up living in a shack on the beach giving legal advice to the natives in exchange for rum. And regret every day of my life that I let you get away."

Her fist tightened on his chest and her brow puckered. "I don't like that one. Make up something else."

"Okay." He threaded his fingers through hers and opened her hand across his heart. "Summer will end. The winds will come, blowing the roofs off houses and freezing the water in the fountains. Our favorite restaurants will close, the tourists will go home. You'll have to start making your own coffee. You'll hate it here. You'll start talking about what the weather is like in Southern California and it'll make me crazy. We'll have a fight. You'll call your dad. He'll send you a ticket home. I tell you to go, you faithless little wench, and you'll storm off to the airport, dragging that great big rolling suitcase of yours behind you. You'll be approaching the boarding gate when you hear someone call your name, and you turn around and see me, pushing past security, running toward you . . ."

Her fingers tightened on his. "Oh, please don't tell me you get mowed down by a security guard with an AK-47."

He chuckled. "No, they're in a good mood that day. You start running toward me, and I sweep you up and twirl you around, right there in the middle of the Rome airport, and I ask you to come live with me in a shack on a beach in the South Pacific."

She turned and propped herself up on her elbows, looking down at him. "And I say yes," she whispered.

"And we have three kids . . ." he murmured, as her face came closer to his.

"But no nanny." She kissed him, long and sweet. And then she murmured softly against his lips, "Ah, Kevin. What is going to happen to us?"

He took her face in his hands, his fingers tangling in her hair. He looked into her eyes and all he wanted in the world was to make those eyes smile, to wipe away all her worries, to promise her everything was going to be all right and to spend the rest of his life keeping that promise. But all he had to offer her was the truth.

"Sweetheart," he said simply, "I don't know."

She sighed, and wrapped her arms around him, and they both discovered, after a time, that it didn't really matter much at all.

CHAPTER SEVEN
ᘏᘄ
There Should Have Been Belly Dancers

Never in the history of engagement parties, everyone would agree later, had there been a more memorable one than the engagement party Paul and Derrick hosted for Lindsay Wright and Dominic DuPoncier at the Hummingbird House B&B on the evening of October 8. The drive was lined from the street to the parking lot with colorful Japanese lanterns, and the parking lot, which had been extended to include a good portion of the west side of the property, was overflowing. Valet parking was of course provided, because when Paul and Derrick gave a party, it was done right.

"On the other hand," Paul confessed to Lindsay with a faintly worried frown on his face as he air-kissed her at the door, "we might have left a tad too many of the details up to Harmony. She has a tendency to drive a theme into the ground. I completely put my foot down about the belly dancers, though," he assured her. "And the fire walkers."

"Now that," remarked Dominic with every appearance of seriousness, "is a shame."

The slightly atonal strains of Moroccan music

drifted through the house from the back garden, where a band dressed in the traditional caftan and fez was set up under a striped canopy with exotic looking instruments and colorful drums. "I hope they know something by the Stones," Dominic murmured to Lindsay, which made her laugh.

The night was crisp and clear, just cool enough to make the warmth of the dancing fire from the brass braziers and the thousands of candles that lined the paths welcome. The entire garden was alight with swaying flames and twinkling lights, and a perfect harvest moon hung overhead, as though it had been special-ordered for the occasion—which, Lindsay speculated later, it might well have been, given Paul's propensity for perfection. Gauze-draped canopies were set up across the landscape, highlighting various stations along the Moroccan buffet—appetizers on miniature skewers served with individual dipping sauces, rich roasted meats, and exotically flavored fried sweet potatoes, a dessert station with gooey honey pastries and bright fruits floating in champagne. There was a flower-draped arbor with a bucket swing made for two, full-length mirrors in gold frames set at precise angles along the paths to reflect the lights and the gaiety, and, in the center of the patio that overlooked the koi pond, an astonishing life-sized photo poster of Dominic and Lindsay had been placed, dominating the crowd. It was clearly a candid shot, with the two of them holding hands against a blurred back-ground of green, looking into each others' eyes and laughing.

Lindsay stared at it, hardly knowing what to say. "How did they . . . ?"

"I really can't imagine," Bridget said, but looked far too innocent to be convincing.

"It's . . . spooky." Lindsay didn't seem to be able to take her eyes off of it.

Dominic's eyes twinkled. "I like it," he said. "Maybe they'll let us take it home after the party."

"I can't imagine why they wouldn't," said Cici, and her tone reflected the kind of horrified fascination that was in Lindsay's eyes.

"Marvelous, isn't it?" Harmony, sweeping by in an elaborate purple and red silk caftan with a matching turban headdress, blew her a kiss. "All of your friends will write their good wishes on it before they leave, and you can keep it as a souvenir!"

Lindsay happened to notice Derrick standing a few feet away just then, and he rolled his eyes to the heavens in a gesture of helpless apology. Lindsay grinned. "Thank heaven it was Harmony's idea," she told Cici. "I was starting to think something had gone terribly wrong with the boys' taste."

"I think it's just what you need over the mantel

at Ladybug Farm," Dominic said, and Cici slapped his arm playfully.

Seventy-two people wandered through the garden, sipping wine and sampling the buffet, laughing and chatting and embracing the happy couple. Many of them were friends Lindsay hadn't seen since she'd left Baltimore, and the Hummingbird House was filled to capacity with overnight guests. They snapped photographs of the elaborate décor for their social media pages and caught up on old times, and when they went home they would take memories, stories, and recommendations to friends and colleagues for the eclectic and elegant little B&B in the Shenandoah.

"Say what you like about Harmony," observed Cici to Derrick as she paused to fill her glass from a champagne fountain that flowed from the mouth of a lion into a sparkling blue tiled table-top pool, "and we have said plenty, but she does know how to make the most of her marketing dollar. This party is going to be tweeted and retweeted for weeks. You won't be able to keep up with the reservations."

"That's true, I suppose." He tried not to look too worried. "I just hope it isn't too over the top. We had hoped for something a little more . . . dignified." Then he cheered. "But the buffet is incredible, isn't it?"

"Out of this world," Cici assured him. "And how many times does anyone in this county get to taste Moroccan food? You boys have definitely taken the quality of life around here up a notch since you moved in."

He looked pleased. "Do you think so? That's sweet of you to say. We do try. Oh, there's George and Arianna. Did you speak to them? My," he added confidentially, "she's put on weight, hasn't she?"

He hurried off to welcome his guests and Cici was still chuckling when Bridget came up beside her. "Oh my goodness, is that champagne?" She stretched across Cici to get a glass and filled it from the lion's mouth. "Isn't this fun? It's just like the old days back on Huntington Lane."

"I was just thinking the same thing," Cici agreed. "It's good to see old friends. Although I can't actually remember Paul and Derrick ever giving a party with a turbaned fortune-teller, even on Huntington Lane, and they gave some pretty outrageous parties."

"Lindsay seems to be having a good time."

"I don't know why she was so worried about trimming back the guest list for the wedding. She should have known Paul and Derrick would outdo themselves for her. And now the people we didn't get to invite to the wedding got to come to a Moroccan feast, even some of Dominic's friends from the university."

"The important thing for a second wedding is to be flexible," Bridget said, sipping her champagne. "It's really silly to try to have a traditional wedding at this age, even if you *are* wearing Vera Wang."

And then she glanced at Cici, her expression a little hesitant, as though she were embarrassed to ask the question. "Do you ever feel . . . I don't know, jealous of Lindsay? Just a little?"

"Do you mean because of Dominic?"

Bridget ducked her head in assent. "And the wedding. And . . . well, yes, the husband."

Cici thought about that, but not for long. "Not really. In the first place, I like Dominic a lot, but he's really not my type."

"That's not what I mean."

"Well, it would make a difference," Cici insisted reasonably. "There's nothing worse than two women interested in the same man, especially if he's only interested in one of them."

"I suppose," Bridget said. "But I'd certainly like to think that grown-up women would have better sense."

"There's nothing sensible about romance, no matter what the age. But the truth is, I've got nothing to be jealous of Lindsay about—except maybe that dress. She's happy, and I'm so glad, but she's no happier than I am. I love my life. I wouldn't change a thing." Cici looked at Bridget, but even before she asked the question, her smile understood the answer. "What about you? A little jealous?"

Bridget nodded. "Sometimes. Just a little. I loved being married, and I wasn't ready for it to be over. I miss my husband. Sometimes I think it's not fair. But then I realize that if Jim hadn't died when he did, I wouldn't have what I have now. Ladybug Farm, and you and Lindsay, and The Tasting Table and the winery and the animals and the garden and even Ida Mae . . . pretty much everything I've ever dreamed of. So yes, I'm happier than I've ever been, or ever expected to be . . . but sometimes a little sad too."

"And that," said Cici, touching her glass to Bridget's, "is perfectly okay."

"Good evening, my ladies," said Dominic, coming up beside them. He smiled and lifted his glass to someone across the garden before adding, "Are you having a good time?"

Bridget laughed. "The important thing is, are you? This is really off the charts, isn't it?"

"Lindsay has some amazingly generous friends," he admitted, glancing around for the hosts, "and they know how to pick good wine. This, however . . ." he nodded toward the champagne fountain, "I wouldn't drink at gunpoint."

"It's not that bad," Cici said.

Bridget added, "It has bubbles, that's all that matters. I'm so glad so many of your friends could make the trip, Dominic."

"I think they feel like the lucky ones. Apparently there's a waiting list for reservations at this place, except for this weekend. The guys cleared the schedule for people who were staying over after the party, and they're providing free transportation to the Holiday Inn for the overflow."

Cici smiled. "That's just like them. And there's nothing they wouldn't do for Lindsay."

His eyes crinkled with a smile. "Then I'm lucky to be joining the family." He gazed over the crowd thoughtfully. "You know, next week we really should schedule a meeting with Paul and Derrick to talk about coordinating some events between the winery and the B&B. Tours, tastings, pairing dinners, that sort of thing. It would be good for both businesses."

"That's a fabulous idea," said Bridget, her eyes lighting up. "We could have farm-to-table dinners at The Tasting Table served with Ladybug Farm wines! Just like they used to do in the old days of Blackwell Farms."

"Of course," Dominic pointed out, "back then, farm-to-table was just called dinner. Who knew eating real food would turn out to be trendy one day?"

"Maybe," Cici said with a pointed look at Bridget, "it would be better to have the meeting after the wedding. We still have an awful lot of work to do."

"Oh," Bridget said, remembering that she still had two walls to paint Wedgewood blue, not to mention two hundred miniature crab puffs to bake and freeze. "Oh, yes, that's right. Food and stuff."

Dominic said, "Come to think of it, I have to meet with the lawyer about the sales contract next week. The buyers want to do a long-distance closing so . . ."

"Closing?" Cici repeated. "Dominic, did you sell your house?"

He looked confused. "Didn't Lindsay mention it?"

"That's wonderful!" exclaimed Bridget. "We'll help you pack. When are you bringing the horses?"

"She must've forgotten," Cici said. "You know how it is with all the wedding chaos. She probably thought she'd mentioned it already. But congratulations!"

He said, "Thanks. As a matter of fact . . ." But his attention was caught by something over Cici's shoulder and he smiled. "Excuse me, ladies, my lovely bride-to-be is waving me over. Someone she wants me to meet, I see. I'll catch up with you later."

Cici watched him go with a faint, puzzled frown. "I wonder why Lindsay didn't tell us about the house?"

Bridget had no answer.

Eventually the band, which was as versatile as it was talented, switched to more familiar Western instruments and contemporary music, and the main patio became a dance floor. Lindsay loved to dance, and couldn't believe her good fortune in finding a man who enjoyed it as much as she did.

"If we lived in the city we could take ballroom dance lessons," she told Dominic.

The music was slow and easy; her arms were around his neck and his were around her waist. He bent his forehead to touch hers briefly. "I don't want to live in the city. Do you?"

"We could go on cruises with all the other old people, only we'd be the best dancers."

"I don't want to go on cruises with old people. We probably should have talked about that."

Lindsay looked up at him, smiling. "Thank you for being such a good sport about this party."

"What's there to be a good sport about?"

"It's a little bizarre. Most engagement parties are all about hearts and flowers and champagne and diamonds."

"Boring," he scoffed. "Besides, there was champagne. Of a sort."

She laughed. "Anyway, thank you for being nice to my friends."

"I like your friends. All of them. I can't bear to think what my life would have been like if you all hadn't moved here."

They finished the dance in tender silence, and turned to applaud the band when it was over. Dominic said, "Sweetheart, why didn't you tell Cici and Bridget my house had sold?"

She avoided his eyes. "Didn't I? I could have sworn I mentioned it." Then, "Oh, look! Harmony is reading palms. Let's go get ours done."

Harmony had set up a table layered in fringed scarves flanked by standing iron chandeliers, their flames bobbing and weaving in the breeze. A brass dome incense burner was centered on the table, and a stream of blue, patchouli-scented smoke curled upward from it. Cici was in the guest chair across the table from her when Lindsay and Dominic arrived, her hand extended palm up while Harmony studied it.

"And three grandchildren," Harmony was saying, and Cici looked alarmed.

"Not anytime soon, I hope," she said.

A small crowd had gathered and everyone laughed. Harmony just smiled complacently. "In good time," she said. "Everything in good time."

Then she looked up at Lindsay and exclaimed, "Oh, there's our bride! I've been just dying to get my hands on you! Literally!" She extended her hand across the table to Lindsay. "Sit down, sit down. I'll read your palm. Every woman should have her palm read before her big day."

Lindsay had never known quite what to think about Harmony. At first she'd been concerned for her friends, who—if one were completely frank—could so easily be taken advantage of. And then she might have been a little jealous at how easily this strange woman had insinuated herself into their lives. Eventually she had confirmed that Harmony was neither a con artist nor a criminal and that, in fact, she might care as much about Paul and Derrick as Lindsay did. And despite her strangeness, Lindsay had grown to like her.

Lindsay took Cici's seat, who sighed, "They'll be Italian."

"Who?"

"The grandchildren."

Harmony made a small production of clearing her spiritual plane with elaborate hand gestures, waving the smoke around the crowd and into Lindsay's face. Lindsay coughed a little and blinked her watering eyes, and Dominic grinned and put a hand on her shoulder. "Better you than me, sweetheart."

Paul and Derrick joined the crowd that was watching, sipping their wine and looking cautiously pleased with how well everything was going. "Not too much?" Paul whispered to Cici.

"Not a bit," she assured him.

Harmony cleared her throat and the show was ready to begin.

"There you go," Harmony said appreciatively, her fingertip tickling the center of Lindsay's palm as she traced a line. "Lovely long life line, filled with accomplishment. One marriage, early in life, very brief. One child, late in life, but hundreds of other children whose lives you changed."

Lindsay lifted an appreciative eyebrow. "I was a teacher," she agreed, even though she knew that Harmony had to have known that.

"Oh, look," exclaimed Harmony, "your friendship line! You are truly blessed there."

"I couldn't agree more," Lindsay said.

"I see a major change in midlife," she went on, "a grand adventure. And here, love and destiny intersect! There couldn't be a more propitious sign for a bride. And here is the point of your union . . . another adventure . . . a sudden surprise . . ."

Lindsay glanced up at Dominic, eye twinkling. "Maybe I'll get my honeymoon after all!"

"As soon as the harvest is done," he assured her.

"What's the surprise?" Bridget wanted to know, peering down at Lindsay's open palm as though she could actually find the answer there.

"More grandchildren?" suggested Cici.

And someone from the back of the group suggested, "More children?"

There was a lot of laughter and teasing and adamant denials from the engaged couple, and no one except Paul noticed the way Harmony's face changed as she stared into Lindsay's palm. He nudged Derrick, who noticed as well and said, rather loudly, "Well, of course we all know this is just in fun. Am I right, Harmony?"

Harmony smiled quickly, but her eyes were dark and troubled for those who cared to look.

"Of course," she said. "Nothing I say is meant to be taken seriously."

"Oh, that's too bad," Lindsay said. "I was really looking forward to that honeymoon. So what else do you see?"

Harmony's smile faltered, and then almost by force of will, deepened. "Destiny," she said. "The man you are about to marry is your destiny. And your marriage will bring you nothing but joy for all your life together."

There were speeches and toasts and a few teary moments. Lindsay lingered long after the party was officially over, embracing friends and thanking Paul and Derrick over and over. "I can't imagine the wedding party will be any better," she said, "I really can't. What would I do without you? Thank you so much!"

Dominic was finally able to pull her away just as the last candle was snuffed, and before the cleanup crew started stacking chairs.

Paul and Derrick saw them safely to their car, and then walked back to the house. They found Harmony in the foyer, sipping a glass of wine and watching through the window. Her smile was quick and false when she saw them. "Well, fellows," she declared, lifting her glass in salute, "another triumph. Well done!"

Paul said, very seriously, "What did you see in Lindsay's palm?"

And Derrick added, "We saw your face."

Harmony hesitated just a fraction of a second too long, and then she cast a brilliant smile at them. "Oh, please, fellows, I just make this stuff up as I go along. You know it's all in fun."

And both of them knew she was lying.

Lori and Kevin sat beside the fountain where they had shared their first gelato, basking in the autumn sun and absently tossing crumbs from the hard roll that remained of their lunch to the pigeons that clustered around their feet.

"Mom's e-mail said everyone from the old days was there," Lori said. "Imagine that. It would have been fun to see them. There were supposed to be belly dancers and sword-jumpers, but Uncle Paul nixed that. Figures. If *I* had been there, there would have been belly dancers. Don't you ever miss home, Kevin?"

"In Italian, sweetie," he reminded her.

With only a slight roll of her eyes, because she had been the one who had begged him to teach her Italian in the first place, she took out her phone and activated the app. It took her a few minutes, but she finally pieced together an Italian version of her question. Kevin frowned when he heard it.

"Let me see that thing." He took her phone. "You just asked me if I require forgiveness for abandoning my mother."

She retrieved her phone. "Let's skip the lesson for today."

He scattered the last of the crumbs for the birds and watched them peck around at his feet as he asked her, "Do you ever mention anything to your mom about us?"

She glanced at him cautiously, but was unable to read anything on his face. His eyes were shuttered by sunglasses. "Do you? To your mom?"

"I couldn't even tell her I lost my job."

Her brows drew together in a mixture of hurt and puzzlement. "Is it the same thing? Are you ashamed of me?"

He looked at her swiftly. "No! God, no." He turned away for a moment, gazing across the square. "I don't know what to say to her." He glanced at her. "Do you?"

She shook her head mutely.

Both were quiet for a moment. Then Kevin said, "Why do you suppose that is?"

Lori looped her pinky finger around his, her expression thoughtful, her tone soft. "I think . . . I don't know, I think for now I want it to be just us. All our lives everything has been about family, and now I want some time to figure out what it means to be us. Does that sound stupid?"

"I think it sounds pretty smart." Smiling, he turned her face to his and kissed her. Fountains in Italy seemed to be made for kissing. As did street corners and cafés, taxicabs and castle ruins; in fact, almost anywhere when you were in love. In Italy, everyone smiled at lovers.

When they parted, Kevin stroked her cheek. His tone was gentle, but serious. "We can't stay here forever," he said. "You know that."

She was quiet for a moment. "I know I talk about home too much." She laced her fingers through his. "I also know I can't go on bumming off you—"

"Hey," he protested.

"Or your credit cards," she went on determinedly, "forever."

"As long as your dad keeps you in Prada, I'm okay," he said, but he couldn't get her to smile.

Lori said, "You probably won't believe this, but I'm pretty insecure. I think it has to do with growing up a fatherless daughter."

He could tell she was serious, so he nodded soberly.

"I mean, my mom was great, and so was my dad—long distance. But I worry about things, probably more than I let on."

He squeezed her fingers. "Baby, I know."

She sighed a little. "Yeah. I guess you do. It's just that . . . I don't want to take any chances with this, with us. I want to keep it safe as long as I can, just like this. I know we can't stay here forever," she said, searching his face, "but what if we go home and—there's no 'us' there? Oh

Kevin, can't we stay for just a little while longer?"

He said, "Mia amore, we can stay as long as you want to."

She leaned her head against his shoulder. "So," she said, "if you *did* chase me down at the airport, and if I *did* agree to live with you in a shack on an island in the South Pacific . . . what do you suppose would happen next?"

He smiled and drew her close, entwining one of her curls around his finger. "Well, I'll tell you one thing," he said. "There would definitely be belly dancers."

CHAPTER EIGHT
ಌ
A Woman's Place

Lori grinned as she checked her messages. "Hey, Mom says they bottled the crush. They only broke six bottles, which is pretty good considering this is the first time they've used the machine, except for a few bottles we experimented with over the summer." But her delight faded as she added, "She also says Dominic wants to offer me a job as soon as my apprenticeship is over."

Kevin glanced up from his own phone. "That's good news, isn't it?"

Lori's expression was glum. "It would be if there was an apprenticeship."

"Oh, what a tangled web we weave." Kevin did not look too happy himself as he pocketed his phone and picked up his coffee. "My mom wants to know what I've heard about the interview. It's only the fifth time she's asked."

They were having breakfast at a café a few streets down from the hotel, which was a favorite place of theirs not only because of the flakey spicy panforte that had quickly become one of Lori's addictions, but because of the free Wi-Fi. The proprietor, a plump, rosy-faced woman who wore a different colored flowered apron every day, had become so accustomed to seeing them that she brought their order now without asking. Kevin always said something sweet to her in Italian that made her blush and shoo him away with her apron, which was no doubt why she always took a little extra care to make sure his coffee was always prepared exactly the way he liked it.

Lori sighed. "What happened to the good old days when news from home was supposed to make you smile?"

"Finish up," Kevin said, standing. "I think I have an idea that will make you smile."

She watched him skeptically as he went to pay the bill, lingering as he always did to pass a few words with the lady behind the counter. He returned looking very pleased with himself, and extended his hand to her. "Come on," he said. "I want to show you something."

She gulped down the last of her cappuccino and let him tug her out of the bakery and around the corner toward the narrow alley between buildings. "Whoa," she said, pulling back. "I thought we were going to a museum today."

"Life is more than museums and train rides, kiddo, even in Italy," he said. "Keep an open mind."

He started up a set of metal stairs, and Lori, mindful of her open-toed shoes and looking around warily for rats, followed a little less enthusiastically. At the top of the stairs there was a door with peeling pink paint, and he surprised her by taking out a key and opening it. With a flourish, he gestured her inside. Lori entered cautiously.

It was a big open room with dusty marble floors and two tall palladium windows, coated with grime, on the longest wall. Half-moon clerestory windows dotted the room at ceiling level, which was so high that Lori had to tilt her head back to make out the very faintest impression of a faded fresco there. The floors were scattered with crumpled newspaper, and there was a cardboard box filled with what looked like mechanical parts, but otherwise the room was empty save for a tiny electric stove and an even tinier icebox at one end of the room. At the opposite side of the room was a giant claw-foot tub. A single thread-bare dishtowel hung on a bar beside a galvanized sink. Lori peeked into a small closet and found a toilet. The whole room smelled like sugared cinnamon.

She said, a little stunned, "Wow."

"It's half the price of the hotel room," he pointed out. Looking around, he added, "But I think I can negotiate it down to a third. And it has free Wi-Fi."

Her footsteps echoed as she walked over to the window and saw a small balcony with another set of stairs leading up. "What's this?"

"It leads to the roof. It would be like having our

own deck looking over the city. All you do is walk out the window." He twisted a metal handle on the window and pushed. Then pulled. He twisted the handle the other way. He pushed harder. Nothing happened. "Maybe I'll work on that," he said.

She thrust her hands into the back pockets of her jeans and turned full circle. She said again, "Wow."

Kevin said, "The language school is always looking for people to teach English. It's not much, but it's enough to live on."

Lori said hopefully, "I could work in the café."

He took her shoulders, his expression gentle but stern. "Honey, you're in one of the richest wine-making regions in the world. You have a college degree, references from two wineries, and you work cheap. You're going to stop feeling sorry for yourself and go out and get a job at a winery, just like you came here to do. Vacation is over."

She scowled and pulled away. "I don't need you to save me, Kevin."

To which he replied, "Somebody has to."

"Yeah, well what about you? You think teaching English part time to people who barely even read and write their own language is a proper use of *your* talents?"

"I think," he replied coolly, "it pays the bills. Eventually I'll get a better job. In a university, maybe, or with an American company in Rome or Milan."

"So why don't you do that now?" she shot back.

He said, "Because you're here."

She had already drawn a breath for a retort before he finished speaking, but now she let it out wordlessly. She looked at him for another moment with a mixture of disgruntlement and tenderness, then she walked back over to the window that wouldn't open, twisting her head to look out and up. "We could put some pots up there and grow flowers," she said noncommittally. "Maybe even tomatoes. That would be fun. Assuming you could get the window open, of course."

"I'll buy a screwdriver."

She turned and looked around the room again, trying to appear thoughtful. "I don't know, Kev. Moving in together is a big step. I hardly know you."

He came up behind her and looped his arms around her waist, resting his chin atop her head. "It'll make a great story to tell our grandchildren. How we lived above a bakery in Italy and slept on a mattress scavenged from the trash . . ."

She looked up at him in alarm and he assured her, "We won't get it from the trash."

She leaned back against him and he went on, "And watched the sun set over the Tuscan hills from our roof, drinking wine and eating bread and cheese for supper."

"Men are such romantics," she observed indulgently, caressing his crossed wrists with her fingers. "And just where are we when we're telling this story to our grandchildren?"

"We are . . ." He thought about that for a brief moment. "Sitting in front of our fireplace in Sonoma, in a big Tudor-style house in the middle of fifty acres of vines, owners and operators of our own multi-million dollar winery called . . ." He tilted his head toward her inquiringly.

"Heart of the Vine," she supplied.

"That'll do for now," he allowed. "A little sappy, but we'll work on it. I'm in my big leather chair, the one you're always wanting to throw out because it's so old, and the leather is starting to crack in places, but I like it because it's just now getting broken in. I'm looking good, if I do say so—white hair, neat beard, a really sharp dresser—not all shrunken up and slumped over like a lot of old dudes. And you are hot, for a sixty-year-old grandmother of eight."

"Eight?" She nodded in satisfaction. "That's impressive."

"Damn right. Our kids are heirs to a dynasty. They know how to do their duty. But . . ." He took her in his arms and turned her to face him, dropping a kiss on her nose. "That dynasty is never going to happen if you don't get off your butt and get a job."

"I've got news for you, lover," she said, draping her arms around his neck. "You don't get kids, or grandkids, by making wine. Drinking it, maybe."

He kissed her, and she murmured, "That's a start." And then, as he bent his head toward hers again, she said, "What if I can't get a job in a winery? What if no one wants me?"

"I want you," he assured her.

"Oh, good. That's a relief. I can just hang out here and stay busy making curtains while you're out making a living."

"This place could definitely use some curtains," he agreed. "And you know what they say. A woman's place is in the home."

She looked at him skeptically. "Oh yeah? And just where is your place?"

Kevin caught her hair in his fingers and pushed it gently back from her face. He looked into her eyes. He said, "By your side."

She said softly, "I love you, Kevin."

He said, "I love you, Lori."

She searched his eyes. "Is this what we're going to do, then?"

"For now . . . Yes. I think so. If you want to."

She sighed, "I want to. I really do." And she melted into him as though there had never been another place where she belonged.

"I wish I knew," Bridget said, frowning as she used a biscuit round to cut pastry dough into two-circles, "what it is about Italy that makes children forget how to use a phone. Kevin hasn't answered a single one of my e-mails."

Cici came behind her with a pastry bag, squeezing a dollop of Bridget's top-secret proprietary crab puff mixture onto the center of each circle. "Well, he did e-mail he'd met Sergio's family. And that Lori looked good. It was nice of him to go all the way out there."

"He hasn't said a thing about the job," Bridget complained. "*Or* about when he's coming home. Just that he'd be staying 'awhile.' What's awhile?"

"Must be nice," said Lindsay, "to be young and rich, without a care in the world, roaming around Italy just because you can." She came behind Cici with a pastry brush and the egg wash, folding each circle in half, pressing the edges together with the tines of a fork, and brushing them with the egg mixture.

Eight days and counting before the wedding. Dominic had gone into Staunton to review the preliminary paperwork on his house sale with the realtor. He had complained about having to be away from Ladybug Farm for the day when there was so much to be done, but the ladies were secretly glad to have him safely away while they finished up the painting on the master suite, which they planned to reveal over the weekend. Before that could be done, however, there was still a reception for over two hundred people to prepare.

The countertops were covered with baking sheets, and the baking sheets were covered with crab puffs in various states of completion— cooling on racks, waiting to be baked, waiting to be wrapped, waiting to be packed and placed in the freezer until the morning of the reception. So far one hundred fifty of the delicate morsels of delight had been completed—not counting the tray that Lindsay had dropped when she burned her hand taking it out of the oven. The kitchen was redolent with the aroma of warm baking pastry and tart seafood, but now it was Ida Mae who removed the trays from the oven and Lindsay, her bandaged hand protected by a surgical glove, had been assigned less hazardous duty.

"I don't suppose you've heard anything from Lori," Bridget said.

"Just a thank you for the bath salts." Cici paused to transfer more of the rich crabmeat filling from the bowl on the table into the pastry bag. "Which is more than I usually hear from her."

Ida Mae gave a disapproving *"hrrmph"* and set a tray of steaming golden crab puffs on the counter with a clatter. "It's your own fault, if you ask me." She picked up an unbaked tray and slid it into the oven before closing the door with a squeak. "What do kids know about how to act like a family these days, anyhow?"

"Now, Ida Mae, I don't think that's fair," Cici objected. "Lori and Kevin are good kids, and we raised them to be strong, independent, contributing members of society."

"And that's what you got, didn't you?" returned Ida Mae with a sniff. "They're over there contributing to some foreigner's society while you've got grapes turning to raisins on the vine—"

"They are not turning to raisins!" cried Bridget, then looked at Cici, worried. "Are they?"

Lindsay said, "Dominic knows when to pick the grapes, Ida Mae."

"I thought that girl wanted to make wine," Ida Mae went on, heedless, "and just whose wine is she making now, after we-all put up with her for nigh onto five years? In my day, a family cleaved together, and that's how you got things done. Why, there was a time when this house held four generations, babies crying, young folks courtin', women working together in the kitchen, men out in the fields, all of them pulling together for the family, and that's the way it's supposed to be."

Cici, Bridget, and Lindsay shared a look, because it seemed unlikely that there had ever been a time when the Blackwells, one of Virginia's most prominent families, had ever required their men to work in the fields or their women to work in the kitchen—even though the idea of four generations filling up the rooms of the big old house did have an undeniable appeal.

"Kids aren't like that anymore, Ida Mae," Cici said. "They want to go off and make their own mark on the world, and what's wrong with that? This country might never have been discovered if Christopher Columbus had never left home."

"Leif Erikson," Lindsay murmured absently, slathering egg on the edges of the pastry. "Leif Erikson was the first to discover the Americas."

Ida Mae turned away from the oven to glare at Lindsay. "Where'd you hear a crazy thing like that?"

"It's true, Ida Mae," Bridget assured her. "The Vikings were here long before the Spanish."

Ida Mae gave an entirely skeptical grunt and began removing the pastries to wire racks to cool, muttering, "It's no wonder them kids ain't got no more sense than they do, filling their heads with such foolishness."

"Either way," said Cici, "Erikson or Columbus, I'm sure their mothers would have appreciated an e-mail now and then. Lindsay, you're really making a mess there."

"Oh. Sorry." The gooey egg wash had slopped over the baking sheets and countertops in Lindsay's absentminded haste, dripping onto the floor in places. She tried to wipe it up with her fingers, made a bigger mess, and went to the sink to dampen a paper towel.

"I read an article the other day," Bridget said, "about how social media is actually making us less social."

"I can believe that," Cici said. "No one uses the telephone anymore."

"That's because nobody cares what the other person has to say," Bridget said. "And listening to someone else takes up too much time."

"That's true," Cici agreed, thinking about it. "There aren't that many people outside this room that I'm interested in listening to."

"It's just like with Kevin," Bridget went on. "He lives three hours away but I see him what? A couple of times a year? But he e-mails every week so no one can accuse him of not keeping in touch with his mother. And Katie doesn't understand why I complain about never seeing the girls when she keeps posting pictures of them on Facebook."

"How many more of these do we have to make, anyway?" Lindsay said, scrubbing the counter with a paper towel.

"We're almost done," Bridget assured her.

"Like I said, it's your own fault," Ida Mae said. She snatched the shredded paper towel from Lindsay and put a wet cloth in her hand instead. "A woman gets married, she takes her husband's name . . ." She gave Lindsay a dark look. "She moves into his house, she puts up with his mother, she raises her kids under his roof. 'Raise up a child in the way he should go,' " she quoted, " 'and when he is old he shall not depart from it.' Your own damn fault."

Cici compressed her lips against a smile and Bridget gave an amused half-shrug, but Lindsay looked oddly uncomfortable. She wiped her hands on the cloth. "Um, girls, could I talk to you about something?"

Cici glanced at her curiously. "Sure, Linds."

And Bridget said, "Is anything wrong?"

Lindsay bit her bottom lip briefly, twisting the cloth in her hand. "No. It's just that Dominic and I were talking and . . ."

The phone rang. Lindsay looked relieved. "Never mind," she said quickly, "I'll get it."

Bridget and Cici exchanged a puzzled look as Lindsay hurried to answer the phone. Ida Mae warned, "Y'all are getting behind." She pushed through the swinging door to the pantry, where the freezer was stored, with a basket filled with packaged crab puffs.

On the telephone, Lindsay said, "Oh, hi, Paul!"

Bridget and Cici turned back to filling the crab puffs, and Lindsay said, "Really? That's fabulous! You are an angel! See you in a few."

She hung up the phone and turned back toward them. "That was Paul," she said. "My dress is here. I promised I'd be right over to try it on." She looked in dismay at the trays of pastries. "I hate to leave you with all this . . ."

Bridget hesitated, then smiled. "Go." She waved her on. "We're almost done anyway."

Cici said, "What was that you wanted to talk to us about? Before the phone rang?"

For a moment Lindsay looked troubled, and then she gave a brief shake of her head. "It was nothing. I'll tell you later." She turned for the door, grabbing her keys on the way. "Oh," she called back over her shoulder. "Your dresses are here too! I'll bring them back with me!"

"But," Cici protested, and heard the screen door slam. "I wanted to try my dress on too," she finished, a little forlornly, to Bridget.

Bridget just gave a satisfied nod and picked up the pace with the biscuit cutter. "Thank goodness," she said. "We'll get this done twice as fast without her, and I might even be able to finish painting the room this afternoon. We can start moving in furniture tomorrow!"

CHAPTER NINE

ಌ

A Matter of Perspective

"Oh my," Lindsay exclaimed softly, turning in profile to the mirror, "you can't even tell it was let out! The seamstress is a genius."

"She should be," Derrick said, stroking his chin as he assessed the drape of the train with a critical eye. "She was trained by Vera herself."

"Not entirely," Paul corrected. He snapped the last hook and made a minute adjustment to the bow at the waist. "But she did train under someone who worked for one of the seamstresses in the New York salon. Seriously, you don't think we'd trust it to an amateur, do you?"

He held up the jacket and Lindsay slipped her arms into the sleeves. He pretended not to notice the bandage on her hand.

"Perfect!" exclaimed Derrick. "Love the way the bow fits into the V in back, and those lace panels look like they were custom made."

"They were."

"You know what I mean."

Without taking his eyes off Lindsay, Paul held out his hand and Derrick placed the satin shoes in them. Balancing herself with a hand on Paul's shoulder, Lindsay slipped them on. Paul held out his hand again, and Derrick swept the hat from its nest of tissue on the bed and presented it to him. Paul maintained an intense and concentrated silence as he finger-combed and curled Lindsay's hair, pinned it over one shoulder, and arranged the cloche just atop the opposite ear.

"Perfection," breathed Derrick, pressing his hands together, and Lindsay gave a hesitant, excited smile.

Paul stepped back, examining his work critically. "You have earrings, yes?"

"Oh." Lindsay touched her bare ears. "Yes, they're my something borrowed."

"Nothing on the neck," Paul advised. "It would only take away from your utterly flawless décolletage, and who knows how many more years you'll be able to say that? Ask that gorgeous fiancé of yours to give you a bracelet."

She pointed out, "He's already giving me a ring."

"Who do you have to do your hair and makeup?"

"Well . . ."

Purline volunteered from the door, "My sister does hair."

Derrick said, "We could probably get Georgette to come down for the day."

Lindsay said worriedly, "I really hadn't planned . . ."

Paul said, "Bridget would have to double the

size of the buffet. The woman eats like a horse."

"I kind of thought I'd do my own," Lindsay said.

Purline said, "I knew a woman that gave herself a home permanent once. All her hair fell out and when it grew back it was stone white."

Derrick stared at her, and Lindsay touched her hair uneasily. "I thought I'd just touch up the color. Nothing major."

"Her eyebrows fell off too," Purline said.

Now everyone stared at her and she explained, "She tried to bleach them. Burned them right off."

Paul pulled his gaze away from her and told Derrick, "Call Georgette."

Purline said, "My sister does makeup too."

"Purline," Derrick said, "was there something we can help you with?"

"Oh. Yeah. I'm making rum-raisin pears for Sunday brunch and I need to know how many folks we're expecting."

"Rum-raisin pears?" repeated Lindsay, interested. "That sounds delicious."

"It is," Derrick confided, "out of this world. She uses a streusel topping . . ."

"Which would be better with a sprinkle of cardamom," Paul pointed out.

Purline scowled at him. "Do you know how much cardamom is a bottle? You'd go broke in two Sundays."

"And serves it with whipped cream," Derrick said.

"Which would be better with a smidge of vanilla bean shaved on top," Paul said.

Purline rolled her eyes and Derrick supplied quickly, "Twenty-two. Twenty-two people for brunch."

Purline gave Lindsay one last appraising look and said before she left, "The dress looks real nice. But my mama could've fixed it for you for half the price."

Lindsay grinned when she left. "She's going to be just like Ida Mae in fifty years, you know."

"Lord preserve us," Paul groaned, "if we have to wait fifty years."

And then Lindsay said, bracing herself for the bad news, "So, how much were the alterations? And does she take credit cards?"

Paul waved away the question. "Not a penny, darling. The woman owes me a favor."

"He got her daughter into the Ford agency," Derrick explained. "She's making ten thousand dollars an hour now."

"Has a hideous cocaine problem," added Paul, "but I can hardly be held responsible for that."

Lindsay laughed and hugged him lightly, careful not to crush the dress. "I don't know whether that's true or not, but I love you for it."

He smiled and patted her cheek. "It will all be worthwhile if we can just get you to the altar without breaking a major bone or slashing an artery," he assured her. He spun her around deftly and began unsnapping hooks. "Now let's get you out of that dress before someone comes in here with a glass of grape juice."

Lindsay laughed, mostly at the notion of anyone at the Hummingbird House drinking anything so mundane as grape juice.

"We've decided on traditional cutaways," Paul said, "even though it is a little non-traditional for an afternoon wedding. But this isn't exactly a traditional wedding, is it?"

"I'll wear rose," said Derrick.

"And I'll wear garnet," said Paul.

Lindsay kept a nonjudgmental expression. "Jackets?"

"No, precious, cummerbunds. Honestly, what are we, ringmasters?"

"And for precisely that reason," Paul said with a pointed look at Derrick, "we decided to eschew the top hats."

The way Derrick remained deliberately silent suggested the decision had not been entirely mutual.

Lindsay smiled. "You guys are the best, do you know that?"

"We certainly aspire to be."

"No, I'm serious." She blinked a little at the surprise of the bright autumn sun when they stepped from shade on the dappled light of the path. "Before I came over here I was really starting to wonder if I was making a mistake, you know?"

Paul stopped still, staring at her, horror and outrage widening his eyes. "I do not know! This wedding is perfection. Nothing about it is a mistake!"

Derrick added with a note of panic, "You are *not* getting cold feet. Tell me you're not."

Lindsay raised a calming hand. "Relax. Everything's fine." She started walking again and her companions, watching her cautiously, fell in beside her. "It's just that every time I turn around I'm bumping into something or breaking something, and every decision I make is the wrong one, and everyone is working so hard, and, really, aren't we too old for all of this? Yesterday Dominic spent twelve hours bottling wine and then after supper started hanging the lights in the gazebo because he didn't think he'd have another chance to do it before the wedding, and Ida Mae almost fell off a ladder the other day trying to clean the chandelier, and the girls have been baking and freezing food all week and then going upstairs to work on the master suite, and Dominic sold his house and I was afraid to even tell them because he wants us to build our own place." She ran out of breath then and just stood there for a moment, tracking down her thoughts. "Not that it matters because of course we already planned to live at Ladybug Farm, that was the plan and it's already settled, but my point is, I was really starting to think the whole thing might be just a giant mistake, and *way* more trouble than it was worth. But then I saw the dress, and it was as though the last puzzle piece fell into place. It's perfect. Everything about it is just perfect. And that's the way it's supposed to be. A wedding is just a symbol of what you wish for your marriage—fairy-tale perfect. Of course you know it's not going to be, but for that one day . . . well, having the perfect dress is a symbol, that's all, but it's an important symbol. So thank you!"

They both looked mightily confused, but thoroughly relieved. "Darling, anything we can do," Paul assured her.

"We are completely at your service," Derrick added sincerely. "Completely."

They helped her place the garments in the back of the car, and Lindsay turned to hug them both. "I love you guys, I really do! Thank you so much for everything!"

Kisses all around, and she drove away, delighted.

Without Lindsay's help, Bridget and Cici were able to finish the crab puffs in less than half an hour. They cleaned the kitchen, left the last trays to cool, and were finishing the final coat of Wedgewood blue on the master suite when they heard Lindsay's car pull up. They quickly put aside their brushes, stripped off their gloves, and helped Lindsay carry the garment bags and boxes up the stairs.

Lindsay was too superstitious to try the dress on again, but she did unzip it from its bag and spread it out on the bed, complete with hat and shoes, for Cici and Bridget to admire. Bridget and Cici couldn't wait to try on their own dresses, and Lindsay clapped her hands in delight when she saw them.

"Perfect!" she exclaimed, and Cici and Bridget each returned a small curtsey in her bare feet. Lindsay pressed her clasped hands to her lips, her eyes shining. "Now it's all coming together. How gorgeous are those colors going to look in the photographs against the background of the mountains and the turning leaves? Paul is a genius!"

"A fact with which he'd be quick to agree," Cici said, turning to admire herself in Lindsay's full-length mirror.

"He was right about the pink, too," Bridget agreed, spreading the folds of her skirt. "It's stunning on me."

"That's because it's French rose," Lindsay reminded her, "not pink."

"And this style is classic," Cici added. "Thank you for not picking something ugly and brides-maid-y."

"I would never do that to you," Lindsay assured her. "Now, about the shoes . . ."

"Paul said dyed-to-match is totally out," Cici said. "Come look at the nude pumps I ordered when I thought I'd be wearing them to Lori's wedding." She led the way to her room. "If you like them, Bridget can order a pair. Three-day delivery, free shipping."

They had just reached Cici's room when the phone rang. She went to answer it.

"It's got to be Paul," Lindsay said, "making sure the gown arrived safely."

And then she heard Cici exclaim, "Noah!" She waved the other two over excitedly, and as Lindsay reached for the phone she said, "Hold on, I'm putting you on speaker."

She pushed the button and replaced the handset. Everyone hovered over the microphone. "Hi, Noah, it's me!" Lindsay said, and Bridget added, "And me!"

"Hi, guys," Noah said. "Listen, I don't have long but they wanted everyone to call home and let you know there's going to be a communications blackout for a while. Don't know how long. You're not supposed to worry."

But when the three women's eyes met, worry was exactly what was reflected there. "Why?" Lindsay demanded. "What's going on?"

"Don't know," Noah said. "They don't tell us privates everything, you know. Even if they did," he added truthfully, "I probably wouldn't be able to tell you. That's why there's a blackout."

"But I don't understand," Bridget put in. "How long will this blackout be?"

"Don't know," he repeated. "But until then, no calls, no e-mail. You can send me stuff, though. You know, in the mail. By the way, thanks for all the cool stuff you sent last time."

"You're welcome," Cici said. "But Noah—"

"Gotta go," he said, "really."

"We love you, Noah," Lindsay said quickly. "And call the minute you can."

"Roger that. Bye."

When he was gone, the three women stood looking at each other, their puzzled expressions tempered with concern. "He sounded excited," Bridget ventured.

"I thought he sounded scared," Lindsay said.

Cici said, "I'm sure there's nothing to worry about. It's probably just routine. A drill, or . . ." She trailed off.

Lindsay said abruptly, "I'm going to see what I can find out on the Internet."

She turned for the door and the other two followed. But two steps into the hall Lindsay stopped so abruptly that Bridget bumped into her.

"What?" Bridget demanded.

Lindsay just stood still, staring at the floor. Bridget followed her gaze. Cici edged around her to see what they were looking at.

"Oh, no," she said.

There on the gleaming hardwood floor at Lindsay's feet was a bright smudge of blue paint, and next to it another. Beyond that was another. All of the smudges were shaped like paw prints, and they led, inexorably, to the open door of Lindsay's room.

In united, silent, dry-throated dread, the three of them followed the paw prints down the hall, through the door. There they found the kitten, its paws tinted with blue paint, contentedly curled up on the once-perfect Vera Wang.

"Not a good day," Cici said heavily. She poured a measure of wine into a glass, reconsidered, and poured a little more. She handed the glass to Bridget.

"It's only three o'clock," Bridget protested, but not very convincingly.

"Feels later." Cici poured another glass.

"Well," said Lindsay, coming into the kitchen, "I guess the good news is that I didn't pay full price."

Cici handed her a glass of wine.

Bridget's face was torn with lines of distress. "Lindsay, did I tell you how sorry I am? I thought I had closed the door. I thought I'd covered the paint tray. The kitten wasn't even in the house when I started painting, I swear. I couldn't be more upset."

Lindsay patted her arm reassuringly. "It wasn't your fault, Bridge. It was an accident."

Cici leaned against the counter with her own glass in hand. "I don't suppose Paul had any ideas about the dress?"

"I don't know." Lindsay took a sip of her wine. "I couldn't hear him over the weeping. His, not mine."

Cici winced.

"I got as much of the paint out as I could," Bridget assured Lindsay anxiously, "and I left it soaking in liquid soap and warm water, but . . ." Her tone was dejected. "I don't think it's salvageable."

Lindsay nodded. She seemed surprisingly sanguine about the whole thing. It was a little spooky.

A savory stew simmered on the back burner; their first of the year. Half a bottle of merlot had been used to deglaze the pan; they were drinking the rest. A swirl of yellow leaves danced past the window on a vagrant breeze, and Ida Mae had a covered loaf of wheat bread rising in the warm corner near the range. All were signs of a fast-approaching autumn. They could practically hear the year spinning out.

Lindsay opened the refrigerator and took out a block of cheese. The other two women watched cautiously as she selected a knife from the rack, and began to slice the cheese onto a platter. "Do you remember," she said, "when I first started planning the wedding and I was so worried about all the other wedding problems that we'd had here? And then I started having all those stupid accidents and you thought it was because I didn't want to get married?"

Bridget nodded mutely. Cici said, "Be careful with that knife, Lindsay."

Lindsay put the knife down and offered the platter of sliced cheese to them. They each shook their heads. She picked up a slice of cheese and bit into it thoughtfully. "I think we both were right," she said. "I never should have planned a wedding here, and I really didn't want to get married."

"Oh Lindsay, don't say that—"

"You're just upset about the dress—"

But she gave a quick short shake of her head to silence them. "I mean, of course I *wanted* to get married, I'm wild about Dominic."

Bridget and Cici looked relieved, and Lindsay took a sip of her wine. "But the thing is, weddings are for brides and I'm really not a bride. I am a grown-up woman who came of age in an era where choosing a man over your women friends was practically an act of treason against the creed of Gloria Steinem, and don't tell me you don't know what I'm talking about because you do."

Cici nodded, sipping her wine. "Men come and

men go, but a good friend is hard to find." Bridget looked a little confused, so she added, "It's a feminist slogan."

"So I think," Lindsay said slowly, piecing together the logic as she spoke, "the problem was that I was trying to be something I wasn't, and that made me do things I didn't want to do. Because here's the thing." She looked at them calmly. "Ida Mae was right. A wife's place is with her husband. But Dominic wanted to build us a house of our own, out of the folly, and I told him no because I didn't want to leave this house. Or you guys, or the life we have here. I should choose him. I should always choose him. But I didn't. Do you understand what I'm saying?"

Bridget's voice was quiet and filled with dread. "No. I don't understand. But it doesn't sound good."

Cici put in, "Lindsay, listen. Maybe you shouldn't overthink this. It's been a rough day. Why don't we just finish our wine and not think about this anymore? Everything will look different in the morning."

Lindsay smiled softly and shook her head. "Everything is already different, that's what I'm trying to say. Actually, that's what I've been trying *not* to say since I decided to marry Dominic, but once I did, everything changed and I need to stop pretending it didn't. That it won't. I'm not upset about the dress. It's actually kind of a relief.

It wasn't until I saw the dress, all . . ." Here she paused a moment, allowing herself a moment of regret for what might have been. "All ruined," she went on, "that I realized I'd been obsessing about the wrong thing. It's the marriage, not the wedding, that's important. You'd think a person my age would know that."

She took a deep breath and let it out again, looking quietly pleased with herself, and also a little sad. "So as much as I love you guys, and appreciate all the work you've done, I choose Dominic. I choose to live with him in a little house in the woods, and I choose to try to take our two grown-up, complicated lives and try somehow to twist them together into this one semi-cohesive unit. That's my first job. As for the wedding . . ."

The phone rang and Lindsay, who was closest, held up a finger. "Hold on."

"That's got to be Paul again," Bridget said with a wince.

"And if you think he was upset about the dress," Cici answered in a near whisper, "wait until she tells him she's calling off the wedding."

They heard Lindsay say, "I'm sorry you must have the wrong . . ."

Bridget's eyes flew wide. "She wouldn't!"

"What do you think this has all been leading up to?" Cici whispered back. "She was a complete wreck before this and now she doesn't even have a dress. She'll get married at the courthouse, you mark my words."

"But . . ."

Lindsay said, "What? What did you say?"

Something in her tone made them both turn to look at her. Her head was bent and she gripped the receiver so tightly her knuckles shone white. The distress in every line of her body was so intense that Cici and Bridget could feel it radiate across the kitchen, and they straightened up, bracing themselves against it.

Lindsay said hoarsely, "Yes. Yes, I understand. I'll be right there. Thank you."

There are words that need no follow up, moments that need no interpretation. In an instant they change your world, and you instinctively know that even while you wait, hopeless and hopeful for the answer to the question you do not want answered: *What's wrong?*

Lindsay replaced the receiver. Cici put down her glass. Bridget, frozen in place, just waited. Lindsay turned to look at them, and then she stood there for another silent eternity, her eyes dark smudges in an otherwise white face.

She said, "That was the hospital in Staunton. It's—there's been an accident. It's Dominic."

CHAPTER TEN
‭ॐ‬
Love Changes Everything

There had been other days, other nights, other drives to other hospitals that had been just as terrifying. The time that Kevin, eight years old, had been hit by a car. The time that Lori, barely two years ago, had broken her leg at college. The time that Cici had fallen off the roof. The time that Lindsay had crashed her car into a telephone pole one icy night.

The night that Bridget's husband had died.

None of those drives into the abyss of the unknown had been made alone, and this one was no exception. Cici drove. Bridget held Lindsay's hand. For a while Lindsay babbled in a determined, though slightly incoherent way. "It can't be too bad, right? I mean, he told them to call the house, to call us, and he had to be okay to remember that, right? Otherwise, I mean, they routinely call the contact person on your emergency card, which I'm sure would be one of his children. The nurse said they were admitting him, but if it was really bad he'd have a team of surgeons, right? So it must be okay. They're just being careful." She gave a decisive, self-reassuring nod of her head. "Right?"

"Absolutely," said Bridget, squeezing her hand. "Did the nurse say anything else? You know, about what happened, or what his injuries were?"

Lindsay seemed to shrink before their eyes, like a balloon slowly deflating. "I didn't . . . she didn't . . . I should have asked. I didn't ask." She looked at Bridget with eyes that were dark and stunned and were slowing filling with horror. "It could be bad, couldn't it? They don't tell you when it's bad." She gripped the seat and leaned forward. "Cici, how much farther? Can't you go faster? I'll pay the ticket. Just go faster."

Cici glanced at her in the rearview mirror. "We're almost there. And they always tell you when it's bad, Lindsay. Just hold on. Everything's going to be okay."

And because they had all been through this together so many times before, they knew that it would. One way or another, everything would be okay.

"Everything looks good so far," the young resident —who couldn't have been older than Kevin— said, and it wasn't until those words were spoken that any of the three of them were able to take a deep breath. "Three broken ribs and a fractured wrist, some ligament damage in the right knee. We'll be watching for pneumonia and keeping an eye on that head injury, but if all goes well he should be ready for discharge in a couple of days."

"I can see him, right?" Lindsay was already moving past him toward the room.

"He's a little groggy," the doctor cautioned.

"Do you know what happened?" Cici asked.

He consulted his electronic tablet. "Swerved to avoid a deer, it looks like."

"Damn fool thing," Dominic muttered when Cici and Bridget cautiously pushed open the door to his room a few minutes later. It was unsettling to see the man they were so accustomed to thinking of as vital and unstoppable lying injured in a hospital bed, a purplish bruise creeping down one side of his face and a spot of blood on the gauze bandage that wrapped around his forehead. He was propped up against the pillows and the lines of his mouth were set against the pain, but still he tried to smile when he saw them. "Couldn't have happened at a worse time, eh, my ladies?"

Lindsay, who sat on the bed beside him, squeezed his hand. Her eyes were red and puffy and she had a tissue clenched in the other hand, but her smile was filled with adoration and relief. "There would never be a good time."

"Don't you worry," he assured her. He seemed short of breath, but that was to be expected. "I'll be out of here and walking on two feet in plenty of time for the wedding. Meanwhile . . ." He cast a labored and apologetic look around the three of them. "I've left you short-handed with too much work to do."

"Don't be silly," Bridget said, "we're great in an emergency. It's what we do best. We're just glad you're okay."

"You really scared us," Cici added with a smile. "But Bridget is right—the one thing we know how to do is rise to the occasion, so don't worry about anything at home. Now, tell us about the accident. Where's your truck? Do you need us to get anything from it? Do you want us to call your kids?"

It was decided that there was no point in alarming the children at this point, and the officer who had worked the accident had told Dominic he could call the station to find out where his vehicle had been towed—not that it mattered, because there was very little of it to salvage. He made a list of things that needed to be done at the winery before he got back, and Bridget assured him that they would go by his house twice a day to take care of the animals. They could tell he was getting tired long before the nurse came in to check his vitals, so they wished him a restful night, assured him everything was under control, and reconvened in the hallway.

Bridget hugged Lindsay, just because she looked as though she needed it. "Are you okay?"

Lindsay nodded, swallowing hard. "Still shaking a little. From relief mostly."

"Me too," Bridget admitted.

Cici said, "I think we're all entitled. Thank God, Lindsay," she said, pressing Lindsay's hand. "Just . . . thank God."

Again Lindsay nodded, unable to speak. For another moment the three of them just looked at each other with eyes brimming with residue of terror and the depths of gratitude, and then, with almost a single breath, they broke apart.

"Let's get you settled for the night," Bridget said.

"We'll bring back your car and some clothes in the morning," Cici added. "We'll pack a bag for Dominic too."

Bridget said, "We'll need a key to his house."

"Have you got cash for the vending machine? I'll bring up a tray from the cafeteria for you before I leave. I know you don't feel like eating now but you know you won't leave Dominic to go down later."

But when they consulted the nurse's station about making accommodations for Lindsay to stay with the patient during the night, they were told that, regrettably, that would not be possible. "Non-family members are asked to observe regular visiting hours," the duty nurse said. "It's hospital policy."

"But he doesn't have any family in the state," Cici objected.

"And I'm his fiancée," Lindsay insisted.

"When Lori was in the hospital in Charlottesville we all took turns staying with her," Bridget said.

"I know," the nurse said, though her expression was sympathetic. "I just can't make an exception. Confidentially, I'm not a fan of the policy, but it is what it is. It's too bad you're not already married."

"Because if we were there wouldn't be a problem," Lindsay said.

Again, the nurse gave her an apologetic, sympathetic look. "I'm really sorry. I have to get back to my patients."

Lindsay turned to her friends with such a familiar look of stubborn determination around the set of her lips that they knew instantly it would be futile to point out that it was only for a couple of days, and that she would probably be of more use to Dominic if she came home with them and got some rest, or, failing that, the sofas in the waiting room looked moderately comfortable. Instead Bridget said, "I'm sure the hospital administrator is still in his office."

And Cici added, "Or we could talk to the doctor. He can write an order or something."

Lindsay said, "This is what I want you to do." Her tone was calm and very reasonable, but the glint in her eye was dangerous. "I want you to call Reverend Holland, and ask him to come to the hospital."

"Of course," Bridget said, looking relieved. "He's our pastor. Of course he'll come. And people listen to him."

But Cici watched Lindsay, waiting for the other shoe to drop. It did.

"Tell him," Lindsay said, "to bring our marriage license."

"Oh, Lindsay," Bridget said softly.

Cici's brows drew together in concern. "Lindsay, are you sure? Don't be impulsive. It's one night, two at the most. Is that really enough to abandon your whole wedding for?"

"We can fix the dress," Bridget went on urgently, "you know Paul is not going to give up until he does. And the flowers are ordered and the cake is baked and you've worked so hard, Linds. Are you sure? Cici's right. It's one night. Is that worth canceling everything for?"

Lindsay just shook her head fiercely. "One *hour* with him would be worth it, one minute. Don't you see that? When I heard that voice on the phone everything changed. On the ride over here I bargained my whole life to God if only Dominic would be okay. And I kept thinking about what you said, Bridge, when we were sitting on the porch and I was being so silly about setting the date. We're not promised tomorrow. And you know something? That's a good thing, because it means that every minute of every day is already the best time of our lives. I don't have to wait for my wedding day. It's already here. And now, if you'll excuse me . . ." she caught each of their hands in hers and gave a grateful squeeze, "I need to go ask the groom if he's up to getting married tonight."

The bride wore jeans and a tee shirt smudged with blue paint, and she carried a bouquet of white roses that Bridget had bought from the gift shop, stems wrapped in adhesive tape to keep them from dripping. The bridesmaids tucked in their shirts and put on lipstick. And the groom, with a rose pinned to his hospital gown, just looked delighted. When Reverend Holland called for the ring, everyone looked momentarily confused, but then Bridget stepped up to the occasion, donating her own gold band with a whispered, "Something borrowed. And I want it right back."

Afterwards, they toasted the happy couple with orange juice and bran muffins from the cafeteria. Some of the hospital staff brought homemade cookies to the party, and they laughed and they talked until the lengthening of Dominic's silences reminded them all that he was in the hospital for a reason. Bridget retrieved her wedding band with the promise to find the rings Dominic had secured in his top dresser drawer and bring them with her in the morning when she returned. Bridget and Cici walked out with Reverend Holland, thanking him profusely, leaving Lindsay with a comfortable fold-out chair and her own blanket and pillow next to Dominic's bed.

It was long past dark by the time Bridget and Cici finished the chores at Dominic's house and their own. They each took a cup of butternut squash soup from the pot Ida Mae had left warming for them on the stove and sat on the porch in the dark, wearing their heavy sweaters against the crisp night air, warming their hands on the big soup mugs. The only light came from the pools that were cast by the windows. It was cold. It was quiet. Even Rebel had found his bed, and the malicious kitten—whose name would forever-more be Paint—was snoring softly on Bridget's pillow. Every bone, every muscle in their bodies ached from tension and fatigue. They were so tired, so stunned and battered, they could barely lift the mugs to their lips. But they were drawn to the porch, to the clean crisp air that washed the smell of the hospital from their lungs and the fear from their pores; to the ritual, to the serenity of home.

"Wow," said Cici after a time. "Lindsay's married."

"And did you ever, in a million years, picture it like this?"

"Never."

Bridget sighed a little. "Her beautiful wedding."

"*Our* beautiful wedding," Cici corrected, gazing

into her soup. "I think we may have gotten a little more caught up in it than we should have. Kind of like we did with Lori."

"I suppose. But that's what women do, isn't it? We celebrate each other."

"I've never seen her so happy."

"Dominic seemed glad they decided to do it this way too."

"We have a lot of phone calls to make tomorrow. Un-planning a wedding is going to be almost as hard as planning it."

Bridget said tiredly, "Good thing we're up to the task."

They were silent for a time, warming their hands around the mugs, listening to the quiet of the night.

Bridgett said softly, "Do you know what I'm remembering? The first night we spent here. There were a billion stars in the sky, remember? Just like tonight. I'd never seen so many stars. And we sat on the steps and felt small and scared and wondered if we'd made a mistake."

"I remember," Cici said.

Bridget leaned back in her chair, tilting up her head to see the stars beyond the roofline of the porch. "I never said anything, but that night I felt as lonely and lost as I've ever felt in my life."

Cici said, "I know."

"Kind of like I do tonight."

And Cici said softly, "I know."

They sat in silence for a time, rocking and sipping their soup. The porch felt empty without Lindsay, without Dominic. And yet sorrow, after the great tragedy they had so narrowly escaped, seemed self-indulgent and vain.

"It will be different now," Bridget said. "I mean, I'm so happy for Lindsay and Dominic, and I love them both, but it will be different."

"Well, they won't be moving into the folly for a while," Cici pointed out. "It's going to take a lot of work to turn it into a real house. And even then, they'll still be here."

"But it will be different." Bridget's words were almost a sigh.

"We're not promised tomorrow," Cici reminded her.

Bridget said after a time, "I just wish they were here, both of them. Right here on the porch sipping wine and rocking with us. That's all I wish."

Cici smiled sadly to herself in the dark. "Yeah. Me, too."

Bridget and Cici arrived early the next morning at the hospital with two overnight bags and a basket of muffins that Ida Mae had arisen at 5:00 a.m. to bake. The horses had been fed and the golden retriever had been comforted and played with. Bridget announced her intention to ask Dominic's permission to bring his dog home with them to Ladybug Farm that evening, and to start moving in the cats the next day. Cici argued that the cats would fare better than the horses or the dog without supervision, and that they needed to prioritize. They were still debating the question when they reached Dominic's door. Cici knocked, and Bridget called, "Yoo-hoo!" They pushed open the door.

Lindsay was standing beside the empty bed, and when she turned to them, she looked stricken. A kind of cold fear rose off of her in waves, and it was something they could feel as they walked into the room.

"Lindsay." Cici's voice sounded hoarse, and she stared at the empty bed. "Where's Dominic?"

Bridget put down the bag she was carrying and looked around anxiously. "Lindsay, what happened? Is everything okay?"

Lindsay held open her arms for them wordlessly, and started to cry.

Signora Bastioni, their landlady, had felt sorry for the young lovers and had donated a mattress that Kevin and Lori dragged, pushed, folded, and manipulated up the stairs and into their new apartment. They found two folding wooden chairs and a table that was not quite big enough to hold two plates—which was just as well because they did not have two plates—and Lori covered it with one of her colorful scarves and

259

set it before the window. With his first paycheck from the language school, Kevin bought a lamp for the table, because the days were growing shorter, even in Italy. Lori got a job as a cellar worker in a winery half an hour away—all it had taken was one phone call from Signor Marcello —and although it was temporary, backbreaking work with no promise for employment after harvest, and paid wages that wouldn't have kept her in biscotti without Kevin's help, she was as pleased as though she had landed a position as president of the company. And now that she was actually interested in what her coworkers were saying, she found that her Italian was improving noticeably.

Kevin fixed the window lock and Lori planted flower seeds in terra cotta pots and placed them on the roof. It didn't matter that winter was coming. She was convinced the flowers would bloom in the spring. In the evenings they sat on the roof with a bottle of wine, sometimes with a blanket wrapped around their shoulders to protect them from the chill, and watched the stars and the lights from the village and talked. They never got tired of talking, even when—sometimes especially when—the conversations took the turn of the quick hot arguments that were so inevitable between them, and that were just as inevitably, passionately, and quickly forgiven.

As her days and nights grew full with the intense

joy and wonder of her own life, Lori talked less and less about Ladybug Farm, although there were moments, such as this one, that always took her back. The Tuscan sky was painted with the brilliance of a gold and rose sunset that seemed to go on forever, and the vintner had rewarded all the cellar workers for a particularly difficult week with a bottle of surprisingly good wine. She and Kevin made a picnic of bruschetta with fresh pesto from the shop down the street, and a sweet orange panforte that the signora had left outside their doorstep before she closed the shop for the day. Now they sat on the roof sipping the wine, bathed in the radiance of the sunset and the simple presence of each other.

Lori said, snuggling into the curve of his shoulder, "Do you think we'll ever get tired of this?"

"I think," replied Kevin, kissing her hair, "that anyone who could get tired of something this beautiful doesn't deserve to have it. And yes, I mean you, not the sunset."

She smiled and sipped her wine. "Of course you do. You know how to treat a lady."

"My mama raised me right."

"Oh, crap." She put down her wine and sat forward, digging her phone out of her back pocket. "I had a message from Mom at lunch. I didn't get a chance to check it."

She turned on her phone and gave a small grunt

of surprise when she saw the screen. "Two voice mails and three e-mails," she said, scrolling through. "I guess I forgot to check last night too. Boy, is she going to be mad."

She was silent as she retrieved the e-mails, and Kevin, whose fingers were lightly stroking her back, felt her change. She sat up straighter, her muscles stiffened. He sat forward to better see her face. "Lori? Everything okay?"

She turned to him with eyes that were dark with distress. "We have to go home," she said.

CHAPTER ELEVEN
 roa
Hopelessly Devoted

To: Cici@LadybugFarmLadies.net
From: LadiLori27@locomail.net
Subject: Re: Dominic

Hi Mom,
Any news? Landing at Dulles at 6:00 a.m.
We'll be in Staunton around noon. Should
we stop at the hospital?
L
PS Forgot to say that Kevin is on the same
flight

To: Bridget@LadybugFarmLadies.net
From: KSTLawguy@hotmail.com
Subject: See you soon

Hi Mom,
I was with Lori when she got the news from
home & could tell she was upset. Decided
to fly home with her and help with the
drive. Needed to get back anyway. I'll talk
to you when we get there. Hope everyone
is holding up okay. Keep us informed.
Kevin

To: LadiLori27@locomail.net
From: Cici@LadybugFarmLadies.net
Subject: Re: Dominic

Hi Sweetie,

Apparently it was a pneumothorax (sp?) from the broken rib that punctured his lung. He's out of surgery now but in ICU and it's touch and go. The head injury complicates things. I didn't mean for you to come home. Please be careful driving after flying all night. We'll be at the hospital. Even Lindsay's not allowed in to see him. Did I tell you they got married already? Sorry, haven't slept. I love you.

Mom

PS Did you say Kevin is coming too?

To: KSTLawguy@hotmail.com
From: Bridget@LadybugFarmLadies.Net
Subject: Re: See you soon

Oh, Kevin, how sweet of you—and what a surprise. Thank you, darling. I'm afraid things are not going too well here. Don't say anything to Lori, but we may have bad news by the time you land. We all care so much for Dominic, and to see Lindsay like this is breaking my heart. It will be so good to have you here. I wish it could be under better circumstances.

Love,
Mom

To: Bridget@LadybugFarmLadies.net
From: KSTLawguy@hotmail.com
Subject: See you Soon

Me too.

Love,
Kevin

Lori put her phone away as her suitcase came up on the carousel, pointing it out to Kevin. "Mom said there's no change," she said. She wore no makeup, and her normally pale complexion was pasty in the light-flooded airport, emphasizing the dark circles under her eyes and the frizzy curls that escaped from her untidy topknot. "She was trying not to cry, but I could tell . . . it's pretty bad."

Kevin lifted her suitcase off the carousel and set it beside his on the floor. "Seeing you will make her feel better. Seeing both of us, really. Sometimes all it takes is a break in the routine to change the way you look at things."

"But," she said, looking at him helplessly, "it can't change *things*."

"Not usually," he agreed, and gave her shoulder a gentle squeeze of reassurance.

She snapped the handle on her rolling suitcase in place and looked at him with concern. "Are you okay to drive? Did you get any sleep?"

"A few hours." He hoisted his duffle. "Seriously, Lori, you didn't leave your car in long-term parking for four months."

"Cheaper than taking a cab."

And, even considering the cost of having the airport's auto service jump-start the battery, he supposed it was.

"It's weird," Lori observed softly when they left the Beltway and pointed the car west, toward the rolling hills of the Virginia countryside. "It's like you close your eyes in one world and wake up in another. You take a breath, and before you exhale everything has changed."

Kevin said, "There's not much more to life than that, if you think about it."

Her brow puckered a little as she gazed out the window. "All the time I was gone, this place was going on without me. The leaves were turning, the grapes were ripening, the grass was growing . . . and now, back in Siena, it's as though we just walked out of our lives there." She looked over at him. "Do you think Signora Bastioni will remember to water the flowers? Do you think they'll bloom next spring, even if we're not there?"

"Sure they will."

She was quiet for a moment, clearly not believing him. "Everything even looks different here. Not like I expected."

"For me too," Kevin said. "Of course, it was summer when I left."

The trees were about a week past their brilliant yellow and orange peak, but there was still plenty of color on the branches, and in the background a swath of multicolored pastels defined the area between sky and earth. There were bright coral and yellow and rust colored mums planted around mailboxes and in pots on suburban porches, and as they drove deeper into the country, the occasional tendril of smoke could be seen wafting from a chimney.

"It's more than that," Lori said thoughtfully, looking around. "It's like . . . all this time I had a picture in my mind of what coming home would feel like, and this is not it."

"These are not exactly the best of circumstances," he reminded her.

"I suppose that's true."

"Also . . ." He glanced at her as he made the turn onto the highway ramp. "You're not the same woman who left here."

She smiled, a little tiredly. "That's very true."

"Try to get some rest, baby. We've got a couple of hours."

She turned her head against the headrest and

closed her eyes. "Wake me if you get sleepy."

"I will."

But they had barely gone ten miles before she turned her head toward him again and said, "Do you know what I was thinking on the flight? I was thinking . . ." Her voice grew tight, and a little high, as though she were speaking through a curtain of tears. "What if that text hadn't been from Mom? What if it had been from Aunt Lindsay or Aunt Bridget and it had been my mom in the hospital or—or worse? And then I was thinking that one day that call will come. It will. And I don't know if I can stand it. Do you ever think about that, Kevin?"

He was quiet for a moment, watching the road. When he spoke his voice was somber. "When my dad died, it was like somebody had pulled the rug out from under me. The thing you thought would go on forever suddenly . . . didn't. I didn't even know how to feel. Maybe I was afraid to feel because it hurt so much. After the funeral, I knew my mom needed me, but I didn't know what to do for her. So I just left. I could have had two weeks off. HR wanted me to take the time off, but I went back to work."

"You were only twenty-four," Lori defended him. "You had just started a new job."

"I wasn't a very good son to my mother," he said. "I want to be a better one now."

She reached across the seat and closed her

fingers around his. "Is that why you came back with me?"

He shook his head slightly. "I came back because of what you said."

"What did I say?"

"When you got the text from your mom, you didn't say 'I have to go home.' You said '*We* have to go home.' I always knew that one day, when it was time, that's what you would say. We're a 'we' now. Whither thou goest, babe."

Lori smiled and closed her eyes. She slept the rest of the way, holding his hand.

Kevin and Lori were directed to the Intensive Care waiting room when they arrived. It was the most dismal, terrifying place Lori had ever seen, a tiny beige room dotted with the bleak faces of hopeless people, blankets draped across chairs, a coffee machine in one corner, a door marked "No Admittance" in the other. Lori flew to her mother when she saw her and hugged her with the kind of ferocity she had not known since she was seven, clinging to her mother as though for dear life and trying with all her power not to burst into sobs. Kevin hugged his own mother, and then they both hugged Lindsay and there were probably a few tears then, on all the women's parts.

Lori couldn't help thinking how old they all looked.

And then Cici, pushing aside the wet tendrils of hair from Lori's face, said, "You look so much older, sweetheart. Are you okay?"

Lori just hugged her again. "Mommy," she whispered, "I'm so glad to be home."

Then, somehow, she managed to pull all the pieces of her scattered energy together, to straighten her backbone, and to turn to Lindsay. "Tell me," she said.

Lindsay had lines around her mouth and her eyes, and her usually lustrous red hair looked lank and dull, twisted back at her neck with an elastic band. Even her clothes fit differently, her tee shirt sagging on her shoulders and her jeans clinging to her hips. She twisted a ring—her engagement ring, Lori realized—around and around on her finger as she spoke. "I got to see him for a few minutes. He wasn't aware, of course, and there's a ventilator . . . they're going to remove that tonight, and if all goes well . . . The doctors seem more optimistic than they did this time yesterday." Her eyes clouded over. "It's just that . . . it was so sudden, you know? We didn't think it was all that serious. We were so happy. We got married, did your mom tell you that? And . . . it just happened so suddenly." She seemed to banish despair with an effort and smiled bravely. "I'll tell him you're here, Lori. He'll be so pleased."

Suddenly Lori felt her throat and her eyes go

hot and she couldn't speak. She blinked hard to control the tears, and Kevin came forward. "What do you need us to do, Aunt Lindsay?"

"Oh, Kevin." She smiled at him weakly. "I didn't expect you to come. It's so sweet of you."

"We're here now," he said strongly, "and we're your arms and legs. So make a list. We'll get it done."

Lindsay looked as though she might burst into tears then so Lori spoke up quickly. "What about Noah? Do you need me to call him?"

"Oh . . . I didn't want to bother him until I knew something definite . . ."

"I'll call him," Lori said.

"There's a communications blackout . . ."

"We've got this," Kevin assured her. "Do you have your cell phone? We'll have him call you here."

Lindsay's eyes were swimming with tears so Bridget said, "That would be great, Kevin. Noah has the number."

Lindsay pressed her fingers briefly to her lips, cleared her throat, and said, "Dominic's children are coming in tomorrow morning. I thought I should call them, but I didn't want to make it sound worse than it was, but I forgot they were coming in for the wedding anyway. Paul and Derrick are putting them up at the B&B . . ."

She looked suddenly as though she had lost her train of thought, and Bridget put an arm around her waist. Cici spoke up gently. "Paul and Derrick are going to stay with Lindsay tonight, and then the children will be here, so as soon as . . . well, as soon as we know everything is okay, Bridget and I are going to drive back. We promised to take care of Dominic's place, and . . ."

Kevin said, "What needs to be done?"

Bridget said, surprised, "Oh, Kevin, you don't even know where his house is."

Lori said, "I do."

"But there are horses and a dog and—"

"We'll take care of it."

"But you've both been flying all night and . . ."

Lori repeated firmly, "Mom. We've got this. I know what has to be done at Ladybug Farm. We'll take care of the horses. I'll call Noah. It's okay. Don't worry about anything. We'll see you when you get home."

There were more kisses, more reassurances, and a frantic list of things to check on. When they were gone, Bridget and Cici stood looking after them with a faintly puzzled look on their faces. "How did they grow up so fast?" Bridget asked.

Cici gave a small shake of her head. "You know that moment every mother dreads? When the child becomes the parent?"

Bridget looked disturbed. "We're not there yet, are we?"

Cici said. "We're getting closer every day."

Then with an uncertain look toward the door by

which the two people left, Cici added, "Bridget, this may sound strange, but did you notice anything . . ."

She let the question trail off, and Bridget just looked curious. "About what?"

Cici gave a shake of her head. "Nothing. It was just nice of Kevin to come back with her, wasn't it?"

"They're good kids," Bridget agreed, smiling, "both of them. But . . ." The smile faded. "He didn't say a thing about the job."

"Neither did Lori," Cici said, noticing that for the first time.

And then, wearily, she smiled and went to get Lindsay another cup of coffee.

It was almost dark by the time Kevin and Lori finished everything on their mothers' lists, along with the additional chores barked out by Ida Mae, who didn't blink an eye at seeing them both back at home but took full advantage of the extra labor. "It won't be the first time I nursed a sick man back to health in this house and it won't be the last," she said, "but I won't be doin' it flying up and down them stairs. So you all can get that bed set up in the sunroom like we had it when you was laid up with your leg, Little Missy, and scoot up in the attic and bring down that folding table and chairs so's I can serve them their meals in there proper like. I reckon she'll be wanting to move in there with him, now that she's up and married him, so no point in making things hard on myself."

Kevin said gently, "Miss Ida Mae, maybe it would be better to wait and see if . . ." He glanced uneasily at Lori. "What I mean is, there's a chance that . . ."

Ida Mae just glared at him. "Waitin' and seein' just lets the devil in the door, mister. Now you do as I say and you do it quick so I can get back to my kitchen. I've got a pie in the oven."

So they moved furniture. They fed the chickens and the goat and the dog and the cat. They made phone calls. After a certain amount of confusion, they even folded up the drop cloths, put away the painting supplies, and returned the furniture that was stacked in the hall back into the big empty room that once had been a combination of Lori's room and the guest room. Kevin put his suitcase in Noah's room across the hall. Lori put hers in the blue room. And they smiled regretfully at one another as they did so.

Kevin showered and changed, mostly to try to wake himself up, and went looking for Lori. He noticed the light that was shining through the window of the winery office, but when he crossed the lawn and entered the office, it was empty.

He glanced around the space—the dark computer screen, the piles of papers scattered across the desk, manila folders filled with receipts on a low shelf, an old-fashioned card-file rolodex with a few cards turned forward, as though someone had just finished making a call. It was cold inside the room, made even colder by the harsh fluorescent light, and a little creepy. He called, "Lori?"

When he had visited the winery before, Dominic explained that the original entrance to the cellar had been via a trapdoor in the floor, which the ladies had intended to remove in favor of a more traditional staircase. That had proven too expensive, however, so they had simply put up a half wall and a gate around the pit in the middle of the floor, and left the stone staircase intact. Kevin went through the gate and down the stairs. The fluorescents were on in the cellar, too, and Lori was checking a gauge on a piece of some kind of equipment. She glanced up distractedly when she saw him.

"Hey," she said. "Did you get hold of the Red Cross?"

"Yeah. They promised to get a message to the unit commander within twenty-four hours."

"It just seems strange to me that the whole unit would move without telling anybody."

"It's wartime. That's what a communications blackout is for."

She looked up from making a note on a clipboard, her expression worried. "That means they're fighting, doesn't it?"

"Not according to Red Cross," Kevin assured her. "The military is very careful about revealing troop movements, even if they're just moving to a new duty post."

Lori's lips compressed briefly. "Still . . . maybe we'll just tell Aunt Lindsay Noah's not allowed to call out for a few days."

Kevin nodded. "That's what I thought."

There was a small bitter twist to her lips. "We're getting to be experts at lying, aren't we? Good thing we're here to do the dirty work."

And then, before he could respond, she said, "Good news from the hospital though. Mom said everything went well with the procedure and that she and Aunt Bridget are on their way home. They couldn't talk Aunt Lindsay into leaving though, even for just a few hours. I guess she's too scared."

Kevin said, "Ida Mae is holding supper for them, but she said to tell you to come fix a plate if you're hungry."

Lori shook her head. "I'll wait."

He glanced around. "What are you doing?"

She gave a brief shake of her head. "This couldn't have happened at a worse time. The grapes are still on the vine, we've got new wine in bottles, and a hundred gallons in reserve that have to be monitored. I don't know what Dominic had planned to do about the harvest, and who's going to work the cellar? And did you see that desk? Who's been doing the paperwork around here, anyway? I don't even know where to start."

Kevin walked over to a wall of racked bottles. "Is this the new wine?"

She shook her head. "No, that's what we put up this summer as a test run." She came over to him and took down a bottle. "See, we didn't label it. It's not for sale. I guess they were going to serve it at their wedding." She smiled a little, looking down at the dusty green bottle. "I remember we did a tasting at Noah's going-away party. It was young, of course, but it was *good,* you know." Her eyes were bright with pride and pleasure as she looked up at him. "It had real promise, even I could taste that. And it felt so amazing to see something I had worked on go from an idea to a wine, I mean a real wine . . ."

Suddenly the brightness in her eyes started to glisten, and spilled over in wet splotches onto the bottle. Kevin lifted a hand to her but Lori dashed away the tears with an angry gesture. "No," she said tightly. "No, I'm okay. I'm just so freaking mad at myself. I had a chance to learn from a classical winemaker, one of the best teachers in the world, and he was *right here,* right here all the time and he *wanted* to teach me, but I let the chance slip away because I was too embarrassed to tell the truth. Too proud to come home. *Damn it.*" She sniffed and blotted her eyes with her fist. "Just . . . damn it."

Kevin said gently, "There's no point in beating yourself up, honey. And it sounds like there's a chance Dominic will be okay, maybe even back to work before too long. It's not over, yet."

She looked at him helplessly. "But it is, Kev, don't you see? Those months that I should have been here, that I could have been here . . . they're over. They won't come again. And I wasted them."

She turned and put the bottle back on the rack. "I've got to get cleaned up," she said wearily, "and put on my happy face for Mom. This day isn't even half over. And I have a feeling the hardest part is yet to come."

They walked back across the dark lawn toward the house, not touching.

"And so *then,*" Cici said, leaning back in her chair with her wine glass cradled to her chest, "Paul and Derrick came sailing in with these two big hampers outfitted with enough supplies to go on a luxury safari. We're talking gourmet food . . ."

"Smoked oysters," put in Bridget, "and gouda with water crackers and a whole chicken that Purline had roasted that afternoon."

"And inflatable pillows and those silk travel blankets that fold up into the size of a pocket square—"

"And even a collapsible cot!"

"And a half bottle of wine that will get Lindsay

thrown out of the hospital if she doesn't have the good sense to drink it in the bathroom," Cici confided. "Of course the nursing staff was fit to be tied, but what could they do? The boys had brought gifts to share with everyone in the waiting room, not to mention perfume and Godiva chocolate to bribe the nurses, and bouquets of flowers for the families of every patient in ICU. When we left it looked like an English garden party in there, and I swear it was the first time some of those people had smiled in weeks."

Ida Mae gave a derisive sniff as she set the warm apple pie on the trivet in the center of the table. "You ask me, the only thing you need in a place like that is a Bible and a prayer partner."

"Reverend Holland was there, too," Bridget assured her. "He was crazy about the smoked oysters."

They were all gathered around the kitchen table, enjoying a ground beef casserole with a flakey biscuit crust while one of the first fires of the season danced on the raised hearth. Lori, whose Italian wardrobe consisted mostly of jeans and summer dresses, sat closest to the fire, her bare arms covered by a sweater borrowed from her mother's closet, her freshly shampooed hair drying in loose curls around her shoulders. Kevin sat next to her, and their mothers were across the table. Sometimes Kevin dropped his hand to Lori's knee under the table, because touching her, when she was this close, was simply not optional, but no one noticed. Ida Mae, who rarely consented to join them for family meals, agreed to sit down for "just a bite," mostly, everyone knew, so that it would be easier for her to hear all the news.

"We weren't allowed to visit, of course," Cici said, "But Lindsay told Dominic you were here, Lori. He was still kind of out of it, but she said that made him smile, and he gave her a thumbs-up." She smiled. "It's so good to see you, sweetheart. Thank you for coming."

"And thank you both for taking care of every-thing this afternoon," Bridget added. "I don't know how we would have gotten it done without you."

"It wasn't a problem." Lori waved a hand casually. Then she cast a sideways glance at Kevin. "Well, until we discovered Kevin is afraid of horses, that is."

Kevin scowled uncomfortably. "What's not to be afraid of? They're wild animals ten times bigger than humans with teeth the size of fence pickets."

"Thank heavens," said Lori, "for all those riding lessons I had as a kid or those poor horses would still be standing in a corner of the field wondering where their dinner was."

"Yeah, well, I can sing all four parts of *The Mikado*," Kevin retorted, and refilled her glass.

Everyone laughed, and Bridget began to slice the pie.

"I think we should bring the dog back here," Lori said, digging into the slice of pie Bridget passed her. "He can stay in the house until Rebel gets used to him."

Bridget cast Cici a mildly triumphant look.

Kevin said, "I think you need to hire an armed guard for that border collie. And take out more insurance."

"And what happened to my room?" Lori inquired. "Not to mention the guest room. Kevin put his stuff in Noah's room. I hope that's okay."

"Oh, sweetie." Cici looked momentarily nonplussed. "We didn't think . . . It's a long story. But we'll get a bed set up for you . . ."

"It's okay," Lori assured her. "We already moved the furniture back in there. But seriously. A girl goes to Italy for a summer and you destroy her room. What's up with that?"

Bridget and Cici both laughed weakly, and without much humor. "Like your mom said," Bridget said, "it's a long story."

"Does that mean you're planning to stay awhile, sweetie?" Cici asked. Her smile was cautiously hopeful. "Did you tell the Marcellos when you'd be back?"

"Actually . . ." Lori focused on her plate. "Things didn't work out like I expected there. So I guess I won't be going back."

"Oh." Cici waited, but Lori did not offer to explain further. "I'm so sorry."

Then, because the silence that followed was growing awkward, Cici changed the subject. "If everything goes well," she said, accepting her own slice of pie from Bridget, "they'll be moving Dominic into a private room tomorrow and I know he'd like to see you."

"I'd like to see him too," Lori said, perhaps a bit too eagerly. "Do either of you know who he's hired to harvest the grapes? Because they really can't stay on the vines more than a week now without going sour. And I know he must have contracted with a distributor for the new wine but I can't find the papers, and does anyone know if you're entering anything into a show because, seriously, you can't introduce a new wine into the market without some press and Dominic knows that."

Bridget and Cici just looked at her blankly.

"Hey," Kevin said softly, and she felt the pressure of his fingers on her knee beneath the table. "Maybe a little bit too much for a guy who just started breathing on his own a few hours ago."

Lori lifted her wine glass and took a huge gulp.

"Y'all gonna want coffee?" Ida Mae inquired from across the room. "Cause it's getting kinda late and my show starts in ten minutes."

Bridget said, "Thank you, Ida Mae, but no. We'll take care of the dishes."

"Lindsay loved the muffins," Cici added, turning in her chair. "She told me to thank you."

Ida Mae said, "Hmph. I got some good dried bloodwort for that young fellow to make into tea when he gets home. Good for the constitution. Y'all don't wake me when you get up in the morning."

Cici said, "Thank you, Ida Mae," as she shuffled off toward her room.

Kevin lifted an eyebrow in mild distaste when she was gone. "Dried bloodwort? Really?"

"Actually," replied Bridget, "it's a known immune system builder. I saw it on the Dr. Oz website. Sometimes these home remedies aren't as silly as you might think."

She placed a slice of pie on a dessert plate and passed it to Kevin. "Now," she said, "tell us about the job. When do you have to be back?"

Kevin hesitated, and if he glanced at Lori it was only for half a second. But an unspoken signal passed between them when she dropped her eyes to her plate, and he said, "It's a really long story, Mom, and I'd rather tell it when everyone isn't so tired. But I can stay for a while if you want me to, and help out until everything gets back to normal. As long as it doesn't involve horses, of course." He smiled and cut a bite of the pie with his fork. "This looks great. The last time I had apple pie was here, just before I left, remember?"

Because Bridget looked as though she wanted to ask more questions, Lori spoke up quickly, deftly turning the conversation toward matters domestic, the people she knew in the community, the things that had happened since she'd been gone. When they finished their pie, she started gathering up the dishes, and Kevin volunteered to help while Lori shooed Bridget and Cici off to bed. Cici smiled wearily and demanded, "Who are you and what have you done with my daughter?" but neither she nor Bridget put up much of a real protest as they climbed the stairs to their rooms.

At the top of the stairs, Bridget looked back to make sure neither of the young people was within hearing distance, and then she said quietly, looking worried, "Kevin's hiding something."

Cici nodded, dragging out the elastic band that held back her hair. "Lori is definitely not telling the whole truth about her job at the villa."

Bridget cast another uncertain look back toward the stairs. "Don't you want to know what's going on?"

Cici was thoughtful for a moment. "You know something? Sometimes the kindest thing a child can do for her mother is to lie."

Bridget considered that for a moment. "We have very kind children," she decided. She smiled tiredly. "Good night, Cici."

" 'Night, Bridge."

• • •

Lori closed the door to Kevin's room silently behind her and tiptoed quickly across the floor, her bare feet stinging with the cold. He rolled over when she approached, peered at her blearily in the dark, and then sat up abruptly. "Lori!" She pressed her fingers against his lips and he changed to a whisper. "Are you crazy? What are you doing here?"

"All my winter clothes are packed away in the attic and I'm freezing," she whispered back. "I can't sleep."

He was wearing a sweat suit and was buried under a mound of quilts. She hugged her arms in the flimsy sleep shirt she had brought from Italy and shivered. He threw back a corner of the covers and she climbed in beside him. He drew her into his arms, and then winced. "Your feet are like ice."

"Sorry. There's a fireplace in my room but no wood."

"It's cold in here too. I guess they've been too busy to do whatever it is they do to turn on the furnace. What time is it?"

"About three."

"You can't stay."

"I know." She pulled the quilt up over her mouth and nose and snuggled deeper into his circle of warmth. They held each other for a time, sharing heat and listening to the sound of each other's breath. Lori turned over in his arms, gazing up at the dark ceiling. "We're never going back to Italy, are we?"

"Sure we will. On our tenth anniversary. We'll leave little Oscar—"

"Sebastian."

"And Gertrude—"

"Gabriella."

"With our moms and we'll do the whole European tour. We'll stop in London first . . ."

"We should have told them, Kevin," Lori said.

He lifted one hand to stroke her hair. "Not tonight, we shouldn't have."

"Then when?"

"Soon."

"Do you mean when you can frame it in a happy ending?"

He looked down at her in the dark, but could see only the shine of her eyes, not the emotion there. "Are we going to have a fairy-tale ending, Lori?"

She was quiet for a moment. "I figured out why everything looked so different from what I expected when we were driving home. Lying awake in my room, freezing, I was thinking about it, and . . ." She turned her face toward his. "It was because you were with me. Because all that time I was worried that if we came back here there wouldn't be an 'us' I didn't realize that I would be part of us no matter where I went from now on. That's why Aunt Lindsay is camped out in a hospital waiting room to be close to a man she barely even knew a year ago and has only been married to for a couple of days . . . because when you're part of an 'us' you forget how to not be that. And when I got home and everything felt so different to me, it felt right, too, just like it did in Italy. It felt right when we were doing chores together and it felt right to look across the table and see you there, and even though everything was different, it was *right* because you were there. Does that make sense?"

He kissed her hair tenderly. "I couldn't have said it better."

She said, "What do you think we're going to do?"

He was quiet for a time. "One thing is for sure. You can't leave here. You've worked too hard to get back here and . . ." he turned in her direction, and she could see the flash of a teasing smile in the dark. "Right now you're the only one with a job offer."

"We'll see how Dominic feels about that when he finds out all I learned how to make in Italy was really bad coffee."

"I've been thinking about it. I'm a pretty good teacher. And I was surprised how much I like it."

"You could teach at UVA," she said, and her expression was cautiously excited in the filtered dark. "It's practically next door."

"Maybe, after a while. I'd have to get a doctorate degree. Meanwhile, we've got to pay the bills."

"Don't worry. I'll support you."

"Sweetheart, I appreciate the offer, but I got a quick look at the books this afternoon, and on what the winery can afford to pay you, you can't even support yourself—and that's with free room and board."

He was thoughtful for a moment. "I can get a teaching certificate, high school or middle school level maybe. Of course, this time of year it won't be that easy to find a job opening." He glanced down at her. "It might mean I have to leave for a while. Maybe even go out of state to find the right graduate program *and* job. It wouldn't be for long. Two years max. And I'd be back here every chance I got."

She was silent for a time. Then she reached for his hand, and laced her fingers through his. "Since you pulled me out of that bar in Siena, you've done nothing but worry about how to make my dreams come true. Do you really think I wouldn't do everything in my power to help yours come true now? Whither thou goest," she whispered.

He brought her fingers to his lips. "We're going to figure this out, babe."

"I think we already have."

They were quiet for a time, holding each other,

and then he dropped another kiss on her hair. "I can't believe I'm saying this, but you really have to go."

"I know." She smothered a groan and turned over, reluctantly pushing back the covers. "It's got to be forty degrees in this room. The window is covered with frost."

"Here, take my sweatshirt."

He started to sit up to pull the shirt over his head, but Lori suddenly bolted upright beside him, staring at the window. "It's covered with frost," she repeated, and she forgot to whisper.

"Lori, what . . ."

She leapt out of bed and raced to the window, pressing her hands flat against the glass. She whirled back to him, her face streaked with distress. "The grapes!" she cried. "They're still on the vine!"

Before he could stop her, she rushed past him into the hall, down the stairs, and out of the house.

CHAPTER TWELVE

ตฌ

Rising to the Occasion

By the time Kevin got his sneakers and his glasses on, Cici and Bridget were already in the hall, squinting in the lights Lori had turned on in her wake and looking as confused as he was. The front door stood half open and the dog was barking wildly. "Something about the grapes," was all he could offer, and he bounded down the stairs and into the cold night air, calling after her.

He followed the glow of Lori's flashlight down the path to the vineyard, followed closely by Cici and Bridget. A thin layer of patchy snow scattered across the grass, dusting the vines and the bushes. He found Lori, in her nightshirt and a pair of cowboy boots, standing stock-still at the edge of the path, the flashlight pointing straight down at the ground. She was staring at something that looked like a pebble in her hand. She lifted the flashlight and opened her hand to reveal a single grape. When she transferred it to him, it was ice cold and as hard as a rock.

"Frozen," she said dully. "They're all frozen."

"Lori, for heaven's sake!" Cici had a flannel jacket in her hand, which she quickly wrapped around Lori's shoulders. "It's got to be twenty degrees out here! What's the matter with you?"

"The grapes!" Of all of them, Bridget was the first to figure it out. She was out of breath from running, shivering in her robe and slippers, and her face was marked with horrified disbelief as she looked around the darkened rows. "We forgot about the grapes!"

Kevin took the flashlight from Lori and directed the beam to cluster after cluster. Amidst the yellow, withered leaves, the grapes were so shiny they were like wax, plump with juice and sugared with snow. It was clearly too late to save them.

Cici's hand went slowly to her throat. "The temperature must have fallen after midnight," she said. "I haven't listened to the forecast in days."

"Are they all like that?" Bridget said a little desperately. "Surely they can't all be frozen! We never have a hard freeze this early in the year! How could it have gotten so cold so quickly? I mean, there are valleys and temperature pockets and . . ."

"Why didn't I listen to the forecast?" Cici's voice was tight and high. "We might have saved some of them."

"Why this on top of everything else?" Bridget sounded as though she might cry, and Kevin put his arm around her shoulders. "Why is it always, *always* something?"

"Well, it's too late to do anything now," Kevin

said. His breath frosted on the air, and the cold crept down the neck of his sweatshirt. "Let's get back inside."

Lori murmured, "Twenty degrees."

Cici reached for her. "Come on, Lori, you're going to freeze."

Lori spun suddenly to her mother. "Mom," she said quickly, "there's a weather radio in Dominic's office. Run turn it on, and see how much longer it's supposed to stay below freezing. And find a thermometer—make sure it really is twenty degrees out here!"

"What?"

She turned quickly to Bridget and Kevin. "Open the doors to the cellar and drag the press as close to the entrance as you can get it. We'll have to de-stem outside and get the grapes directly into the press. The tractor has lights, doesn't it? Does anybody know how to drive that thing?"

Kevin said, "I can drive anything with wheels, but—"

"Then hurry!" She gave him a small shove. "Hook up the wagon and drive it around to the far side of the vineyard. We'll start with the Cabernet Franc and work our way up."

"Lori, honey." Cici took her arms, her expression filled with compassion and regret. "It's too late. The grapes are gone. There's nothing we can do."

Lori pulled away. "Mom, please! You're wasting

time! We've only got a couple of hours before the sun hits those vines!" She started running toward the winery.

Cici cried, "Lori, what are you doing?"

Lori called back, "Making ice wine!"

They worked with knit gloves on, cutting, plucking, and de-stemming, not to protect their hands but to keep the heat from their fingers from thawing the grapes. They sweated in their polar jackets and fleece pants, then shivered when the cold air dried their sweat. By the time the rising sun shot rays of gold through the knotty lines of vines, they had harvested a little over half the grapes and Lori insisted they abandon the effort.

"But all those grapes!" Bridget protested, shouting over the chug of the tractor engine. "We worked so hard—Dominic worked so hard—we can't just leave them!"

Lori shook her head adamantly. She was wearing a pair of her mother's sweatpants, rolled up at the waist and stuffed into her boots, and one of Bridget's wool jackets with a knit cap pulled down to her eyebrows. "The radio says thirty degrees by nine o'clock," she called back. "We've got to get these grapes into the press while we still can!" But when she cast a glance around the remaining rows, so forlorn and abandoned-looking in the yellow-gray shadows of dawn, her expression was almost as bereft as Bridget's.

The wagon was almost full, despite the partial harvest, and they stood outside the winery with frozen feet and chapped lips, fingers clumsy with cold and fatigue, to strip the frozen fruit off the stems and into five-gallon buckets, which they transferred as soon as they were full to the big basket press just inside the open door. The radio forecast changed to thirty-five degrees by nine a.m., thirty-two in low-lying areas. Kevin moved the wagon to the shadow cast by the open doors and they worked faster.

"Just be sure not to get any bruised or damaged grapes in the mix," Lori said, sifting through a double-handful in the bucket. "I know it was hard to see the good clusters in the dark."

"What difference does it make?" Cici said wearily. "They're frozen. When they thaw they're going to turn to sour mush, anyway. Lori, honey, are you sure about this?"

Lori didn't look sure at all as she turned to lug another bucket of grapes to the press. It was Kevin who pointed out simply, "I don't really see that you had any choice."

The press, which was designed for a full harvest of crushed grapes, was filled to capacity when they poured in the last bucket of hard frozen grapes. Kevin helped place the metal plate and Lori screwed it down. Hugging her arms and shivering, Cici looked at it anxiously. "What do we do now?"

Lori said, "We wait."

Bridget said, teeth chattering, "Do you think it would be okay if we waited in the house?"

Cici started toward the press. "Lori, nothing is happening. Are you sure you know how to work that thing?"

"Mom, it's okay." Lori adjusted the pressure with another half-turn of the screw. "That's the whole point of pressing frozen grapes. The water is left behind as ice crystals and all you get is a few drops of concentrated juice from each grape. It will take a while to see any juice flow."

Bridget stared at her. "A few drops? Do you mean we did all of this for a few drops?"

"No, of course not. We'll get ten or twenty gallons if we're lucky."

"Ten gallons?" The astonishment on Cici's face slowly turned to horror, and then, inevitably to despair. "But . . . we need two hundred gallons to break even this year. I know I heard Dominic say that! Oh, Lori, all this work. Why didn't we just take the loss?"

Kevin looked at her oddly. "Aunt Cici, do you know how much ice wine sells for?"

"No, it's okay," Lori said quickly, "she's right. It's a risk. It might not make at all." She adjusted the pressure again. "Why don't you all go back to bed? There's nothing more you can do here."

Cici looked at her for another moment, and then said wearily, "Sounds good to me."

"The lights are on in the kitchen," Bridget said, turning toward the house. "Ida Mae must have breakfast ready."

Cici dropped her hand onto Bridget's shoulder and leaned against her as they started up the path. "I don't even care."

Bridget glanced back. "Kids? Aren't you coming?"

"Right behind you," Kevin said. "I'm just going to put the tractor away." He looked at Lori questioningly.

"Go to bed," she told him. Her smile was tired. "You can't help. I have to stay and watch the pressure."

Cici turned back to her. "In the cold?"

"It won't take long," she assured them, trying to look confident. "Really, go on. The hard part is done."

And so, looking reluctant but too weary to fight very hard, one by one they left her alone.

Ten minutes later Lori looked up from adjusting the pressure again to see Kevin crossing the lawn with a large basket in his hands. "Ida Mae sent you a care package," he said when he reached her. He set the basket on the ground and began to unpack it, first bringing out two medium-sized rectangular objects wrapped in dishtowels. "Hot bricks," he said.

"For my feet?"

"To sit on. Save one for me." He put them on

the ground and handed her two smaller, foil-wrapped objects that smelled like bread.

"Breakfast?"

"Hand warmers," he replied. "Actually they're hoe-cakes. Confederate soldiers used to put them in their pockets in the morning before they went on maneuvers to warm their hands and keep their trigger fingers nimble. When lunch time came around, they ate them. Trivia courtesy of Ida Mae. She said you're supposed to put them in your gloves."

Lori did so, and breathed a small moan of appreciation. "Oh, that's nice. I'd forgotten what my fingers feel like."

He took out two more foil packets, but this time handed only one to her. "Breakfast," he said, and the last thing he took out was a thermos of coffee.

"I guess Ida Mae has done this before," Lori said.

"She didn't have any questions about what we were doing out in the vineyard all night, if that says anything. I get the feeling there's not too much that woman hasn't seen before."

They unwrapped their ham biscuits and sat on the warm bricks in the doorway, facing the press. Kevin poured coffee into the thermos cup and passed it to her. Lori took a sip, and handed it back to him. "I've been trying to think how we could have saved the rest of the grapes. Even if we'd filled every freezer in the house it wouldn't have meant more than a couple of bottles."

He nodded toward the press. The sound of dripping grape juice was slow—very slow—but steady. "So. What do you think?"

"I don't know." Her voice was heavy. "Maybe we did waste our time. It really needs to be below zero for a good ice wine, and this was a freak freeze, the temperature is going to be back up in the sixties this weekend, which will affect the fermentation, and there are really only a couple of other wineries that even make Cabernet Franc ice wine, and what do I know about it anyway?" She sighed. "Even with the best case scenario, Mom might be right. We might not break even."

He sipped his coffee, and handed the cup back to her. "I'll try to get into the computer this afternoon and run some figures. It might not be as bad as you think."

She took the cup. "I don't think my mom has much faith in me."

"Honey, one day they'll erect a statue to you. Meantime, they're both asleep."

Lori sighed. "I feel bad about waking them up and making them work all night. I hate to say it, but I think they may be getting too old for this."

Kevin bumped her shoulder lightly. "I hate to say it, but I think *I'm* getting to old for this."

She smiled.

They ate ham biscuits and sipped coffee from a shared cup, and listened to the ping-ping-ping of grape juice into the metal trays. Twice Lori got up to adjust the pressure. She blinked and strained and struggled to keep her eyes open, even though her feet were like blocks of ice and her cheeks were raw with cold. And then Kevin said softly, "I get it now."

She looked up at him questioningly, mildly surprised to see that the sun had risen high enough to paint his face in shades of gold. He took her chin in his fingers, and turned her face away from the cold interior of the winery and toward the vineyard, where the rising sun had painted a winter fairyland across the frozen vines. Melting snow sparkled like diamonds on the curve of the vines and the grass. A few cumulous clouds hung low on the horizon, their bottoms painted pink and outlined in gold against a cerulean sky while the mist that breathed off the thawing hills and vines rose upward to meet the light. The profile of the vineyard was graceful and strong, even as the hills seemed to melt into the horizon. The air tasted as fresh and new as Christmas morning, and against the permeating background scent of grapes there was an acrid smell of a wood fire mixed with something wonderful baking in the kitchen. Lori said softly, "Oh, my."

She leaned against him, and together they watched morning come to Ladybug Farm.

• • •

"Ice wine, you clever little minx," Dominic said, grinning. "Of course you did. What was your yield?"

"Twenty-five gallons," Lori said, though she looked a little uncertain. "It was more than I expected. I'm afraid some of it may be water."

"Did you watch the temperature?"

"I stopped pressing at thirty degrees."

"Then you're fine."

"I'm worried about the sugar."

"We can adjust that with yeast. But let it sit for a few more weeks, then test the brix." He smiled. "My, you look good to me, girl. It's good to have you home."

Lori relaxed for the first time since coming into the room, and she grinned back. "You look good too. When are they letting you out of here?"

Dominic's hospital room looked more like a cheerful little apartment now, with colorful quilts from home and bright cushions brought by Paul to "cozy up the place," books and magazines, baskets of fruit and baked goods, and of course the perennial clusters of get-well balloons and potted plants. There was even a giant poster print of Dominic and Lindsay in one corner, scrawled with the signatures of well-wishers. Though his face was perhaps not as tan as she remembered, and no one looked particularly robust in a hospital robe with his arm in a sling, Lori had been relieved to see that Dominic was much further along the road to recovery than she imagined.

"Tomorrow is the plan," he replied, "and it can't be too soon for me." He gave a small shake of his head. "I've been feeling like such a damn fool since this happened, lying up here in a hospital bed being fussed over while everything we worked for all year went to ruin . . . but sometimes things do have a way of working out, don't they? If I'd been there I would've harvested early last week. It wouldn't have occurred to me to leave anything on the vines for ice wine. You don't do that in Virginia, and who could have predicted a freak freeze like that in the middle of October?"

"I could have," Lindsay said, coming into the room with two coffee cups in her hand. There was a vending machine down the hall that made sweet frothy caramel lattes and even added whipped cream, and she had become addicted to them. "If there's one rule about Ladybug Farm, it's that anything that can go wrong, will."

She offered one of the lattes to Lori, who declined politely. She just couldn't get used to the sugary flavor of American coffee after Italy. "More for me," Lindsay said, setting one of the cups on the nightstand and carefully removing the lid from the other. "I can't believe you all were out there picking grapes at night in the cold." She sat on the arm of the big chair where Lori was sitting, and when Lori started to get up and offer her seat, Lindsay waved her down again. "I feel just awful that I wasn't there to help."

Lori cast a sideways grin at her. "I'll be sure to tell Mom and Aunt Bridget how bad you feel."

Lindsay sipped her latte, oblivious. "The only thing I don't understand—well, one of the things, anyway—is how we're going to get six hundred bottles of wine out of twenty-five gallons of juice."

Dominic looked amused. "We're not. We're going to get two hundred half bottles of ice wine and sell them for five times as much."

"Of course, we'll have to hold it longer," Lori added, "and there are extra bottling expenses. Kevin is running some projections for you," she added to Dominic. "Also a cost analysis and P&L. They'll be ready for you to look at when you get home."

"Well now," Dominic lifted an eyebrow, impressed. "She not only makes wine, she brings her own accountant."

Lori said, "Actually, Kevin's a . . ." She broke off and corrected herself easily. "Kevin's a real workaholic. He was looking for something to do, and he's pretty smart about things like that. We got the receipts filed and the bookkeeping up to date, too."

Dominic said, "Maybe I should break some more ribs. That would give you time to get the office painted and cut back the vineyard."

Lori said, "Don't even joke about that." And Lindsay said at the same time, "Not funny!"

Changing the subject, Lindsay said, "Did your mom tell you Noah called yesterday? Gosh, it was good to hear from him! What I could hear, that is," she added with a small frown. "He said something about being in transit and the connection was just awful. He didn't say where he was in transit to, or maybe he did and it got cut off. I told him everything was okay here and he said something about talking to me Saturday. That's tomorrow—although, oh dear." Her frown deepened. "I'm not sure if he meant Saturday his time or Saturday our time." She abandoned the effort to figure it out with a smile. "Anyway, thank you for everything you did to get in touch with him."

"It was Kevin's idea to call the Red Cross," Lori said.

"Well it sure lifted my spirits to hear his voice," Lindsay said, "even parts of it."

"That's what the Red Cross is for," Dominic said. "Although, of course, there was never any real emergency."

Both women stared at him, and Dominic lifted a single finger in self-defense, smiling. "Even though I'm very grateful that everyone else thought differently. Not only did I get to spend my honeymoon in a luxury suite with round the clock attendants, but I got a nice long visit with all my children and I got the help in the winery I've been asking for. So all in all, it worked out pretty well, I'd say."

They laughed, and Lori delivered the remaining messages from everyone at home, said her good-byes, and got up to leave. Lindsay walked her out.

"So that's pretty cool," Lori said, "that Dominic's coming home on the day that was going to be your wedding day."

"Is it?" Lindsay looked surprised. "I'm afraid I lost track of the time."

"I guess the 'for better or worse' part came a little sooner than you thought it would."

Lindsay smiled and gave a small shake of her head. "You probably won't understand this, and I hope in a way you don't, not for a long time anyway. But I was so proud of myself the night I finally let go of the wedding fantasy and just married the man, you know? It was as though the accident was a wake-up call, and now we had our second chance and it was nothing but happily ever after as far as I could see." She paused, and even her steps slowed as she chose her words. "Twelve hours later he stopped breathing. He almost died on the operating table. Twice in one day I lost him, and twice I got him back. And now every minute I get to spend with him is the happiest minute of my life. Because when you love someone it all feels like the better part, even when it's the worse."

Lori's brows drew together faintly, and she said, "Yeah."

They reached the elevator, and Lindsay hugged Lori. "Thank you, honey, for coming home. Dominic was his old self today for the first time since the accident, and it was all because of you. And knowing that you'll be here to help out with the winery takes such a load off his shoulders, and mine."

Lori looked uncomfortable. "I'm glad to help," she said. "But the thing is . . . well, I'm not sure how long I'll be able to stay."

"But your mother said things didn't work out in Italy." Lindsay looked at her closely, confused. "I thought you weren't going back."

Lori nodded. "It's just that . . ." She didn't know how to finish.

"Are you going back to school? But you won't be able to enroll until winter quarter at the earliest, and . . ."

"Aunt Lindsay," Lori blurted, "I'm in love with Kevin."

Lindsay stared at her.

"My mom doesn't know, neither does his, but he has to find a job and so do I and I just can't promise anything right now because I don't know what's going to happen to us, or where we'll end up."

A dozen questions raced through the shock in Lindsay's eyes, and at least another dozen emotions flickered across her face before she inquired cautiously, "Does Kevin love you back?"

Lori drew in a gulp of air, and nodded. Her response came out as barely above a whisper. "Desperately."

Lindsay smiled, and took Lori's face in her hands. "Then what in the world," she demanded gently, "are you doing here with me?"

"It was really very sweet," Lindsay said. She sat beside Dominic on the bed and opened the second latte. "And kind of sad. Poor Lori. She's had such a troubled love life, and I remember how I was at that age, so certain that every man I met was The One, and getting my heart broken every damn time." She licked a froth of melted whipped cream from the top of her coffee. "And then it turned out I had to wait thirty years, when I was totally out of the mood to get married, before I actually found The One."

Dominic, who had been flipping through a trade journal his daughter Cassie had brought, removed his reading glasses and smiled. "Well, let's hope our young Romeo and Juliet fare better, shall we?"

"I don't know. It's weird, thinking about them as a couple. I mean, they practically grew up together. And what if it doesn't work out? Cici is going to flip. And Bridget . . . I can't even imagine what she's going to think."

"Friends usually make the best lovers," Dominic pointed out. "And I think you may underestimate the ladies, not to mention their children. After all, a man doesn't fly across an ocean to be with the woman he loves only to break her heart on his mother's doorstep."

Lindsay smiled. "You know what else is weird? That I'm talking about this to you instead of Cici. But I kind of like it. In fact . . ." She swung her legs up onto the bed and propped a pillow behind her back, snuggling close to him. "I think I'm really starting to like this whole marriage thing."

"I am delighted to hear it," said Dominic. "Because I did hope we could give it more than a trial run."

He kissed her, and when she settled back against the pillow again she was smiling. "Lori pointed out that tomorrow is the day we were supposed to get married originally. I hadn't even thought about it."

"Is it now? We should have a party."

She knew he was teasing and she was about to make some flip remark when suddenly she sat up straight, staring at him. "Oh my God," she said. "I think we already are."

Kevin glanced up from the computer as Lori came into the winery office. "Hi, baby," he said, a little absently. "Listen, I found about a half dozen invoices that hadn't been mailed so I sent them out. It's going to be a lot easier to collect revenue if you actually invoice for product. And I went ahead and filled out the quarterly tax forms, but they can wait 'til the deadline to write the check. Fortunately, with no income you don't pay much in taxes. Honey, I don't mean to criticize, but this is not a one-man operation. They're going to have to hire somebody to run this office, even if it's only part time. Maybe if the ice wine works out there'll be enough in the budget for it next year. You need to talk to Dominic about that. Oh, and I found a bunch of credit card payments in receivables for ticket sales, but I don't know how to apply them. Do you know what that's about?"

She came over to the desk, turned his chair around, and sat on his knee. He looked up at her, his concentrated expression slowly fading into pleasured welcome as he caressed her back. "This is different," he said.

She kissed him. Inevitably, he kissed her back, gently at first, and then with rising passion. Finally, reluctantly, they broke apart. "Okay," he murmured, letting his hand slide from her waist to her hips and back again. "This is a test, right?"

She said, "We can't go on like this, Kevin."

"I'm one hundred percent onboard with that, sweetheart." He settled his hands on her waist and kissed her throat. "So why don't you tell me what you have in mind? And keep an eye on the window. If one of our mothers walks in and finds you like this there'll be more than one person in the hospital."

Lori said, "It's time to tell them the truth."

He leaned back, studying her face. "All of it?"

She nodded. "I know that ever since we got here we've been telling ourselves we were protecting them by avoiding the subject, but you know we were really just protecting ourselves. Because if we told them about us, we'd have to tell them how we got to be us, and that would mean you telling about losing your job and me telling about Sergio and lying about the apprenticeship."

He nodded. "I know."

"They're going to be mad. They might even cry. And . . . they might not like that we're together. It will be hard for them to get used to. But sometimes you just have to stand up and do what you have to do, and be ready to pay the price if it goes wrong." She thought about that for a moment and added, "Just like with the ice wine."

He smiled. "I love you, do you know that?"

She smiled back. "Yeah. Actually, I do."

He tightened his hands on her waist and pushed her gently to her feet. "Let's go then. No time like the present."

She said, "A kiss for luck?"

He slipped his arms around her and drew her into him, and suddenly her eyes flew wide, and she stepped back. "Did you say ticket sales?" she demanded.

"I can't believe we forgot the burning of the vines party!" Bridget said, looking around the kitchen in a mixture of panic and despair. "We've been planning it for over a month!"

"We didn't forget it," Cici insisted, annoyed. "We just didn't know it was *tomorrow*. Anyway, with everything that's been going on around here this past week, we're lucky to remember our names." She pushed back her hair with both hands and winced with embarrassment. "No wonder Dominic's daughter sounded so surprised when I called to invite them all to dinner tomorrow. They thought they were already invited!"

"Well, don't look at me," Ida Mae muttered, slamming the oven door on an herbed chicken she had just put in to roast. "It ain't my job to keep up with your doin's." But she looked more than a little disgruntled to realize that she, like the rest of them, had been too busy preparing for the arrival of the invalid to remember something so important.

"You sold less than a hundred tickets," Kevin pointed out. "And they were all on credit cards or through online payment services. If we refund the money today you'll be clear of Internet fraud."

Bridget's eyes grew even bigger. "Fraud!"

"It's not just the tickets," Cici said. "It's all the people who were going to pay at the door, and the drop-ins from town, and all our friends."

"You could put a sign at the end of the driveway that says it's canceled," Lori suggested. "Don't most people know about Dominic's accident any-way?"

"Maybe an announcement on the radio," Cici said worriedly.

"That takes twenty-four hours," Bridget said. "Remember when Paul and Derrick were trying to find homes for all those dogs? And besides, not everyone listens to the radio."

"Y'all got a freezer full of food," Ida Mae pointed out grumpily. "Two freezers. What're you expectin' to do with that?"

"And," suggested Lori hopefully, "you've got plenty of wine."

"But we canceled the band," Cici said.

"And the flowers. And we were going to have tents for the food and rent chairs to set up in a circle around the bonfire . . ."

"Well, it's too late to rent tents or chairs," Kevin said. "But if you just canceled the band this week they probably don't have another gig."

"I'll call them," Lori volunteered. "Where's their card?"

"But," Bridget said anxiously, "we were going to have garnet tablecloths and monogrammed rose napkins, and runners made of grapevines, and candles . . ."

"That was for the *wedding*," Lori pointed out. "This is a tasting. You don't have to have

311

tablecloths. You just have to have glasses. And I saw boxes of them stacked up in the barn."

Bridget looked mildly insulted at the thought of serving food without tablecloths, then said thoughtfully, "The layers for the wedding cake are already frozen. I suppose if I frosted them and displayed them separately it wouldn't look so much like a wedding cake."

Cici said, "We'd have to set up the parking lot and get someone to direct traffic . . ."

"I could do that," Kevin said.

"And I can take the money and pour the wine," Lori said. "We'll set it up in The Tasting Table just like we did for the blessing of the vines. We'll open both doors and the traffic will flow through directly into the gardens and the vineyard."

Bridget closed her eyes and released a slow weary breath. "I just don't know that I'm up for this," she said. "Every muscle in my body still aches from picking grapes."

"And I don't know if I'll ever get full range of motion back in my shoulder," said Cici, wincing as she rubbed her right shoulder. "We've hardly slept at all this past week and you have no idea how much there is to do for something like this. The lawn is a mess and the chrysanthemums are all dead and the paths have to be swept and the windows washed . . ."

"And we still have finger sandwiches to make, and the cheese straws and the harvest soup . . ."

"I'll help," Lori said.

"So will I," said Kevin.

"And so will I."

They turned to see Lindsay standing at the door. Bridget and Cici exclaimed in surprise and Lindsay rushed to them, hugging them each hard. "I left you alone to deal with the grape crisis," she said, "but there was no way I was going to let you do this by yourselves. Dominic's children are with him now and they're all going to help him pack up and bring him home in the morning. So I'm here for the duration. Now." She stepped back, holding one of Bridget's hands and one of Cici's, looking pleased and determined. "Where do we start?"

Bridget looked at Cici. Cici looked at Bridget. They both looked at Lindsay, and their faces broke into reluctant smiles. "Well," said Bridget, "maybe we can do this after all."

They mowed the lawn and raked the leaves. Lindsay drove into town for fresh chrysanthemums to replace the dead ones and spruced up the ravaged flower beds with mulch and colorful decorative cabbage plants. They dragged out two big iron kettles from the barn and filled them with ivy and yellow daisies, and placed them on either side of the entrance to the winery. Paul and Derrick drove over with their cars loaded with the outdoor candelabra they had used at the engage-

313

ment party, a box of leftover candles, and the surprise delivery of garnet-colored tablecloths and rose napkins, monogrammed with Lindsay's and Dominic's initials entwined like vines.

"They were ordered too late to return," Paul explained. "We were going to save them for your first anniversary party, but this is so much better."

Kevin cut grapevines and dug a fire pit. Lori moved the tables in The Tasting Table to form an L-shaped buffet, and Paul arranged coils of grapevines and candles in miniature terracotta pots down the center of each one while Derrick carried the big serving dishes down from the house and placed them just-so upon beds of colorful autumn leaves. Dominic's two sons arrived on orders from their father, and pitched in hanging lights and flower baskets, washing windows and cutting vines for the bonfire.

They washed glasses and unpacked two cases of wine. Lori made a display at the pouring table describing the virtues of each bottle and clearly quoting the price per case. Kevin remembered the cash box and they pooled their resources for change. Bridget set out the frozen layers of the cake to thaw, and unpacked the decorations. Tomorrow each layer would be frosted and decorated with white chocolate roses and fondant grapes. Trays of frozen delicacies were set out to thaw in the cold pantry. A hundred fifty finger sandwiches were assembled, wrapped in damp paper towels, sealed in plastic bags and stored in the refrigerator. Everyone grated cheese for the cheese straws, which needed to sit overnight before being sliced and baked in the morning.

When all that remained were the last minute details that had to be put together before the guests arrived the next day, they all shared a supper of roast chicken and potatoes with green beans, and Ida Mae's ice box lemon pie. Derrick and Paul left to return to the Hummingbird House, along with Dominic's sons. Lindsay talked to Dominic on the phone. Kevin went upstairs to take a shower while Lori helped Ida Mae clean the kitchen. And because they all knew the danger of cluttering up Ida Mae's kitchen once she had declared the day was done, Cici, Bridget, and Lindsay were left with nothing to do except pour themselves a glass of wine, pull on their sweaters, and go out onto the porch to bask in the last pale shades of a setting sun.

"Oh, Lindsay, I do like Dominic's boys!" declared Bridget. "I can't wait to meet their wives."

Lindsay beamed as though they were her own. "All his children are wonderful," she said. "Wait until you meet Cassie. She's the kind of person you want to give your house key to and say 'make yourself at home.' And so smart. Lori's going to love talking to her about the wine business. Of course," she added easily, settling into her rocking chair, "I should have known I would like them. After all, Dominic raised them."

"All that energy!" Cici said, smothering a small groan as she sat down. "Not just the boys, but Lori and Kevin too. Were we ever that young?"

"Not in recent memory," said Bridget. "But my goodness, look how much we got done in one afternoon!" She smiled at Lindsay as she took her chair. "It was like old times, all of us working side by side again. I'm so glad you were here."

"It feels strange to be away from Dominic," Lindsay admitted, and she smiled as she sipped her wine. "But my, it's good to be home."

"It was awful without you," Bridget said. "And Dominic, too. The night the grapes froze—I've never felt so helpless."

"We're all lucky Lori and Kevin were here to help," Lindsay said. "Maybe even luckier than we know. Dominic seemed to think that Lori's idea for ice wine could save the winery."

Cici looked surprised, and impressed, and cautiously proud. But then she frowned a little. "You know, though, Bridget's right. We were completely unprepared. And when Lori started asking all those questions about the wine, and Kevin was asking about which papers were where and what forms had been filed with which agency . . . we didn't know the answers." She glanced at Lindsay, then at Bridget, looking embarrassed. "It's our winery, our business, and we didn't know. It was just so easy to let Dominic take care of things. That's not like us, and we can't do it anymore. If we're going to be a team, we all have to pull our weight. We can't depend on Dominic to take care of us. It's not fair to him, or to us."

Bridget nodded. "I think it's a bad habit women fall into, whenever there is a man around. To just let him take care of things."

Lindsay said, "I think we all took Dominic for granted, and I'm no better than either one of you. Or at least I was. I know better now." She slid a glance at Bridget. "Speaking of guys who take care of things, that Kevin sure is a hard worker."

"Who knew he could drive a tractor?" Cici put in. "Or swing an ax? I always thought of him as the kind of guy who didn't like to get his hands dirty."

Bridget smiled. "There's not much Kevin can't do. He just never showed much interest in doing it around here before."

Cici sipped her wine, watching the sky fade to a pale winter yellow over the dark profile of the mountains. "I wonder what changed his mind?"

Lindsay said, with studious innocence, "You know what I was thinking this afternoon? What a cute couple Kevin and Lori make."

Cici laughed. "Seriously? All they did as kids was fight."

"Lori used to pester him to death," Bridget remembered fondly, "and Kevin tormented her.

Of course, she was half his age, and no boy is going to put up with a baby girl following him around all day."

"Well they're not fighting now," Lindsay pointed out. "And when you're six and twelve the age difference is a lot bigger than when you're sixty and sixty-six. Or twenty-four and thirty."

Cici and Bridget exchanged an amused look. "Well, that I'd like to see," said Cici.

Bridget added, chuckling, "We could be grannies together."

The door opened and Lori came out, a notebook in one hand and a pen in the other. She shivered in her tee shirt and jeans. "It's cold out here," she said.

"Oh, honey, will you go inside and put on some clothes?" Cici said. "Weren't you supposed to get your things down from the attic today?"

"No time," said Lori. She pulled up Dominic's rocking chair so that it closed in the circle with the other three chairs and sat down. "Now," she said, "this is how I see it going. The band sets up at three, we open the gates—figuratively speaking, that is—at four. Aunt Lindsay, you're going to get some signs directing people to parking, right? They need to be up by two at the latest. And I called the girl at the newspaper. She said she'd try to get out to take some photos and do an article so will one of you *please* study up on what's going on at the winery so you can

318

do an interview? I just don't think it's right to ask Dominic, it being his first day home from the hospital and all." She paused then and shivered, rubbing her bare arm with one hand.

"Lori, at least go put on a sweater. There's one hanging by the door."

She waved a hand, trying to keep her teeth from chattering. "That's okay. So we should start bringing the food out a little before four—Uncle Paul and Uncle Derrick said they'd help, so you guys can act like hostesses and you don't have to get all sweaty and flustered at the last minute. It's going to be sixty-five tomorrow afternoon, which is perfect for an outdoor event, but fifty after the sun sets. So I figured we'd light the fire around five-thirty . . ."

The door opened again and Kevin came out, his hair still damp from the shower, wearing jeans and a sweatshirt and carrying a sweater in his hand. Lori smiled when she saw him. "Hey, Kev. We're just going over the details."

He came over to her and draped the sweater over her shoulders. "Seriously, kiddo? It was right by the door."

And there it was for anyone to see: the tenderness in his touch, the warmth in her eyes. The way he looked at her, the way she smiled at him.

He added, with a look that none of them could understand because they were too nonplussed by what they had seen—or imagined they'd seen—

pass between the two young people only a moment before, "Do you think you could finish this later?"

Lori held his eyes for a moment, nodded, and said, "Sure." She stood.

Kevin turned to Bridget, his expression somber. "Mom, there's something I need to tell you."

Lindsay started to rise. "Maybe I should—"

"No, Aunt Lindsay, Aunt Cici, both of you stay," Kevin said. "I want you to hear this."

Cici cast a concerned look toward Bridget, and Bridget tried to smile. "You're starting to worry me, honey."

Kevin glanced at Lori. She moved closer to him, clutching the sweater around her shoulders. She said, "Actually, Mom, I guess I have a few things to tell you, too. About Villa Laurentis, and my apprenticeship. But Kevin wanted to go first."

Kevin said, "This won't be easy for me to say. You won't want to hear parts of it. Parts of it will hurt you, and maybe make you ashamed of me."

"Oh, Kevin," Bridget exclaimed, "how can you say that? You're my son and I'm always on your side! But now you're really scaring me. Please, what is it?"

"It's kind of a long story," Kevin said.

Lori said softly, "But it's worth it." She wrapped her hands around Kevin's arm and pressed her cheek to his shoulder, looking up at him. "Because it has a happy ending."

CHAPTER THIRTEEN

∽

The Happy Ending

"Seriously, Cici," Lindsay said the next morning, "I don't understand you. You were up all night worrying and fretting and trying to talk her out of it when Lori got engaged to Mark, but now you don't have a thing to say?"

"I know," replied Cici, biting into an orange. "It's weird, right? Maybe I'm in shock."

They kept their voices low because the two young lovers were still sleeping—in separate rooms, as far as they knew—and because, more importantly, so was Ida Mae. Bridget even used the whisk to beat the egg whites for the frosting to avoid waking her with the electric mixer, because once Ida Mae was up the domain of the kitchen was automatically surrendered.

Lindsay poured cereal into a bowl and cast Bridget an inquiring look. "Bridget? You're taking this awfully well."

"Are you kidding? I'm so glad my only son is not wearing an orange jumpsuit in the federal penitentiary that everything else he does for the rest of his life will receive nothing but a standing ovation from me." She paused in her work with the whisk, a little out of breath. "You know," she added thoughtfully in a moment, "I don't think we really appreciate how much pressure we put on our children without even realizing it. We want them to be perfect. We want their lives to be perfect. I think maybe the reason Kevin got into the situation that he did was because he was always so driven to live up to the expectations his dad and I had of him. He didn't understand that all we really wanted was for him to be happy." She picked up the whisk again. "The thing is, when I saw the way he looked at Lori last night, when he came out and put the sweater on her shoulders, it hit me for the first time—he looks happy." She smiled at Cici. "That's all that matters."

Cici smiled back, then shifted her glance to Lindsay. "What she said." She reached for another orange segment. "Of course I'm worried about them. But it's not like it was with Mark. I mean, I've loved Kevin all his life, and I still love him. I've loved Lori all her life and I still love her. It's almost as though . . . I don't know, it just feels okay to me."

Bridget smiled. "What she said."

Lindsay sat back at the table, cradling her cereal bowl against her chest contentedly. "Well, then. We may not be having a wedding at Ladybug Farm today but we've got plenty of love to go around." Suddenly she grinned. "Hey, you know what? If things *do* work out with Kevin and Lori, and if they *do* get married some day, when they come back to visit they can have that master suite you worked so hard on! Then it won't be wasted."

Bridget said, smiling to herself, "He wants to be a teacher. His dad would be so proud. Not," she added quickly, "that I won't be proud of him if he decided to dig ditches the rest of his life."

"I'd be very proud," Cici said, "if he decided to dig those ditches around Ladybug Farm. Dominic says the irrigation system needs to be overhauled." She made a face. "*That* I remember. Couldn't remember where the insurance forms were or that we were giving a party for two hundred people today, but I'm all over the irrigation system."

Bridget put down the whisk and blew out a breath, staring at the soppy mess of partially foamed egg whites. "I give up. How does she do it?"

Cici got up to retrieve the electric mixer from the pantry just as Ida Mae came up the stairs from her suite. She was already dressed for the big day in flannel lined jeans, steel-toed boots, a plaid jumper with a black turtleneck, and a red cardigan. She gave them a sour look and announced, "Company's coming."

They shared a puzzled look. "This early?"

Cici went to the window. "It's a cab."

Bridget stood behind her. "Oh dear. There's a policeman. What's wrong now?"

Ida Mae peered closer. "That ain't no police-man. That's a soldier."

But Lindsay had already flung open the back door and was racing around the porch, down the steps, to the drive, and Cici and Bridget were close behind her. "Noah!" she cried, and flung herself on him. "Noah!"

"Noah, what are you—"

"Where did you—"

"How—"

There were hugs and laughter and exclamations all around, and then Noah, looking at Lindsay with a slightly puzzled look on his face, said, "I told you I'd be here today. Did you forget?"

Lindsay just kept staring at him, as though hardly able to believe the evidence of her eyes. "Do you mean—on the phone? But I couldn't hear you! I didn't think you meant in person!"

He said worriedly, "Listen, is everything okay? Because the Red Cross said—"

"Oh, Noah, everything is perfect now!" said Lindsay, holding on to his hands. Her face was radiant and her eyes glowed with delight and wonder. "Like I told you on the phone, it was touch and go for a while but everything is okay now."

"I guess I couldn't hear you very well either," he admitted. "I thought that's what you said but not a lot of it made sense."

The driver came around with Noah's duffle and stood by patiently.

"Noah," demanded Cici astonished, "is that how you got leave? They let you come all the way back here because of one phone call?"

"That's what I was trying to explain to you on the phone," he said. "I wanted to tell you earlier but that's when the unit got word we were being redeployed to Egypt—"

"Egypt!" exclaimed Lindsay in dismay.

Bridget said anxiously "What's going on in Egypt?"

Noah lifted a shoulder. "I'm just a private. Anyway, that's why you couldn't find me, because just as we were getting ready to ship out my transfer came through . . ."

"Transfer?" Bridget look lost. "You requested a transfer?"

"Not exactly. Kind of. The thing is, I applied to the communications school—it's a really cool program and when you're done you're all set with everything there is to know about satellites and radios and all kinds of technology—but it's kind of new to the Corps and hardly anybody gets in, especially new recruits, so I didn't want to say anything until I found out. Well, I guess I scored pretty high on the test because the next thing I know I've got new orders. The only problem is it turns out the school is in Washington, can you believe that?" The downturn of one corner of his lips reflected a mixture of disbelief and disgust. "I'm practically right back where I started. Too bad, too. I really wanted to see those pyramids."

Lindsay laughed out loud with delight and Bridget and Cici joined in, applauding and hugging him again. "Noah, we couldn't be happier!"

"This is what we've prayed for!"

"You'll practically be close enough to come home on weekends!"

"Don't get too excited," he cautioned, "I don't even start the program until my promotion comes through in December. Meanwhile, I'm assigned to a unit that guards monuments and sh—stuff. Boring duty. Anyhow, the school only lasts six months, unless they decide to advance me to the next level of training . . ."

Lindsay shared a look of triumphant certainty with Cici and Bridget.

"And after that I'll probably be assigned to an aircraft carrier. Now that will be cool." He rubbed his hands together in anticipation, or perhaps to ward off the cold. The cab driver, standing by, shuffled his feet and cleared his throat, but no one noticed.

"I still don't understand how you ended up here," Lindsay said.

"Well that's where it gets a little confusing," he admitted. "As far as I can figure out, your first message about a family emergency got to my old unit commander a couple of days after the Red Cross tracked down my CO at the new post. I guess the Red Cross really gets pissed when they lose somebody because they didn't even wait for me to report to my new duty station before some chaplain is meeting me at the airport in London with a new set of travel orders and talking about two weeks' compassionate leave. That was when I called you from the plane. Glad to hear there's not any emergency after all but, hell—I mean, heck, I'm not about to turn down two weeks' leave. So here I am." He looked from one to the other of them. "So what's been going on?"

Bridget laughed and pressed her hands to her cheeks. "I wouldn't know where to begin!"

Cici said, "It's a really long story."

Lindsay slipped her arm through his. "We'll tell you inside, out of the cold. I have a feeling you could use one of Ida Mae's good country breakfasts."

"Sounds great," he agreed enthusiastically. He picked up his duffle and looked apologetically at the driver. "But first, does anybody have any money to pay this fella?"

Lori let the curtain drop and turned away from the window. "Well, what do you know about that? It's Noah!" She grinned. "I guess your call to the Red Cross worked."

"Is that right?" Kevin sat up in bed and stretched out a hand for her. "Better late than never, I guess. And keep your voice down."

She laughed, took two running steps, and bounced on the bed beside him. He pretended to grimace, but then caught her against him, burying his own laughter in her shoulder. "Seriously," she demanded, "do you really think anyone would think we went through all that last night just so we could continue to *not* sleep together? Our moms are not that stupid."

"Mothers have a way of seeing only what they want to see," he assured her, "and we owe them the courtesy of allowing them to deceive themselves as long as they possibly can." And then he tightened his arms around her. "I missed you, babe."

She whispered back, "Welcome home, Kev."

She kissed him, long and slow, and when she was settled warm in his arms again, her head resting on his shoulder, she said, "How do you think they took it?"

"Better than I expected." He frowned a little. "It was a little spooky, in fact. I guess I really underestimated my mom."

"Parents can fool you sometimes."

"Right." He kissed her temple. "Just when you think you've got them figured out, they hit you with that love thing."

She gazed around the room contentedly. "I really like what they did with my room. It's nice with the fireplace. I could stay here all day."

"Me, too." He tucked a kiss behind her ear.

She smiled, lacing her fingers through his and bringing them to cradle her cheek. "What do you think is going to happen to us, Kev?"

He drew her closer. "Don't know. Don't care. Because . . ." He kissed her. "This is enough."

"Yeah," she said, smiling as she looked into his eyes. "It really is."

When Dominic arrived with his daughter Cassie at noon, he had more than one surprise waiting for him. The first was when the car turned into the drive and he saw a horse trailer parked behind the barn, and two familiar-looking horses munching grass in a corner of the pasture beyond. Lori, after teasing Noah about his buzz cut and admiring his service uniform, had demanded, "Now, go get on some real clothes. You're not afraid of horses, are you?"

To which Noah, with an air of resignation that accompanied every party the ladies had ever given, replied, "It beats washing dishes." And, with the help of Dominic's sons, they had managed to get the horses in the trailer and into a cross-fenced corner of the pasture only moments before Dominic was scheduled to arrive.

His second surprise was when he opened the car door and a big golden retriever came bounding toward him, tongue lolling, eyes shining happily. Rebel barked furiously from the barn. "Because," Lindsay explained, running to intercept the dog's enthusiastic greeting before more harm was done to the recovering patient, "we clearly don't have enough chaos around here!" She embraced her husband while the dog tried to wriggle between them, and she added, "And because Lori insisted on everything being perfect by the time you got home."

He laughed, guarding his injured ribs as he stooped to return the dog's greeting with an equal amount of enthusiasm. When he looked up he got his third surprise. Private Noah Wright stood square-shouldered and tall, his hand extended in greeting.

"Welcome home, sir," Noah said. He added, "I'm glad you're okay. And congratulations."

Dominic shot a glance of amazement and delight to Lindsay, whose smile could not get any broader. He straightened up and shook Noah's hand in a firm grip. "I could say the same to you, Private. On all counts."

Lori came bouncing down the steps from the house, her hair in a curly ponytail, the sleeves of her turtleneck sweater—which she had finally found time to retrieve from the attic—pushed up to the elbows. "Welcome home!" she called. "I was going to make a sign but Mom thought it would be too much. Lunch is all ready, but we're not having much because we have *got* to start setting up for the party. Ida Mae says you have to have yours on a tray in the sick room, but I wouldn't listen to her if I were you. You can't let her start bossing you around or you'll never have a chance around here. Hi," she said, extending her hand to Cassie. "I'm Lori. Are you Cassie? Aunt Bridget says for you to come right in and have lunch and leave the boys to unpack the car. And when you get a chance, I want to talk to you about the California Riesling."

Dominic and Lindsay laughed. Cassie assured Lori she couldn't wait to talk about Riesling with her, and the three of them started toward the house just as Kevin came down the steps to help unpack the car. Lori took a potted plant from the backseat and handed it to Noah, who passed off a suitcase to Kevin. Lori went back in and carefully edged the giant poster print out of the car. Kevin looked at it skeptically. "Somebody's idea of a joke?"

"I like it," Lori said, thrusting another potted plant toward Noah. "Take these to The Tasting Table," she advised. "We need more decorations. Put them on either side of the back door." She handed the poster print to Kevin. "Put this in the sunroom with Dominic and Aunt Lindsay."

Noah said, "Good to see you're still as bossy as ever." Then he said, "So are you two getting married or what?"

Both Kevin and Lori stared at him.

He frowned. "What? Everybody's talking about you guys. It's not like it's a secret or anything. Anyway, let me know what you decide

331

because I need to know where to put my stuff."

He carried the potted plants toward the restaurant and Kevin, with a twinkle in his eye, turned to Lori. "So," he said, "are we getting married or what?"

Lori lugged a box full of miscellanea out of the backseat and looked at him, balancing the box on her hip, her head tilted beguilingly. "Of course we are," she said. "Otherwise little Sebastian, Gabriella, and—"

"Ishmael," he supplied.

"Nathaniel," she corrected, "will be at a disadvantage when they try to enroll in private school. So when do you want to?"

He juggled the poster and the suitcase to look at his watch. "Well, let's see. It's noon now. How about five o'clock?"

"Today?"

"I am not," he told her sternly, "going to spend another night sneaking into your room. Besides, Noah needs to know where to put his stuff."

Lori looked at him for another moment, fighting with the corners of a grin, and then she said, "Well then. We'd better hurry."

"We don't want to make a big deal out of it," Lori rushed into the stunned silence at the lunch table five minutes later. "Just something quick and simple after the party, or maybe even during it if we have time."

Cici choked, "If you have *time?* You'll get married if you *have time?*"

Lindsay kicked her under the table.

"We really hope we have your blessing," Kevin went on, looking from Bridget to Cici, "but if we don't, we hope to earn it. Meantime . . ." he glanced at his watch. "It's Saturday, and the County Clerk's office closes at two so we have to get into town and get the license."

"Kevin's kind of a stickler about legalities," Lori explained, and she did not appear to be joking.

"But Kevin," Bridget said helplessly, "you don't even have a . . ."

Lindsay kicked her under the table.

Lori said, "Really, we don't want to cause anyone any stress. It's just that everyone we love is already here and the party is ready to roll and we knew you'd be mad if we eloped—"

Bridget and Cici gave muffled exclamations of agreement.

"So this just seemed like the easiest way. We have to go into town for ice anyway," she added, "so we might as well pick up the license. Does anybody need anything else while we're out?"

Into the stunned silence that followed, Kevin said to Lori, "Baby, we'd better get going. There's an awful lot to set up for the party before four."

Lori said cheerfully, "Okay, back in an hour.

Don't worry about a thing—we've got it under control!"

And they were gone before anyone could draw another breath.

Bridget sank back in her chair weakly. "What does a heart attack feel like?"

"It's not that I object to the marriage," Cici began.

"Of course not!" Bridget put in quickly. "I love Lori. It's just so sudden—"

"We didn't even know they were dating until last night!"

Noah said, "Could somebody pass the potato salad?"

Dominic did so politely. "Great roast beef," he said.

"Sure tastes like home," Noah agreed.

Neither Bridget nor Cici appeared to have heard them. Cici's face was torn with distress. "It's just that—it's her wedding! She doesn't have a dress, or flowers, or music, and don't you kick me!" She glared at Lindsay.

Lindsay said mildly, "Ladies, have we learned nothing?" She gave that a moment to sink in, and then added, "It's Lori and Kevin's wedding. These will be their memories." She glanced at Dominic and smiled. "And sometimes the best memories are when everything doesn't go perfectly. Meanwhile, Lori's right. The party is in place. We've got flowers everywhere, and plenty of food, and we've already hired the band . . ."

She looked suddenly at Bridget. "Bridget, what happened to my dress?"

Bridget fluttered her hand distractedly, trying to focus. "Oh, Lindsay, I'm afraid it's ruined. The whole bottom front is kind of a faded blue . . ."

Lindsay said, "What if we cut off the ruined parts?"

Bridget's eyes widened. "Cut up a Vera Wang?"

Cici objected, "We can't make a wedding dress! We have signs to make and food to stage and—"

"I can sew," Cassie volunteered. "I'd be glad to give it a try."

"Come on." Lindsay pushed up from the table. She turned back, kissed Dominic's cheek, and commanded, "Rest, or I'll sic Ida Mae on you." She grabbed her sandwich and gestured to Cassie. "I'll show you the sewing room. Bridget, where's the dress?"

Cici got up to follow. "Lindsay, are you sure you want to . . . ?"

Bridget hurried after them. "You know, it's really only the bottom eight inches . . ."

When they were gone, Noah helped himself to another sandwich. "Do you reckon that Kevin fellow knows what he's getting into?"

Dominic just grinned. "Son, I don't think it would matter."

The first guests were thirty minutes away from arriving when Kevin came into the winery office.

335

The golden retriever woofed softly from underneath his master's chair, then laid his head between his paws again. Kevin stopped short when he saw Dominic. "Oh, hi. I didn't know you were out here. Lori sent me for another case of wine. She likes to be over-prepared."

"To tell the truth, all that busyness up at the house was wearing me out," Dominic said, removing his glasses. "I got more rest in the hospital and that place was a zoo. There's a nice case of white merlot I was saving for a special occasion," he added, "and I guess this is it. It's behind the New York cabernet."

"Great, thanks."

"Getting nervous?" Dominic asked when Kevin returned from the storage room with the case of wine in his arms.

Kevin set the box on the conference table and smiled. "No sir, I'm not. I'd be more nervous if we weren't getting married. I know it caught everyone else by surprise, and probably seems a little impulsive, but you know how people talk about the overnight success that only took twenty years of hard work? Well, for us this is an impulsive marriage that was our whole lives in the making and I'd feel like the world's biggest idiot if I waited another day."

Dominic smiled. "I know exactly what you mean." He nodded his head back toward the desk. "I appreciate all the work you did while I was gone. I'm afraid I'm not much of one for paperwork. When I worked for the county I had an assistant who did all that for me, and I haven't quite gotten used to having to run the back office myself." He kept his expression bland. "I'd kind of hoped Lori would be able to help me out on that end when she got home, but I guess now you all have other plans."

Kevin said, "Excuse me, sir, but that would really be a waste of Lori's talents. She's way too creative to be stuck behind a desk. You need to put her in the field when she's not making wine. She'd make a hell of a saleswoman and marketing is second nature to her. I'd hire an office manager if I were you, even if you could only afford one part time. Maybe Aunt Lindsay could learn to do it, or Mom or Aunt Cici."

Dominic looked skeptical. "I don't mean to diminish any of the ladies' considerable talents, but this is specialized work. You need a background in business management." He held Kevin's gaze steadily. "Maybe even law."

Kevin smiled a little uncertainly. "I know you don't want to lose Lori, and I'm going to do everything in my power to keep her here because that's what she wants too. But we have to think about our future, and . . ."

Dominic raised a hand to stop him. "I understand. But it's an offer. This is a family business, and for the first few years most of your salary would be in stock. You've seen the figures. You know what we can afford to pay. But the office job would only be part time, and if you're interested in supplementing your income I have a little pull with the head of the Business Management Department down at the junior college."

Kevin looked interested. "Really?"

Dominic nodded. "I talked to him this afternoon. It happens he's looking to replace an instructor winter quarter."

A slow grin crossed Kevin's face. "You really *do* want to keep Lori."

Dominic said simply, "It's a family business."

"Sounds like I'm lucky to be marrying into this family."

"My friend," replied Dominic, smiling, "we both are."

"Oh, my darling girl!" exclaimed Paul when all the hugs and congratulations were finished. "It's not that we're not just ecstatic for you, but . . ." he stepped back and eyed her critically, his index finger pressed to his lips. "Aren't you going to do anything with your hair?"

"Love the hair," Derrick defended her, beaming like a proud parent. "All wild and woodland nymph. However, the manicure could use a touch-up."

Lori glanced distractedly at her nails and then gave herself a shake. "Thanks, Uncle Paul, Uncle

Derrick. But if we don't get the bar set up I won't even have time to take a shower."

They were in the restaurant, where platters of cold hors d'oeuvres and sliced cheese had already been set out, the candles lit, the warming trays plugged in. Lori was behind the table that flanked the door, still in her jeans and sweater, unpacking glasses and uncorking bottles. It was three forty-five. Through the open doors they could hear the band warming up.

"But it's your wedding day!" Derrick cried. "You should be in a bubble bath, followed by a massage, followed by a mani-pedi . . ."

Lori looked again at her nails, frowning a little.

Paul said. "Let us do whatever it is you're doing. Go pamper yourself."

Lori said. "Thanks, I will in a minute. I'll tell you what you can do, though." She handed them each a collection of whimsical card stock cut-outs in the shape of wine glasses with suggestions like, "Pairs well with Ladybug Farm Ruby Red" and "Pairs well with Ladybug Farm Crystal Rose" written on them in Lindsay's beautiful scroll. "Go put these in front of the serving dishes."

Paul sorted through his collection. "But we haven't brought down the hot dishes yet. We won't know what to pair."

"Doesn't matter," Lori assured him. "Everything goes with Ladybug Farm wine. That's the point."

"Lori, aren't you dressed yet?" Cici said from the door.

Lori looked up and clapped her hands together in surprise and delight. "Mom! Aunt Bridget! You look so pretty!"

"My girls!" declared Paul. "Look at you! Angels, perfect angels!"

Cici, in garnet, gave a curtsey, and Bridget, in rose, did a little pirouette. "We got to wear our dresses after all," she said. "Although not exactly the way we'd planned."

"They are even more perfect for the mother of the bride," Paul assured them, and added quickly, "and groom."

Derrick pressed his steepled fingers to his lips, fighting back bourgeoning emotion as he looked at Cici. "Our baby is getting married," he said. And then he looked at Bridget and corrected, "Our *babies*." At which point the emotion seemed to win, and he turned away.

Lori looked at her mother with a helpless shrug.

Just then Lindsay peered around the open door. "Is everything about ready in here?"

"Almost," Lori assured her. "We need to bring down the hot food and open a few more bottles. Do you think you could finish up here while I run up to the house and change into a dress or something?"

"Happy to," Lindsay said, and she stepped into the room carrying a garment bag on a hanger.

"In fact, I brought a little something for you to consider changing into." She unzipped the bag.

Paul clutched Derrick's arm as the gown was revealed. "Is that the . . . ?"

Derrick placed a bracing hand on his shoulder. "Hold on to me," he whispered.

Lori came from behind the bar, her expression filled with hesitant wonder and question. "Aunt Lindsay . . . that's your wedding dress. Isn't it?"

"Well, it was," Lindsay admitted. "It's undergone a few alterations."

The exquisitely designed gown had been trimmed to a length of two inches above the knee in the front and two inches above the floor in back. The bow had been removed, and so had the lace panels that had enlarged it to Lindsay's size. It was barely recognizable as the same dress they had started out with. Paul took a single staggering step forward; Derrick tightened his hand on his shoulder. Cici encircled Bridget's waist with her arm, smiling at the expression on Lori's face.

"Wow," Lori said. She turned the dress around to look at the back. Paul smothered a groan. "It's really cute."

"Cassie did most of the sewing," Lindsay said. "It fit you the first time you tried it on, so it should be fine now. But only if you like it," she added hastily. "We're not trying to force anything on you."

Lori examined the gown from front to back

again, thoughtfully. She held it up to herself, molding it at the bosom and waist. "Actually," she decided, "I do like it. And it would be nice to wear something pretty for Kevin." She broke into a smile and hugged Lindsay. "Thank you!"

Cici and Bridget shared a delighted look, and Paul bit his knuckles.

Lindsay hugged Lori hard. "It's your day," she whispered in her ear. "Treasure it!"

She broke away, took Lori's shoulders, and turned her toward the door. "Go get ready. I'll take over here."

Lori took the dress and hurried toward the house, and Paul tried hard not to cry.

The bride wore a strapless Vera Wang in a high-low skirt with a denim jacket and stacked-heel ankle boots. Cici bit down hard on her lip when she saw the boots, but Bridget said, "I think they look cute." Paul was drinking heavily.

Kevin, eyes twinkling when he saw her, said critically, "Is *that* what you're wearing?" And then he lifted her off her feet in a hard embrace and twirled her around while she laughed and pretended to protest. "I've never seen anything so beautiful," he whispered in her ear, and kissed her.

That's when Bridget bit down on her lip. "He's not supposed to see the bride before the wedding," she whispered.

All of this took place on the front porch of the

house as visitors were pulling into the parking lot that surrounded The Tasting Table and following the signs that led to the buffet. Lori gave Kevin a playful push as he set her on her feet again, and looked around, assessing. "Okay, okay. If everyone is standing around here, who's taking the money? Who's pouring the wine? Is the lady from the paper here yet? Come on, guys, we've got work to do!"

And so for the next hour they worked the crowd, they poured the wine, they handed out brochures. The sound of bluegrass music mixed with laughter and conversation and the food kept coming. At five o'clock the band leader said into the micro-phone, "Ladies and gentlemen, you're invited to gather around the fire pit in front of the winery for a brief ceremony before we light the fire. And bring your glasses for a toast!"

For the first time, Lori looked a little anxious. She removed the apron her mother had insisted she wear while pouring the wine and stepped out from behind the bar. "Okay," she said, smoothing down her skirt, "I guess this is it. Do you think Kevin knows it's time?"

Lindsay smiled. "I think he heard the announce-ment."

Lori glanced around at those still lingering around the buffet table. "We shouldn't leave until everyone is out. And make sure the glasses are filled."

"Derrick and Cassie are pouring," Lindsay assured her. "Come here."

She broke off several small, colorful chrysanthemum flowers from the display by the bar and tucked them into Lori's hair. "There," she declared, stepping back to observe the effect. "You look like a fairy princess."

"And you can't get married without a bouquet," Bridget said. She came through the door with a bouquet of yellow daisies in her hand tied with colorful ribbon streamers. "These were the prettiest I could find. Of course," she added, looking worried, "they're not exactly in the color scheme."

Lori took the bouquet, delighted. "It's perfect! I love daisies!"

Cici stood at the door for a moment, smiling at her daughter, and then hurried forward. "It took me a while to find this," she said. She fastened a gold chain with a single teardrop pearl around Lori's neck. "Your dad gave me this when you were born. I always wanted you to wear it at your wedding. And . . ." She stepped back and smiled, tears glittering on her lashes. "It goes perfectly with your outfit."

Lori surged forward and hugged her mother hard, careless of their dresses. "I love you, Mom!"

She turned to hug Bridget, and then Lindsay, and when she stepped back everyone was a little teary. "Don't ruin your makeup," Lindsay cautioned, blotting her own eyes.

Lori sniffed a little and smiled. "Okay, let's find Reverend Holland and get this show on the road before Kevin thinks I stood him up." She lifted her voice to those still milling about inside. "Come on, everyone! The ceremony is about to start!"

Bridget looked both puzzled and pleased. "Is Reverend Holland here? How sweet of him."

"I haven't seen him," Lindsay said.

Lori said, "Of course he's here. He comes to everything at Ladybug Farm."

A slow shadow of dread touched Cici's eyes. "Not *winery* events, Lori. He's Baptist!"

Lori stared at her mother. "Do you mean the preacher isn't here?"

"Well honey, if you'd only told me . . ."

"I just assumed . . ."

"Oh, Lori, you took care of everything else, we *all* just assumed . . ."

"How can I get married without a preacher?" Lori cried.

"I could run up to the house and try to call him," Bridget volunteered quickly. "I'm sure he'd come out."

"Y'all looking to get married?"

They all turned to see Farley, a plate piled high with finger sandwiches and crab puffs, standing behind them. "Cost you ten dollar."

345

Lori burst into delighted laughter. "Perfect!" she exclaimed.

There never had been a more perfect sunset. A brilliant cerulean sky was streaked with gold-etched clouds in shades of garnet and rose, lighting the mountains on fire in the background. A gentle autumn breeze loosened a few bright yellow grape leaves and sent them scattering over the ground. Lindsay snapped picture after picture. A delighted crowd gathered before the winery while "The Wedding March" was plucked out on banjo and guitar, and the bride, in denim and designer peau de soie, faced the groom. Their mothers, escorted by a nattily attired Derrick and Paul, stood just behind them. Paul dabbed at his eyes throughout the ceremony, and although he insisted later they were tears of joy, it was generally agreed he was weeping over the dress.

Dominic slipped his arm around Lindsay's waist and whispered, "Are you sorry it's not us?"

Lindsay looked up at him with eyes that were filled with absolute contentment and replied, "But it *is* us."

There was only one near-miss in the ceremony, and that was when Farley, in a voice that could command considerable authority when he chose, called for the ring. A flash of panic in Kevin's eyes revealed that the detail had escaped him.

Bridget began to tug at her own wedding band, but Dominic stepped forward and placed a small circlet woven of grapevine twigs in Kevin's hand. "Thought it might have slipped your mind," he said.

Lori's eyes lit up with delight when Kevin slipped the twig ring on her finger. "Perfect!" she whispered.

Kevin and Lori were pronounced husband and wife as the sun slipped behind the mountains, leaving a halo of radiance in the sky. Kevin kissed his bride, and when they moved apart, waving and smiling to the cheering crowd, Noah stepped forward and lit the vines in the fire pit.

Dominic, leaning slightly on a cane to ease the weight on his injured knee, turned and raised his glass. "Friends and neighbors," he called, and the laughter and chatter quieted down. "Friends and neighbors," he repeated, "since ancient times, the burning of the vines has celebrated the end of the season. It reminds us that the past is behind us, and that we are born again with each new year. This . . ." he smiled at Lindsay, "has been a good season." He turned to the bride and groom. "Let's all raise our glasses to an even better one."

There were cheers and applause and the clinking of glasses. The bride's eyes sparkled in the light of the fire and the groom's eyes glowed with pride as they filled their own glasses and drank to each other, to their family, and to their future. Ladybug Farm's first vintage, it was generally agreed, was a resounding success.

The lights came on as darkness fell, twinkling in the gazebo, glowing in yellow pools across the lawn, illuminating the paths. The bonfire shot gentle sparks into the air and scented the night with the smoky taste of autumn. A small black and white kitten could occasionally be seen streaking from shadow to shadow, chasing the glitter of candlelight. Rebel stationed himself in the pasture with the sheep, keeping a wary eye on both his flock and the invaders, while a contented golden retriever snoozed in the office, awaiting his master's return. Lori and Kevin cut Bridget's newly reassembled wedding cake, which was decorated with raspberry roses and fondant grapes, and danced under the lights of the gazebo. The wine kept flowing, the band kept playing. No one wanted to leave.

Cici climbed the steps to the porch and sank down into her rocking chair, kicking off her shoes with a small moan. "That's the *last* time I'm ordering shoes from the Internet," she said.

Bridget sat down beside her, prying one shoe off with the toe of the other, and repeating the process on the other foot. "I don't even have that excuse," she said. "I tried mine on before I bought them."

Cici smiled wryly, massaging her toes. "But we looked good, didn't we?"

Bridget grinned. "You'd better believe it."

Cici sat back, stretching out her feet to the cool night air, and reached for her wine glass. She glanced at Bridget with a mixture of curiosity and amusement in her eyes. "So are we related now?"

Bridget thought about that. "I don't know. I'll have to look it up." She lifted her glass to Cici. "What I do know is that we are going to make great mothers-in-law."

Cici saluted her. "I'll drink to that."

They were quiet for a time, listening to the music, smiling at the activity on the lawn before them. "Did you ever think . . ." they said at once, and then laughed.

"Never," said Cici, shaking her head, "in a million years."

"When we started out on this adventure," Bridget said, "I thought we were leaving so much behind. But now . . . look how much we've gained."

"Everything I ever wanted," Cici said, and when she released a breath it was of pure contentment. "And even more."

Bridget agreed, smiling. "Me, too. Even more."

Lindsay and Dominic came across the lawn, Dominic pretending not to rely on the cane that steadied his gait while Lindsay pretended not to watch him too anxiously. "Another week," he said, passing the cane to Lindsay and using the handrail to steady his progress up the steps. "Another week with this cane and that's it. Although I will admit, my ladies, that chair does look good." He lowered himself into it and added, "I thought the wedding was beautiful."

"I got some incredible pictures," Lindsay said, propping the cane against the wall and setting her camera on the table. "Lori will have a gorgeous album."

Bridget chuckled. "I have a feeling Lori is not a wedding album kind of girl."

"But her mother is," Cici spoke up quickly. "Thank you, Lindsay."

Lindsay sat down next to Dominic and reached for his hand. "What a day, huh?"

"In all the history of Ladybug Farm," Cici began with an incredulous shake of her head.

"This one was just about par for the course," finished Bridget complacently, and they all laughed.

Lori came up the steps, her curls bouncing, her face flushed with dancing and glowing with joy. Kevin was close behind her. Without a word, she bent to kiss her mother, then Bridget, then Lindsay. Kevin did the same. "Thank you," Lori said, clutching Kevin's hand, "for the perfect wedding."

Kevin extended his hand to Dominic. "Thank you for the job offer," he said. "I accept."

Dominic shook Kevin's hand, his eyes twinkling. "I'm glad to hear it."

Lori hoisted herself to the rail. "By the way," she said, "we're moving in. On what you all are paying us, we can't afford our own place."

"It's just for a little while," Kevin put in quickly. He sat on the rail beside her.

The women laughed softly. "No problem," Cici said.

Bridget added, "It's a big house."

Ida Mae came out of the front door with a big trash bag in her hand and made a show of scooping up empty glasses and plates. "Gettin' late," she said. "You need to shoo these folks on outta here."

"It's only eight o'clock," Lori objected, springing down from the rail to take the trash bag from her. "Here, I'll do that."

Bridget said at the same moment, "Ida Mae, leave that. We'll get it in the morning."

Ida Mae glared at her. "You think I want 'coons all over my porch?" And she turned a studious glare on Lori, refusing to relinquish the bag. "And you in your weddin' dress. If you can call that getup a weddin' dress. You need to go fold that dress up in blue tissue before your ruin it."

Lindsay, Cici, and Bridget had to smother quick grins. And Lori confessed, "It's probably already ruined. I sweated all over it, dancing."

Ida Mae gave her a disgusted look and dropped a plastic plate into the bag. "And another thing," she grumbled, "whoever heard of gettin' married on ten minutes' notice without even a preacher *or* a judge? It probably ain't even legal."

"Don't you worry about that, Miss Ida Mae," Kevin said. "I made sure I checked out the ordination certificate. It's perfectly legal." He winked at Lori. "This marriage has to last the rest of our lives, and I'm not taking any chances."

"Besides, I adore Farley," Lori said. "And I thought he did a great job."

Cici chuckled. "Actually, he did. It was very . . . dramatic."

Lori spread out her hand to admire her twig ring. "And I love my ring. I'm going to keep it forever."

Ida Mae gave a disapproving, "Hmmph!" and added, "I'd like to see you wash dishes or change a baby's diaper in that thing, young missy."

Lori just grinned and went to rejoin Kevin on the rail.

Dominic started to push up from his chair. "Please, Miss Ida Mae, come sit down. There's plenty of time to do that once the party is over."

She glared at him with such intensity that he immediately sank back down again. "And you! Gallavantin' around when you ought to be in your sick bed. You'll have us all waitin' on you hand and foot tomorrow, you mark my words."

Dominic murmured, "Yes, ma'am." And there

was a twinkle in his eyes as he glanced at his wife.

"So, Lori," inquired Lindsay innocently, "what did you decide to do about your name?"

Ida Mae listened with interest, but Lori just looked confused. "What about it?"

Cici clarified, "Are you going to change it?"

Lori glanced at Kevin, puzzled, and then back to her mother. "To what?"

"How did you sign the marriage certificate?" Bridget explained. "Gregory or Tyndale?"

"Oh." She smiled. "Both, naturally. Lori Gregory-Tyndale. Our children will be Gregory-Tyndales."

"Has a nice ring to it," Kevin agreed. "Stately."

Cici and Bridget sipped their wine and, wisely, said nothing. Ida Mae grumbled, "Craziest thing I ever did hear." But then she turned the force of her stare on Lindsay and added, "Better than not changin' it a'tall, I reckon." She snatched a plastic cup off the table at Lindsay's elbow and dropped it into the bag.

Noah came up the steps with a plate of cake and a fork in his hand. "Great cake," he said. "I sure have missed your cooking." He glanced at Kevin. "Hey, man, are you gonna get your stuff out of my room?"

Kevin cupped Lori's waist with his hand, drawing her close. "I already did."

Lindsay said suddenly, "Dominic, we should

353

get your children up here and have someone take a big family portrait. Who knows when we'll all be together again?"

"Well, I certainly hope it will be soon," Dominic said. He took Lindsay's hand again and added, "Isn't it odd, ladies, how you never know where a dream might take you?"

"We were just saying that," Bridget said.

"When we decided to buy this house four years ago, we thought it was going to be our last big adventure," Lindsay said. "Now it looks as though that was just the first step in a whole new life of adventures."

"Who knew?" said Cici. "Three months ago this house felt so empty. And now . . ." She smiled at Lori and Kevin, who had eyes for no one but each other. "Now, doesn't it seem nice and full?"

Noah glanced around for somewhere to sit and, finding none, sat on the step to finish his cake.

"Noah," Lindsay protested, "your uniform!"

Ida Mae gave another grunt as she returned to the door with the trash bag. "Y'all are gonna to have to get y'selves more chairs," she said.

Cici looked at Bridget. Bridget looked at Lindsay. They smiled.

"Yes," said Bridget happily, "I suppose we will."

And that's exactly what they did.

Epilogue
ಬಌ

In due time the breath of winter crept across the valley, and the vines slept beneath a blanket of snow while the big house sheltered the dreams of those who slept inside. The windows danced with holiday lights and the halls were filled with laughter and music, with noisy mealtimes and busy days.

Spring brought pale green buds and clusters of tiny grapes that would plump, with time and sun, into a rich ripe harvest. Tractors chugged and hammers swung, and voices called from house to yard and back again. A small house in the glen got a new garden, and a new couple to tend it. Vines were pruned and tied, fruit trees sprayed, tomato cuttings were set out. Baskets of strawberries filled the kitchen with their sweet intoxicating scent, and jars of bright ruby jams and sauces began to line the cupboard shelves once more. When the evening sky pinkened and the shadows lengthened across the lawn, birds fluttered to the feeders that hung from the eaves of the porch. And, like the birds, the family members began to gather, sharing a glass of wine and the best moments of their day, settling in to the comforts of home.

Three days a week Kevin left Ladybug Farm to

teach in Staunton, and every time he made the turn into the drive that led home, he smiled. Lori read about a celebrity chef who was opening a new restaurant in Washington, and she camped out on his doorstep until he agreed to meet with her. She left with a contract in hand, and the Ladybug Farm Red was featured on the grand opening menu.

Dogs barked and raced across the hillside. Roosters crowed. The nanny goat bleated. Cats sunned themselves on the porch. Birds trilled and danced in the trees and returned, every evening at sunset, to the feeders.

Kevin found a herding whistle at the feed store in town and surprised everyone by actually teaching the border collie to respond to it. For the first time since the ladies moved in, they could not only control the sheep, but the sheep dog as well. Noah was promoted twice, completed his training, and was assigned to an aircraft carrier bound for Spain. They kept his room ready for him.

The Ladybug Farm ice wine took a silver medal at the East Coast Wine Maker's Association annual competition. Lori accepted the award on behalf of the winery, but unfortunately could not join in the toast that was drunk in its honor. She and Kevin were celebrating a secret of their own, and the face of Ladybug Farm was about to change again.

Summer turned to autumn, and another harvest season got underway. Trucks backed up to the winery doors and left loaded with cases of Ladybug Farm wine. Cars with out-of-state license plates left a gentle trail of dust along the drive as they made their way to The Tasting Table restaurant, and departed laden with happy passengers, gifts and souvenirs—and, of course, with bottles of wine. The porch of the main house was lined with rocking chairs, and in the evenings every one of those chairs was filled. Occasionally a wife would reach for her husband's hand, or a mother would smile for no reason whatsoever, or a friend would lift a glass to silently toast the passing of another day. The wine, it should be said, was always excellent.

Sometimes the conversation was lively, sometimes it was reflective. Sometimes there were three or four conversations taking place at once. An occasional burst of laughter might demand the attention of everyone else; a stolen kiss might prompt a moment of simple, contented silence. Sometimes, if one listened closely, the voices of the past could almost be heard to mingle with the voices of the present, and—for those who were very discerning—with the happy murmurs from the future. The particularly fanciful might even imagine that the ghosts of the past were looking down on Ladybug Farm with approval, while the laughter of generations yet unborn echoed back through the corridors of time to greet them. And perhaps, in fact, that was precisely what was happening.

Because, as everyone liked to say on Ladybug Farm, you never know where a dream might take you.

ABOUT THE AUTHOR
🙰

Donna Ball is the author of over a hundred novels under several different pseudonyms in a variety of genres that include romance, mystery, suspense, paranormal, western adventure, historical and women's fiction. Recent popular series include the Ladybug Farm series by Berkley Books and the Raine Stockton Dog Mystery series. She lives in a restored Victorian barn in the heart of the Blue Ridge Mountains with a variety of four-footed companions. You can contact her at http://www.donnaball.net.

Center Point Large Print
600 Brooks Road / PO Box 1
Thorndike, ME 04986-0001 USA

(207) 568-3717

US & Canada:
1 800 929-9108
www.centerpointlargeprint.com